A GRACED HISTORY

The Sisters of Mercy of Rochester
1900-2000

Ann Miller, RSM
Kathleen Milliken, RSM

ISBN
© 2005 by Sisters of Mercy of Rochester
All rights reserved.

Photographs from the Archives of the Sisters of Mercy of Rochester.
Cover and text design by Estelle Martin, RSM

PREFACE

Catherine McAuley, an Irish heiress with a tender heart and great concern for the poor of Dublin, founded the Sisters of Mercy in 1831. Soon she gathered a number of women who wished to join her and share in her ministry, professing vows of poverty, chastity and obedience, with a fourth vow of service to the poor, sick and ignorant. Unique among women's religious orders of the time, who were generally cloistered and not visible to the public, the Sisters of Mercy went out daily to minister to the needy.

Mother Frances Warde, American foundress and close friend of Catherine McAuley, brought the Mercy sisters to the United States in 1843 and set up a foundation in Pittsburgh, Pennsylvania. At the frequent urging of Bishop John Timon of Buffalo, she then accompanied six Sisters of Mercy from Providence, Rhode Island to St. Mary's Parish in Rochester, New York in 1857 where they took up residence in St. Mary's Convent on South Street. Frances Warde's Providence foundation in 1851 was the beginning of her establishment of Mercy convents throughout New England.

In *Mercy Comes to Rochester*, first printed in 1985 by the Rochester Sisters of Mercy, Sister M. Florence Sullivan tells the story of these early pioneers and their accomplishments and struggles, covering the years from 1857 to 1902. A former English and history teacher, librarian, and the second principal of Our Lady of Mercy High School, Sister Florence began gathering material on the history of the congregation many years before her retirement as principal. She then became the first full-time archivist for the Rochester community.

It has been a privilege to write Volume II of *Mercy Comes to Rochester*, focusing on the history of the Sisters of Mercy from 1900 to 2000. The twentieth century was a time of tremendous change in religious life; major events occurred that unfolded over years, even decades, in the life of the Rochester community. Rather than trace these events in chronological order spanning many decades, the decision was made to treat them topically, so that each topic would be shaped and developed as a whole. This challenges the reader to understand the timeline within each chapter.

There was a wealth of materials available. The archives of the Rochester Sisters of Mercy are rich with letters, pictures, minutes of meetings, documents, and scrapbooks that record the history of the congregation. Sister Mary Florence and her successors, Sisters Jane Hasbrouck and Jeanne Reichart, deserve great praise for their dedication to this important ministry.

We wish to acknowledge those people who encouraged and supported us through the time of research and writing—the leadership teams, and those sisters who took time to share their stories with us. Special praise goes to the women who were part of the readers group and who offered creative suggestions and new insights: Patricia Donovan, Sisters Dorothy Loeb, Patricia MacDonald, Jeanne Reichart, Patricia Switzer, Marlene Vigna and Janet Wahl. In addition to the readers group, we thank Sisters Jane Hasbrouck and Elaine Kolesnik, who critiqued the first draft. We also want to thank Louise Novros, our expert typist, who outdid herself keeping to the timeline we set for her, with skill, style and good humor. Sister Mary Sullivan proofread with great care each page of the text and offered us the wisdom of her experience as writer. We are deeply grateful for her invaluable assistance.

These pages tell the story of our communal journey as Rochester Sisters of Mercy. Part of this story has been told in *Mercy Comes to Rochester*. We invite you to continue the journey with us into the twenty-first century, knowing that the story is not ended. In Catherine McAuley's words, " . . . it is here that we can most clearly see the designs of God."

Focused by the lens of faith, our communal journey reveals God's presence and mercy through the whole of it —what has been and what shall become our graced history.

Gaye L. Moorhead, RSM, President
Sisters of Mercy of Rochester
July 2005

It commenced with 2, Sister Doyle and I. The plan from the beginning was such as is now in practice . . . We who began were prepared to do whatever was recommended . . . though it was thought the foundations would retard it—it seems to be quite otherwise.

   There has been a most marked Providential Guidance which the want of prudence—vigilance—or judgment has not impeded—and it is here that we can most clearly see the designs of God. I could mark circumstances calculated to defeat it at once—but nothing however injurious in itself has done any injury.

   . . . In short, it evidently was to go on—and surmount all obstacles—many of which were great indeed . . . One thing is remarkable—that no breach of charity ever occurred amongst us. The sun never, I believe, went down on our anger . . . otherwise we have been deficient enough—and far, very far, from cooperating generously with God in our regard, but we will try to do better—all of us . . .

Catherine McAuley
Letter to Elizabeth Moore
January 13, 1839

CONTENTS

January 1, 1900

Sisters of Mercy First Convent and Motherhouse
Rochester, New York

CHAPTER ONE

MERCY WELCOMES A NEW YEAR

J anuary 1, 1900 dawned cold and snowy in Rochester, New York. The Sisters of Mercy who gathered in the community room of their motherhouse at St. Mary's on South Street were in good spirits as they welcomed in a new century. They had just completed a three-day retreat that closed with a renewal of their vows. On New Year's Day, they laughed and shared stories of their Christmas holidays that were soon to end. They had held a Christmas entertainment in their convent for the orphans; St. Mary's pastor, Rev. James R. Kiernan, declared it "very pleasing." Mother M. Teresa Gavigan, the recently elected mother superior, entertained them with an account of her visit to the Mercy sisters in Auburn who were happily and successfully carrying on Catherine McAuley's work in that city. The Auburn sisters had not always experienced such happiness, as Teresa Gavigan remembered very well even though she was only a novice at the time.

Two young novices, Mary Loretto Daly and Mary Clare Dower were to profess their religious vows within the week; there was happy conversation around this anticipated event. Sister M. Stanislaus Brady, principal of St. Mary's School, could not dampen their spirits by reminding them that in just one more day five hundred children would be returning to school, reluctantly perhaps, but with high energy. Sister M. Antonia Desmond, who taught art class, was already looking forward to their return. With her highly praised artistic ability, she loved bringing out the creativity of the students. Twenty-four year old Mary Borgia O'Keefe, the eighth grade teacher, was not so enthusiastic.

Despite their good spirits, so evident on this first day of a new century, the Sisters of Mercy who succeeded those who came to Rochester in 1857 were a small, struggling community who welcomed the twentieth century with only forty-one members in the congregation and who had been invited to staff only two parish schools: St. Mary's in Rochester and Holy Family in Auburn. At that time the Diocese of Rochester had approximately thirty-three parish schools.

Three years earlier, on September 3, 1897, Father James Stewart, pastor of St. Mary's parish and the sisters' "greatest publicity agent" died; two months later, Mother M. Camillus Kelly died suddenly in the last year of her term as superior. Mother Camillus was beloved by the sisters. Twenty-nine of her forty years as a Sister of Mercy had been in the role of mother superior. Her unexpected death had taken its toll on the women in the congregation. Before the new year would come to a close, Father James Kiernan, who succeeded Father Stewart as pastor of St. Mary's, would meet an early death. His successor, Father Timothy Murphy, would die just six months later. These priests were good friends of the Sisters of Mercy and they felt these losses deeply.

In addition, they found themselves in the unenviable position of being out of favor with the bishop of the diocese—Bishop Bernard J. McQuaid. Since its founding in 1868, the Diocese of Rochester has housed two motherhouses of women religious within its geographical area: the Sisters of St. Joseph and the Sisters of Mercy. Over the years, many other congregations of women religious had served the diocese with distinction and dedication, but their motherhouses had been located outside the geographical area of the diocese.

When Bishop McQuaid was appointed the first bishop of Rochester, he quickly announced his diocesan priority: "a parochial school in every parish."[1] He believed his next step was to find or to begin a diocesan community of teaching sisters who could carry his plan to a successful completion. His decision, ultimately, was between the Sisters of St. Joseph and the Sisters of Mercy. With this object in view, he examined the Rules and Constitutions of the Sisters of St. Joseph and found them admirably suited to his plan since the community, according to the advice of its founder, recognized the bishop as its first Superior.[2] The Sisters of Mercy, according to their *Constitutions*, obeyed the Diocesan Bishop "as their principal Superior after the Holy See."[3] Therefore, Bishop McQuaid's choice for a diocesan community of teaching sisters was the Sisters of St. Joseph, to whom "he devoted his closest personal attention."[4]

The Rochester Sisters of Mercy soon realized that if they were to survive, they could not mark time waiting for someone to present them with a future plan of action. They themselves had to undertake service like the apostolic work of their foundress, Catherine McAuley. With Bernard McQuaid as bishop, the prospect of receiving new teaching assignments seemed remote. Mother M. Camillus Kelly had therefore encouraged the sisters to explore other ways of serving the poor of Christ.[5] So, in characteristic good humor, the sisters accepted the advice, remembering Catherine McAuley's advice to her Dublin sisters:

> Let us take one day only in hands—at a time, merely making a resolve for tomorrow. Thus we may hope to get on—taking short careful steps, not great strides.[6]

In *Mercy Comes to Rochester*, Sister M. Florence Sullivan explains, with the objectivity of an astute historian, how Bishop McQuaid first met the Sisters of Mercy. Certainly the sisters would not have chosen the circumstances of the introduction themselves.

In May of 1867, ten years after the arrival of the sisters in Rochester, Father Thomas O'Flaherty, pastor of Holy Family parish in Auburn, New York, asked for Sisters of Mercy to staff a new school in the parish. Father O'Flaherty was very specific in naming the two sisters he wanted: Sister M. Baptist Coleman and Sister M. Raymond O'Reilly. Sister M. Raymond had already moved to Iowa to begin a new foundation. For her own personal reasons, Mary Camillus Kelly did not send Sister M. Baptist who had been the first superior of the Rochester Mercys. She did, however, send five sisters with Sister M. dePazzi Kavanaugh as superior-principal.

From the first days in Auburn, the sisters found Father O'Flaherty unfriendly, and an attitude of distrust arose between the pastor and the sisters. Father O'Flaherty felt perfectly justified in criticizing the sisters publicly. He refused to give them any salary for their work in the school, perhaps with the hope that they would leave and return to Rochester. He gave permission to a lay woman to open a Catholic school that would have a direct impact on the school the sisters were staffing. Unfortunately, these troubling incidents gave the sisters unwanted publicity in the city of Auburn.

This was the situation that awaited Bishop McQuaid's attention as he was consecrated first bishop of Rochester. When he arrived in his new diocese, he was confronted with a file that contained all the documents surrounding the Auburn situation. Later he made the following observation:

> You all remember the trouble in Auburn that met me when I came into your midst as Bishop. Fighting, contention, angry feelings, public meetings against the then pastor, persecuted Sisters of Mercy, disorder and disgrace in the place—these constituted my first welcome to Auburn.[7]

Other incidents, some documented, some passed on by word of mouth, add to the history of the Sisters of Mercy's relationship with Bishop McQuaid. These are carefully recorded in *Mercy Comes to Rochester*, the first volume of this history.

On April 22, 1902, Bishop McQuaid wrote to his good friend Michael A. Corrigan, archbishop of New York, in response to a question about proposed legislation for communities of women religious. In his letter, Bishop McQuaid said:

> There are only two communities of Sisters for which I am at all responsible: Sisters of St. Joseph and Sisters of Mercy.
>
> I know what the Sisters of St. Joseph are; I know very little about the others. Both communities have their Houses of Novitiate.
>
> I know what the Sisters of Mercy are in Ireland; no one knows what they are in this country. I had only two houses in my diocese, until with the addition of

four counties from Buffalo came four houses of the Sisters of Mercy. These last have given me more trouble than all the others in thirty years.

It will be necessary to define their exact status, or they will continue to be a thorn in a bishop's side.[8]

Nowhere in the archives of the Sisters of Mercy is there any history or documentation of the meaning of Bishop McQuaid's words about the "trouble" the four houses of Sisters of Mercy from Buffalo gave him. The events behind these words will therefore always remain a mystery. Even more of an enigma is Bishop McQuaid's reference, "I know what the Sisters of St. Joseph are; I know very little about the others." The "others," the Sisters of Mercy, had been serving in Rochester eleven years before Bernard McQuaid came and thirty-four years under his episcopal leadership.

It is particularly ironic to recall that it was a decision of Bishop McQuaid's that brought the four "troublesome" convents under his jurisdiction. The southern tier counties of Steuben, Chemung, Tioga and Schuyler had been part of the Buffalo diocese, but Bernard McQuaid felt that they rightfully belonged to the Rochester diocese because of their geographical location. Ever since coming to Rochester in 1868, he had petitioned Rome to have them added to his diocese; his request was finally granted in 1896.

As a result of Rome's decision, the Sisters of Mercy in Hornell, Corning, Elmira and Owego who were geographically located within these four counties now had a dilemma: their Batavia motherhouse was in the diocese of Buffalo but they were serving in the diocese of Rochester. The Batavia community had been founded from Rochester in 1862, but two years later Bishop John Timon, acting, he thought, in the best interest of the sisters, had separated Batavia from the parent house in Rochester.

When Mother M. Dolores Clancy, superior of the Batavia community, asked Bishop James E. Quigley, the new bishop of Buffalo, what was the status of the sisters in these four counties, he replied "They belong to Bishop McQuaid."[9]

From 1899 until 1901 these sisters existed as an independent congregation with their motherhouse in Hornell. Eventually, as Sister M. Florence reports, Bishop McQuaid found this arrangement "neither sensible nor practical."[10] In 1901 he visited the Sisters of Mercy in the four southern tier counties and allowed them a personal vote on whether to join with the Rochester community or to return to their original motherhouse in Batavia.

Bishop McQuaid himself counted the votes. After the counting was completed, he announced that twelve sisters had chosen to return to the Batavia community, while the remaining sisters agreed to become part of the Rochester Sisters of Mercy. The fact that their convents and ministries were now part of the Rochester diocese had a considerable influence on their choice. The priests in these parishes also urged the sisters to remain in the Rochester diocese and continue their faithful service. That year the Rochester Sisters of Mercy increased their membership by thirty-five sisters, twenty-four who had entered in Batavia and eleven who had entered in Hornell after the counties were annexed to the Rochester diocese. The Rochester community, at the time, had only fifty members, so this was a day of rejoicing for them. Perhaps Bishop McQuaid's legacy to the Sisters of Mercy was his union of the northern and southern tier motherhouses. One wonders if he was aware of this as he served out the last years of his episcopate.

Bernard McQuaid died in 1909 in his forty-first year as bishop of Rochester. His successor was Thomas F. Hickey, who in 1905 had been consecrated as coadjutor bishop to Bishop McQuaid. Bishop Hickey was a native

Rochesterian and a former student of the Mercy sisters at St. Mary's School in Rochester. With Bishop Hickey, the Mercys were accepted "as trusted auxiliaries in the expanding education work of the Rochester diocese."[11] His installation opened new worlds for the Rochester congregation as the Sisters of Mercy grew in membership and ministries.

Bishop Hickey established ten new schools in the first decade of his tenure. He invited the Sisters of Mercy to staff six of these schools: Our Lady of Mount Carmel (1910), St. Andrew (1915), St. John the Evangelist (1916) in Rochester, and St. Francis of Assisi, Auburn (1910), St. Vincent DePaul, Corning (1913), and St. John the Evangelist, Clyde (1914). In the early 1920s, the Sisters of Mercy were invited to staff three other Rochester schools: St. Salome (1921), St. Thomas the Apostle (1922) and St. Charles Borromeo (1926). With the addition of the four schools acquired in 1901 through the merger of the southern tier counties: (St. Ann, Hornell; St. Mary, Corning; St. Patrick, Elmira; and St. Patrick, Owego) as well as Holy Cross in Rochester in 1906, the Rochester Sisters of Mercy now ministered in sixteen parish schools. This was a significant change from the two parish schools which they had staffed before 1900.

For the majority of sisters at that time, teaching in a parish elementary school was their first mission as a Sister of Mercy, and they worked hard to embody the spirit of Catherine McAuley, their foundress, who believed "It is a special favor of God to be teachers destined to be made the servants of his suffering poor."[12] Education was a high priority for Catherine McAuley, but the work of the sisters was not limited to the schools alone.

Service of the Sick

In the *Familiar Instructions of Rev. Mother*

McAuley, Catherine reminds her sisters that "by our vocation and our sacred vow, we are called to comfort the sick and poor of Christ. This is the principal reason why we are called 'Sisters of Mercy.'"[13]

In 1918 the Rochester Sisters of Mercy certainly found courage in these words of instruction from their foundress, when the influenza epidemic struck the United States. It was the worst epidemic in American history, and before it ended 675,000 people had died. In Rochester, New York, 1100 people died within the first four months. Because of World War I many physicians had been called to duty, so a large part of the care of the sick was placed in the hands of nurses. Just as Catherine McAuley had rallied her sisters during the cholera epidemic of 1832, the Sisters of Mercy joined with other women to nurse the victims of the flu epidemic.

Sister M. Hilary Carroll helped with the epileptic patients at Sonyea Hospital in Mount Morris, while the sisters from St. John's and Mount Carmel convents served in Rochester. Sisters M. Flavia Hanrahan, M. Mechtilde Hart, M. Clement Sheehan, M. Joseph Souliman and M. Antonia Hyde worked with the Red Cross nurses in a temporary hospital in the Baden Street area of Rochester. The sisters from St. Mary's Convent on South Street comforted and cared for the sick in the Troup Street area. The sisters in Owego, New York nursed dozens of their neighbors throughout the epidemic. Sister M. Aquinas Spellacy, a sister nurse at St. James Mercy Hospital in 1918, remembered the epidemic as the worst in her experience. She recalled that "Influenza patients poured into the hospital until every possible space was utilized. Beds were set up in the halls, in store rooms, on porches and even in closets."[14] A public building was opened in Mount Morris with one hundred beds for flu patients. The Sisters of Mercy worked there with the Sisters of St. Joseph.

In the November 8, 1918 issue of the *Catholic Journal*, Bishop Hickey announced that the parochial schools would not reopen until November 11, despite the fact that the public schools were already open. His reason for the delay was that he felt the sisters who had been ministering to the flu patients needed time to rest. In paying tribute to the workers, he said the "priests and nuns have been most loyal with them (the sick), not only in prayer, but also in spiritual and temporal ministrations so faithfully and generously provided for them."[15]

Sister M. Vincent Doyle

Another example of the dedicated women of mercy who served during this era was Sister M. Vincent Doyle (1851-1943), long remembered and revered for her ministry to the poor and needy of Rochester. She was the one most often mentioned by Bishop Hickey when he reflected on his days as a student at St. Mary's School. Sister Vincent, who had entered the Sisters of Mercy in Rochester in 1872, was a teacher at St. Mary's and went on visitations in the parish. From 1883 to 1905, she ministered to the children in St. Mary's Crèche, a daycare operated by the Sisters of Mercy, and visited prisoners in the jail. In 1902 she became director of the Industrial School at St. Mary's and later taught at St. Andrew's School. She was also among the first faculty members of Mount Carmel School in 1909.

In recounting her memories of Sister Vincent, Sister M. Leonard Gavin considered her to be the community's first social worker and a great storyteller. She knew every judge in town and often befriended young boys, especially those who were in trouble with the law. She would bring them food, and they looked upon her as a grandmother.

One small orphaned boy was released into Sister M. Vincent's care. He was adopted by her sister and named Vincent. When he grew up he brought his prospective bride for Sister M. Vincent's approval; she was later invited to their home for the first dinner prepared by the bride. Sister M. Vincent celebrated her golden jubilee at St. Andrew's Convent in 1925. Elected a member of the Board of Trustees of the Rochester Sisters of Mercy, she served in this capacity until her death in 1943 at ninety-two years of age. In her was truly embodied the spirit of Catherine McAuley and the first Sisters of Mercy who went out into the streets of Dublin and ministered to the poor.

Leadership in the Early Twentieth Century

During the first quarter of the twentieth century, Mother M. Irene Consedine, the fifth mother superior of the congregation, greatly influenced the direction of the Rochester Sisters of Mercy. As a result of the merger of the southern tier counties with the Rochester diocese, she was one of the sisters who transferred from the Batavia community to Rochester. Three years later, at the age of thirty-two, she was elected by her new community as mother superior and served in that capacity for seventeen years. Mother M. Irene was elected during Bishop McQuaid's last years, so she experienced some of the frustration that previous Mercy superiors had known in working with the bishop. However, when Thomas F. Hickey, a more congenial friend of the Mercy sisters, was installed as bishop, his relationship with Mother M. Irene was always cooperative and supportive.

During the Christmas holidays of 1916, Mother M. Irene suffered a sprained ankle in the fire that partially destroyed the Rochester motherhouse next to St. Mary's Church on South Street. However, she rallied to the responsibility of relocating the sisters to St. John's Park in Charlotte, which had been previously used by the sisters as a summer residence. The need for a new and larger motherhouse became the dream of Mother M. Irene, but unfortunately she would not live to see that dream become a reality.

In February 1923 she purchased eighteen acres of land on Blossom Road in the town of Brighton from Miss Nellie Tolan, sister of Sister M. Joseph Tolan, a member of the Rochester community. Five years earlier, the Tolan family had given eighteen acres of their land as a gift to the sisters. These transactions would provide the site for a new high school for girls and a permanent motherhouse for the sisters. On August 25, 1927, at a meeting of the Board of Trustees of the Sisters of Mercy, Mother M. Irene was empowered to borrow $125,000 "to be used in part payment for the new school building on Blossom Road."[16] On September 8, 1927, Bishop Thomas Hickey broke ground for the school, with Mother M. Irene standing proudly at his side.

Three months later, on December 18, Mother M. Irene died suddenly of a heart attack at the Charlotte motherhouse, one year before the end of her time as superior—a woman who, in the words of Sister M. Borgia O'Keefe, a member of her council, was "one of those rare superiors whose charity and kindness were far-reaching."[17] Sister M. Evangelist Meyer, a novice at the time, remembered that Mother M. Irene "was a beautiful person inside and out." She vividly recalled that each time Mother M. Irene was going on a trip, "We'd all go to the front hall of the motherhouse, aprons and all, and she'd kiss everyone goodbye." Her death was "traumatic and had a profound effect on the sisters."[18]

Mother M. Irene's body was taken to St. Mary's Church on South Street for the wake and funeral. More than 150 women religious, 100 members of the clergy and hundreds of lay women and men attended the solemn pontifical requiem Mass celebrated by Bishop Thomas Hickey. Many had come to know and revere Mother M. Irene during her seventeen years as superior of the

Rochester Sisters of Mercy.

Our Lady of Mercy High School

Upon the untimely death of Mother M. Irene, Mother M. Liguori McHale, her assistant, became acting superior, and on February 4, 1928, Mother M. Liguori was formally elected superior by a majority of the professed sisters. The new superior had always encouraged Mother M. Irene to put the best building materials and equipment into the new high school. Her theory was that "The best you can buy is the cheapest in the long run."[19] Under her guidance the building progressed rapidly and was dedicated on September 8, 1928, just one year after the groundbreaking ceremony. Reverend William Hart, secretary to the bishop and chancellor of the diocese, presided at the ceremony and blessed the new Our Lady of Mercy High School, dedicated to Mary, the patron of the Sisters of Mercy.

On that date, the *Rochester Times-Union* elaborately described the building which was designed by J. Foster Warner, architect, and constructed by the firm of Leo J. Ribson. *The Catholic Journal* of September 28, 1929 made note of the historic opening day of school:

> The new high school of Our Lady of Mercy on Blossom Road was opened to inspection Monday by the Sisters of Mercy, and many persons were shown through the building, which has about 90 pupils registered for the present semester . . . . Students wore their blue and white uniforms for the first time in honor of the feast of Our Lady of Mercy, the special patroness of the sisters who have charge of the school.[20]

The first faculty members were: Sister M.

Francesca Connor, principal; Sisters M. Florence Sullivan, M. Adolphine Cooley, M. Adelaide Major, and M. Gabriel Oster. The sisters lived on the third floor of the school in the beginning years before the motherhouse was built, and they did all the maintenance work as well as teaching full-time.

On June 23, 1932, the first graduating class of forty-five young women celebrated the completion of four years at Mercy High—another milestone for the Rochester Sisters of Mercy. Three of these graduates entered the Sisters of Mercy: Rita Kast (Sister M. Florita), Irene Gardner (Sister M. David), and Geraldine Georger (Sister M. Agnes Theresa).

Members of the class forged close bonds and established traditions which have lasted through the years: the first school newspaper, *The Quill*; the first May Day; the annual celebration of Field Day; the Catholic Students Mission Crusade, and the Sodality—all have evolved into newer programs, but their influence has lasted. Several surviving members of the first class have described what being a pioneer at Mercy meant to them:

> To me it was like an adventure on paths not yet traveled. We were the explorers and our goal was to obtain a good education. We would learn about unity and involvement, involvement in the school's effort to be the best in all we did. We learned by doing. The "Mercy Spirit" was the special tradition to be introduced. Each successful undertaking gave us so much confidence we would accept the challenges ahead with eagerness! Friendships begun in 1928 have continued to flourish for over sixty-five years.
>
> Margaret Grimes Lynch '32[21]

We had the first Mission Day, began the orchestra,

14

composed the alma mater and were first to plant a tree on the campus on that first Class Day, June 3, 1932. Our Rose Mass and graduates' breakfast were beginners also, the forerunners of happy events that have continued year after year. Best of all we passed on that wonderful Mercy spirit, fostered in us by those first five enthusiastic, loving nuns and reinforced and increased by each of their followers and every succeeding class of Mercians.

Marie Lavelle Hanss '32[22]

Eunice Aman '32 described her years at Mercy as "basically happy years, and I met many nice girls and developed some great friendships."[23] She sent her own daughter to Mercy High School and then had a granddaughter enrolled at Mercy: three generations profited from their Mercy education.

Our Lady of Mercy High School has fulfilled Catherine McAuley's conviction that:

No work of charity can be more productive of good to society, or more conducive to the happiness of the poor than the careful instruction of women, since whatever be the station they are destined to fill, their example and advice will always possess influence, and wherever a religious woman presides, peace and good order are generally to be found.[24]

CHAPTER TWO

THE COMMUNITY GROWS

I n 1929 when the Diocese of Rochester was preparing to welcome its third bishop, John Francis O'Hern, the Sisters of Mercy from thirty-nine motherhouses across the United States were petitioning Rome to form a new governance structure that would be known as the Sisters of Mercy of the Union. The first seven Sisters of Mercy to come to the United States had arrived from St. Leo's Convent in Carlow, Ireland in 1843. These seven women, led by Mother Frances Warde, settled in Pittsburgh, Pennsylvania. By 1929 the seven had grown to 9,308 Sisters of Mercy in sixty autonomous congregations across the United States.

The idea of uniting the various congregations of Sisters of Mercy under one form of government had been considered by the Holy See since 1902. Cardinal Martinelli, apostolic delegate to the United States, was directed by the Sacred Congregation for the Propagation of the Faith to investigate the status of the Sisters of Mercy.

His advice was that the American Sisters of Mercy should be united under one superior. Apparently there was some concern over alleged irregularities and a lack of proper canonical status of some of the Mercy foundations.

The Rochester sisters, having experienced the uniting of the northern and southern tier communities, were not too interested in another Union, and they felt the advice did not apply to them. Their attitude seems to have been that "One amalgamation is sufficient to manage at a time."[1] Over the years, the Sisters of Mercy across the United States met with other Mercy sisters who were interested in amalgamation. The superiors in the Rochester community chose not to attend any of these meetings. Although in the early years of the twentieth century the concept of uniting congregations of Mercys under one mother superior was receiving growing support, the Rochester community was simultaneously dealing with the fire at their original motherhouse in 1916, the need to purchase land to build a motherhouse and a high school in the 1920s, and the unexpected death of their superior, Mother M. Irene Consedine in 1927.

Sister M. Carmelita Hartman, mother superior of the Baltimore Sisters of Mercy, wrote to Mother M. Liguori on April 1, 1928 urging her to respond to the "matter now before the Sisters of Mercy in the United States regarding general government."[2] Four days later, on April 5, Mother M. Liguori's assistant Borgia O'Keefe responded: "Our superior, Mother M. Liguori, desires me to write and say that we are not prepared to take any active part in the proposed movement at the present time."[3] The Rochester Sisters of Mercy wished to remain an independent congregation.

On July 1, 1929, the Rochester sisters gathered together to vote on becoming a part of this new Union of Sisters of Mercy. Rochester Bishop John Francis O'Hern presided at the assembly of sisters. As expected, the vote was not in favor of the amalgamation. Mother M. Liguori wrote a letter to the apostolic delegate, Most Reverend P. Fumasoni-Biondi, informing him of the results of the Rochester vote:

> The votes of one hundred fifty-two Sisters, the entire enrollment of the professed members of our Community, were taken with the following results: One hundred forty two Sisters desired to remain as we are, a diocesan organization, while ten favored the union. All matters concerning the voting were in strict accordance with Chapter procedure—two scrutineers collected and examined the billets [ballots], which were again examined by the Bishop and recorded by the secretary, Reverend Emmett Magee.

> Trusting that this decision will be satisfactory to your Excellency, as well as to the Holy Father, who as we interpreted left the matter entirely to us, I beg to subscribe myself.

> Your obedient servant in J.C.
> (signed) Mother Mary Liguori[4]

It is noteworthy that one of the sisters who lived at the time of the amalgamation observed, "There was a lot of unrest and our sisters voted against it." She also recalled: "In 1929 there was much discussion about the idea of the Amalgamation of the Sisters of Mercy . . . we voted against the amalgamation since we preferred to go on alone for some time to come."[5] Another remembered that "Mother M. Liguori felt we should remain independent because we were doing well at the time; she was afraid the younger sisters might vote for it, however, and that we would be 'swallowed up.'"[6] A sister who was a novice at the time said, "The novices thought it was a good idea, because then we could be sent anywhere, but the sisters voted against it."[7] Another novice realized that the vote on the amalgamation was coming up, and got the idea that "it was a closed issue; there was not much talk about it at all."[8]

It would not be until the latter part of the twentieth century that the Rochester Sisters of Mercy would again consider such a concept, and a new chapter would be written in their history.

Rochester Motherhouse

Despite the looming specter of the depression, the Sisters of Mercy moved ahead with plans for their new motherhouse. At the annual meeting of the Board of Trustees of the Sisters of Mercy, held on February 4, 1930, a resolution was passed empowering Mother M. Liguori, president of the board, to borrow $200,000 to be used as part payment for the new motherhouse to be built on Blossom Road, adjacent to Mercy High School. Plans had already been underway in 1928, shortly after Mother Liguori began her term as superior, since the building at St. John's Park in the Charlotte section of Rochester was becoming increasingly unsuitable for the expanding community. St. John's Park, their former summer home, had been used as a motherhouse since the fire of 1916 when the community numbered 136; there were 194 sisters in 1931. Bishop O'Hern obtained the necessary permission from the Holy See, and ground was broken for the new motherhouse on July 4, 1930.[9]

Bishop O'Hern, shortly after his installation in the diocese, established a commission of laymen to advise him regarding building projects. Raymond J. Curran (father of Sister M. Beatrice Curran), a civil engineer as well as a building contractor, was appointed to this commission. Sister Beatrice shared this memory:

Mother M. Liguori was anxious to build a more adequate structure for the Sisters of Mercy. Bishop O'Hern consulted my father, Raymond J. Curran, the chairman of the building commission, for advice relative to the feasibility of the project. My father had great admiration for the business acumen of Mother M. Liguori, the major superior of the Sisters of Mercy. His words to the bishop expressed it well:

'Bishop, the Sisters of Mercy have never been given the support of the diocese for the work they are doing; they should be given the opportunity to show their ability. My advice is give them the chance to show their talent and dedication. With Mother Liguori in charge they won't fail.'[10]

Bishop John F. O'Hern (left) and Archbishop Thomas Hickey at the groundbreaking of the Blossom Road mother-house in 1930.

Several financial transactions, completed during Mother Liguori's second term in office (1931-34), testify to her keen judgment: the resolution to sell the property at St. John's Park; the sale of property in Corning bequeathed by a benefactor; and the board resolution giving her permission to borrow $15,000 to be used in partial payment for the new motherhouse on Blossom Road. She also negotiated the $15,000 purchase of the piece of land from the Hone estate on Clover Street, extending the Sisters of Mercy property on Blossom Road to the New York Central Railroad. This decision proved advantageous for the Rochester community as time passed and land become more and more sought after in the Brighton area.

The motherhouse was built on land that had once been the site of the first building for Christian worship in the Rochester and Irondequoit Valley area. The structure had been built on these grounds in June 1679 by three Franciscan-Recollect Fathers headed by Father Louis Hennepin, famed in American history for explorations of the Mississippi River. Through the generosity of Herman G. Hetzler, a tablet was erected on the grounds of the motherhouse in 1935 which reads:

A small cabin of Bark of Trees
To perform divine worship therein
Erected June 1679
By Franciscan-Recollect Missionaries

The new motherhouse was dedicated on May 7, 1931. The ceremonies began in the chapel of Mercy High School, and Mass was celebrated at an outdoor altar to accommodate the clergy, sisters, and guests of the sisters. Open house was held for the public during the following three days. After the solemn blessing and dedication of the motherhouse by Bishop O'Hern, a new era began for the Sisters of Mercy "with headquarters established in a structure capably and thoughtfully designed and skillfully built and one well equipped for future development and activity of the Community."[11]

Mercy Celebrates Irish Foundation

Within a few months after the motherhouse was completed, plans began for the celebration of the Centenary of the Sisters of Mercy, December 12, 1931. Because Catherine McAuley, the first Sister of Mercy, pronounced her vows on December 12, 1831, this date is considered the original foundation day of the Sisters of Mercy. The "Pageant Masque of Mercy," written by a Chicago Sister of Mercy, was presented by the students of Our Lady of Mercy High School. Former students from parish schools where the sisters taught joined the Mercy orchestra for the occasion. The production told the story of the Sisters of Mercy in song, dance and speech, from their beginning in Ireland to the pioneer days in America. Sister M. Antonia Hyde, the director, observed: "Neither time nor money was spared to make it a success. The Community entered into this with all the enthusiasm of which nuns are capable, with the result that it was a decided success."[12]

Rochester Celebrates 75 Years

Six months later, in June 1932, the Sisters of Mercy marked their seventy-fifth anniversary in the Rochester area with a three-day celebration: a pontifical Mass at the cathedral with Bishop O'Hern presiding; a requiem Mass at St. Mary's Church for all deceased Sisters of Mercy of Rochester; and the reception of fifteen young women into the community.[13]

The anniversary of the Rochester foundation is June 9, the day in 1857 when Bishop John Timon of Buffalo celebrated Mass in St. Mary's convent chapel for Mother

Frances Warde and the first six Sisters of Mercy to arrive in Rochester. In the foreword to Sister M. Antonia's book, *Mercy*, Bishop John Francis O'Hern praised the sisters as they prepared to celebrate their 75 years in the diocese:

> Their world-record of work, since their foundation by Mother M. Catherine McAuley one hundred years ago, has been one of the glorious pages of the history of Religious Communities of Women in the Church, and their accomplishments for the past three quarters of a century, from the humblest beginnings in the Diocese of Rochester, is a story filled with labors of self-sacrifice, of thrilling love and devotion in the service of God and of God's children. Their growth, like the parable of the mustard seed in the Gospel, has been marvelous throughout these jubilee years, and now has been crowned with the magnificent new Motherhouse and Girls High School on Blossom Road.
>
> +John Francis O'Hern
> Eastertide, 1932[14]

Moving Forward

In 1934 Mother M. Liguori had served for six years as superior of the Rochester community. Since the *Rule* called for a superior to leave office after two three-year terms, she was not eligible for re-election at that time. Sister M. Mechtilde Hart, who had transferred from the Batavia community in 1901, was elected mother superior and served from 1934 to 1937. Mother Mechtilde spent most of her religious life at Mount Carmel School in Rochester as a teacher and principal. Some sisters remembered that Mother M. Mechtilde and those assigned to teach at Mount Carmel in its early years experienced many hardships: walking to and from the school and the motherhouse at St. Mary's in all types of weather; depending for supplies on the kindness of friends; and often feeling inadequate because many students spoke only Italian. Thus, early in their religious life they learned the true meaning of simplicity of life and shared both tears and laughter.

Archbishop Edward Mooney was the fourth Bishop of Rochester, from 1933 to 1937. Mother M. Mechtilde's service to the Sisters of Mercy as superior paralleled his service to the diocese. In some ways, these two leaders were alike: warm, caring individuals who often appeared austere to those who did not know them well. Mother M. Mechtilde gave herself fully to the role of mother superior, and when her term was completed in 1937, she returned to her beloved Mount Carmel School where she taught until 1952.

In 1937 Mother M. Liguori was again elected superior; her third term in office brought the Rochester Sisters of Mercy into the 1940s and World War II. With her keen sense of timing, she oversaw the addition of a new wing to Mercy High School in 1941 in order to accommodate the growing student body. In spite of the continuing national depression and unemployment problems, she had faith that God and the Lincoln Alliance Bank would provide for the welfare of the sisters and their students. She borrowed an additional $300,000 for the new wing.[15]

The addition to Mercy High School included an 1100 seat auditorium, a stage with forty-foot high fly space and a counter weight system for storing lights and scenery over the stage. A new gymnasium, locker rooms, home economics unit, art studio and nurse's office were also added. Eight new classrooms and a library occupied the second and third floors of the new wing, which extended to the east and south from Blossom Road. According to the Brighton town historian, civilian air raid wardens gathered on the roof of this wing, the tallest building in Brighton, to watch for enemy aircraft during World War II.[16]

In the spring of 1945, the Middle States Evaluation committee came to Mercy High School to evaluate the school. Mercy's ratings went so far over the top in every area that the following October the Albany Commissioner of Education came to see for himself what he had heard about. At the end of his day's visit, which had been completely unannounced, he said, "What is happening in this school? I've never seen a busier, happier student body."[17]

History shows that things continued to happen at Mercy High School. In 1990 when Sister Barbara Hamm was principal, Mercy High School opened a middle school department, adding Grades 7-8 to the four years of high school. The building originally built for a college program housed the seventh and eighth grades. The faculty agreed that the middle school students had spirit and traditions that were uniquely theirs, but they were still an integral part of the whole school. Mercy High School introduced a new administrative position in 1990—the role of president. Sister Carol Wulforst served as the first president. Her role was promoting the mission of Mercy through public relations and working for Mercy in the broader community. Sister Carol made friends for Mercy over the years and firmly established an ongoing base of support for the future. Suzanne Klingler Johnston, a graduate of Mercy (1961), succeeded Carol as president in 2004. Suzanne brought many years of experience as both a teacher and an administrator in the Rochester City schools.

On June 24, 2001, ground was again broken and construction started for a new addition to Our Lady of Mercy High School. The new building project was the first major addition to the school since the auditorium and gymnasium were constructed in 1941. This new facility included an enlarged gymnasium, a library/media center, a fitness room, a four-floor elevator, and an atrium area for multi-purpose use. The new wing was dedicated in September 2003, on the 75th anniversary of Mercy High School.

Together these three sisters, (left to right) Sister Patricia Beairsto, Sister Joan McAteer and Sister Teresa Bolha have taught sixty-three years of Theology at Mercy High School.

New Leadership

After Mother M. Liguori's fourth term as superior (1940-1943), and while World War II was at its height, Sister M. Magdalene Schenck was chosen to lead the Rochester community. She had been assistant to Mother M. Liguori during her last term, so she was knowledgeable of the needs and dreams of the community. During Mother M. Magdalene's tenure as superior (1943-1949), the debts incurred during the 1930s and 1940s were paid in full. Mother M. Liguori served as treasurer during that time. Mother M. Magdalene was elected superior again from 1955 to 1961. Other important milestones during her administration included the opening of Notre Dame High School in Elmira in 1955, the centenary celebration of the Sisters of Mercy in the Diocese of Rochester in 1957, and the opening of the new Catherine McAuley College building in 1959.

Mother M. Magdalene always appreciated the dedication of the many lay friends of the congregation: the Mercy Guild, the alumnae of the schools, and the families and friends of the sisters who gave so generously of their time and resources. She worked well with priests, and found both Bishop James E. Kearney, the fifth bishop of Rochester, and Auxiliary Bishop Lawrence B. Casey always supportive in ventures undertaken by the congregation during her time in office. Mother M. Magdalene cared about young people, both in religious life and in society. Sister Dorothy Loeb described Mother M. Magdalene as a "positive influence on subsequent changes in religious life and in the church, having openness to the new, respecting the old. She was a reliable leader and woman of vision." [18]

Mother M. Magdalene's assistant in the 1940s was Mother M. Camilla McGuire, who was elected superior in 1949 and served until 1955. Mother M. Camilla had "a deep love and concern for the sisters and for the congregation. Education was one of her highest priorities and she appreciated the necessity of full-time graduate study for the teaching sisters."[19]   A woman of great intelligence and foresight, she led the community in a needed updating of its Constitutions.

Revising the Constitutions

In her book, *Catherine McAuley and the Tradition of Mercy*, Sister Mary Sullivan develops the history of the preparation and subsequent approval of the first *Rule and Constitutions* of the Sisters of Mercy. She writes,

> Catherine produced a *Rule and Constitutions* for the Sisters of Mercy which, while it is dependent in no small measure on the structure, concepts, and wording of the Presentations Sisters' *Rule and Constitutions*, has nonetheless a noticeably different character from its source. It is more tender in its expression, more humbly stated, and more confident in the good judgment of those who will observe the Rule.[20]

On June 6, 1841, Pope Gregory XVI approved the first *Rule and Constitutions* of the Sisters of Mercy. This text was in Italian, and for about twenty years a variety of handwritten or printed translations were used throughout the English-speaking world. This was the *Constitutions* that governed the Rochester community at its founding in 1857. In 1863, an approved English translation was printed in Dublin and many Mercy communities, including Rochester, began to use this translation.

In 1926 the Sacred Congregation in Rome made a revision of the Mercy *Constitutions* to bring it into harmony with the new *Code of Canon Law* promulgated in

1918. After that the Rochester community followed an English translation of the *Rule and Constitutions* which contained the modifications of the 1863 text.

In a decree issued in Rome on July 16, 1954, approval was given to the Rochester Sisters of Mercy for their request that "the structure of their house be changed into a centralized Congregation of Sisters, in the proper sense of this term, under the authority of a Mother General. The decree noted that "approval is given to the *Constitutions* which have been properly corrected and adapted to this juridical change."[21] It was Mother M. Camilla who led this change in the government structure and the accompanying revision of the *Constitutions*. In 1953 she wrote the following in a letter to the community:

> The adoption of a revised, approved *Rule* does not mean doing away with our original *Rule* or its spirit; it does mean omitting or changing points of the *Rule* which are now obsolete or impossible of execution; this, to the end that the spirit of our holy foundress may be preserved intact . . . [22]

An important change was in the method of electing the superior and the members of the council. The new *Constitutions* called for the election by the professed sisters of delegates who would, in turn, elect the mother general (previously called the mother superior). These same delegates would also nominate and elect the four members of the council. The term of office for the mother general and the council was changed from three years to six years. Moreover, the delegates were, with the mother general, the council and the former mother superior, the only members of the chapter. This was a significant change for the rest of the professed sisters, whose previous *Constitutions* had stated, "the sisters shall meet in Chapter as often as the Mother Superior may think it expedient to have their opinion on matters of importance to the community,[23] including the election of the superior."

The 1954 *Constitutions* were temporarily approved for a period of five years; however, it would be ten years later, in 1964, that the *Constitutions* of 1954 would be formally approved by Pope Paul VI.

Our Lady of Mercy Motherhouse Chapel

Mother M. Camilla was also responsible for the building of the motherhouse chapel. When the motherhouse on Blossom Road opened in 1931, no provision was made for a chapel large enough to accommodate the entire community of Sisters of Mercy. Instead, a small oratory on the third floor was used for private prayer and benediction of the Blessed Sacrament, and daily Mass for the motherhouse sisters was celebrated in a temporary chapel in two converted classrooms on the third floor of Mercy High School. However, ground was broken in May 1949 for a new chapel at the motherhouse, to be built directly opposite the main entrance. Joseph P. Flynn was the architect and Daniel J. Meagher Inc. was general contractor. The chapel was formally dedicated on February 12, 1951, at a pontifical high Mass celebrated by Bishop Kearney. Reverend John T. Callahan, chaplain, assisted, and the sisters' choir provided the liturgical music.

Besides the main altar, there were two side altars made of Italian marble and dedicated to Our Lady of Grace and St. Joseph. The wood furnishings of both the sanctuary and main part of the chapel are of white Appalachian oak and the interior of the chapel is trimmed with Tennessee marble.

The stained glass windows depict eleven of the special patron saints of the order chosen by Catherine McAuley and listed in the first *Constitutions*. One window honors Saint John Fisher, Bishop of Rochester, England, a theologian and martyr who is the patron saint of the Diocese of Rochester. In the west transept there are two small windows over the door leading to the vestry. The first window is a representation of Catherine McAuley, symbolically receiving the initial approval of the congregation of the Sisters of Mercy on May 3, 1835 from Pope Gregory XVI. The second small window is a symbolic representation of Catherine McAuley and the Sisters of Mercy professing their vows on December 12, 1831 after completing their novitiate at the Presentation Convent in Dublin.

The new chapel, which accommodated 350 people, was also furnished with a pipe organ and an electronic bell system. The choir loft afforded an opportunity for the sisters in the infirmary to attend Mass and other services. For the first time since the Sisters of Mercy moved to Blossom Road, they had a beautiful chapel suitable for liturgies as well as private prayer. The inscription above the doorway welcomes all who enter: "Magister Adest et Vocat Te" (The Master dwells here and calls you). Over the years since 1951, thousands have walked through that doorway for Eucharistic celebrations, receptions, professions, funerals, and other ceremonies.

Celebrating 100 Years in Rochester

One hundred years after the first Sisters of Mercy arrived in Rochester, Mother M. Magdalene Schenck, in her second time as superior, took note of "that memorable day" in a letter to friends of the Rochester Sisters of Mercy on March 25, 1957, when she announced the celebration of the centenary:

At that time, even the most optimistic and hopeful of that little group of Sisters could not visualize the service they were to render the people of the

31

diocese in the ensuing hundred years. The Sisters of Mercy now staff twenty-five elementary schools, three secondary schools and a hospital. Their latest contribution to the diocese in the field of education is the founding of a college for the professional training of the young Sisters, the future religious teachers of your children.[24]

Sister Dorothy Schlueter (M. Peter) wrote and directed "The Magnificat of Mercy," a pageant portraying the ministries of the Sisters of Mercy in the Rochester diocese and honoring Catherine McAuley and the American foundress Frances Warde. The pageant, including interpretative dance, choric speech and a musical background, featured hundreds of students taught by the Sisters of Mercy from Mercy High School and five local elementary schools: St. John the Evangelist, St. James, St. Andrew's, St. Rita's and Our Lady of Mount Carmel. Patricia Donovan, who served as stage manager for the production, recalled her memories of the occasion. She reflected on the wonderful selections chosen for the pageant which made the public conscious of the history of the Sisters of Mercy during the Crimean War and the American Civil War.

Sister Dorothy's background in English, coupled with the expertise of Sister M. Pius Keough in speech and drama, helped to make the production a truly professional undertaking. Patricia Donovan later reflected:

> For the first time we realized the corporate reality of Catherine McAuley and Frances Warde nationally and internationally. The pageant made us more aware of the social evils of our time, not just the story of our Catholic schools. 'The Magnificat of Mercy' helped the sisters and the audience to be aware that they were part of something larger than

the Rochester community.[25]

Tribute was paid in the program to Sister M. Florence Sullivan, principal of Our Lady of Mercy High School, "whose untiring efforts have made possible this program" and to Sister M. Margaret Saunders, director of the Glee Club and head of the music department at the high school.[26]

On June 1, 1957, Bishop Lawrence B. Casey celebrated a pontifical requiem Mass in the motherhouse chapel for all deceased Sisters of Mercy. In his homily, the bishop said:

> Fundamentally, the struggles of these pioneers of South Street to develop their life and live up to the ideals of their religious vocation were the same as yours. Human nature doesn't change much in a century, and it must be a source of strength that this goodly company of your nuns who rest in Holy Sepulchre Cemetery trod the same kind of path you are walking—and through the grace of God made a success of their vocation and achieved the ultimate victory.[27]

Bishop Kearney presided at a pontifical Mass, June 15, 1957, at St. Mary's Church on South Street, the birthplace of the Sisters of Mercy in Rochester. Hundreds of religious, priests and lay friends of the sisters gathered for the celebration. The Sisters' choir, under the direction of Sister Dorothy Keefe (M. Joanne), sang an original three-part Mass, "Missa Salve Regina," composed by Sister M. Alexius Wood.

Congratulations came from many people. The Board of Directors of St. James Mercy Hospital dedicated the June 1957 issue of "Mercy Echoes" to the Sisters of Mercy with the words, "The continued success of St. James Mercy Hospital is due to the indefatigable labors of the

Sisters."[28] The medical staff and the women's board also paid tribute: ". . . the Sisters have been an inspiration to the many thousands who enter the hospital to receive medical care."[29] Mr. Frederick J. Shortall, a former pupil of the Sisters of Mercy at St. Mary's School, wrote:

> As I watched the story of the Sisters unfold I could not but relive my share in the drama as some of the scenes recalled vividly many a happy day at Old St. Mary's, class of '25. So the pageant was for me, as it was for so many others, a significant drama.[30]

The school children taught by the Sisters of Mercy gave $14,066 to the centenary fund through baked food sales and other fundraising activities. The hundredth anniversary celebration was the work of many Mercy supporters.

CHAPTER THREE

THE MINISTRY OF EDUCATION

T he story of the founding of the Sisters of Mercy strongly affirms Catherine McAuley's belief that service to the poor, especially women and children, was the highest priority in her life. Catherine could not forget the faces of those in need. "She seems always to have put herself in the position of those who suffer and to have felt their suffering as her own."[1] Visitation of the sick, a soup kitchen, prison ministry, day care for children of working parents, a House of Mercy for young women in need, a free school for poor children— these were some of the ways in which the early Rochester Mercy sisters served the needy of their day. As years passed and the community grew, the sisters identified in greater numbers with the ministry of education. For the immigrant population, education was the key to their adjusting to American life. The development of a strong parochial school system that reached out to the immigrants was always a goal in the Rochester Diocese with each succeeding bishop.

The Sisters of Mercy had moved slowly into the parish education scene. In 1906 and despite Bishop McQuaid's reluctance, they opened the new Holy Cross School in Charlotte at the invitation of the pastor, William Payne, who had come to the parish in 1905. The original school, built in 1887 and staffed by the Rochester Sisters of St. Joseph, was destroyed by a fire in June 1895. Father John Fitzgerald, the pastor, was apparently not anxious to build a new school, so the Sisters of St. Joseph left the parish to serve in other schools.

From 1909 to 1928, during Bishop Thomas Hickey's tenure, the Mercy sisters acquired ten new schools, and from 1950 to 1963, under Bishop James E. Kearney's leadership, nine more parishes invited the Sisters of Mercy to teach in newly built schools.

St. James School in Irondequoit and St. Louis School in Pittsford both opened in 1950. St. Louis School was housed originally in a mansion built on Main Street. This building served as both school and convent for the five pioneer teachers. A new building was not erected until 1956. Eight other schools followed in quick succession: St. Cecilia's in Irondequoit; St. Michael's in Newark; St. Rita's in West Webster; St. Joseph's in Penfield; Our Lady of Lourdes in Elmira; School of the Annunciation in Rochester; Good Shepherd in Henrietta; and Our Lady of Mercy in Greece. From 1960 to 1963 the Sisters of Mercy were invited to staff four additional elementary schools: St. Mary's in Bath, Our Lady Queen of Peace in Brighton, and St. John of Rochester in Perinton; St. Helen parish in Gates requested the Sisters of Mercy to staff the school after the Franciscan Sisters decided to return to their motherhouse in Allegany. By 1963 the sisters were teaching in 31 parish schools in six of the twelve counties of the diocese.

The stories of the women who brought their skills

and influence to the growth of these schools are as varied as the women themselves. In the words of Catherine McAuley:

> The Sisters appointed by the Mother Superior to attend the Schools shall with all zeal, charity and humility, purity of intention and confidence in God undertake the charge and cheerfully submit to every labor and fatigue . . . mindful of their vocation, and of the glorious recompense attached to the faithful discharge of this duty.[2]

Priests and dedicated laity worked side by side with them, but it was the sisters' willingness to move wherever they were needed and to serve for little or no recompense that helped create a parochial school system that in the 1950s enrolled 11 percent of all the students in the United States.[3]

When the new Holy Cross School building opened in 1906, the founding principal was Sister M. Borgia O'Keefe. She had entered the Sisters of Mercy in 1892, the same month she graduated from Holy Child Academy in Philadelphia. Within three months, she was teaching eighth grade at St. Mary's in Rochester. Her teaching certificate was earned on weekends and summers. Mary Borgia served at Holy Cross for seven years (1906-1913). Parishioners described her in these words: "The strength of her influence has been felt throughout the parish. She was director of the young ladies Sodality and greatly interested in the young people of the parish."[4] She also served as founding principal of St. Andrew's School, which opened in 1915. She was later called to be principal at St. Vincent's, Corning; St. John the Evangelist (Humboldt Street) in Rochester; and St. Cecilia's in Elmira. Simultaneously, she was the eighth grade teacher in each school. When she retired, she had taught in parish schools for fifty years. She died at the Blossom Road motherhouse at 89 years of age—still active and engaged in community life.

In 1996, ninety years after it had opened, Sister Carolyn Knipper was the last Mercy sister to serve as principal at Holy Cross School. Unlike Mary Borgia O'Keefe, Carolyn's position was full-time in administration. She had completed a Master's degree in Education and brought a variety of educational experiences to the ministry of administration. Mary Borgia O'Keefe would have been pleased with this development.

In 1916 St. John the Evangelist School on Humboldt Street opened its doors to 118 students and four Sisters of Mercy with Sister M. Sacred Heart Lundergan as principal. By the 1950s when Sister M. dePazzi Connor was completing twenty years as St. John's principal, there were thirteen sisters and 641 students. This parish has always been special for Mercy sisters because of its proximity to the motherhouse. All reception and profession ceremonies for the Sisters of Mercy were held in St. John's Church before the motherhouse chapel was built. When the small convent could not house all the sisters, some lived at the motherhouse and walked to St. John's School. Over the years fifty women from the school or parish entered the Sisters of Mercy. Many graduates of the school still remember Sister M. Anna Failey, who taught primary grades there for thirty-six years. Sister Margaret Caufield also taught music at St. John's for thirty-six years. After Margaret retired, she continued her service to the parish in liturgical and bereavement ministry.

There is a similarity in the stories of three Sisters of Mercy who ministered as elementary school principals in the Rochester diocesan schools. Each of them was a high school teacher before she chose administration in the elementary schools. Sister Mary Alice O'Brien was a home economics teacher and vice-principal of Mercy High School when she decided to join the St. Andrew's School faculty as principal.   When Sister Dorothea Dennis, principal of St. Andrew's for 41 years, welcomed the students, they were mostly white children of German descent; in the 1980s Sister Mary Alice O'Brien welcomed a student body of great diversity: Hispanic, African-American and Caucasian.

Fifteen years later in 1997 Mary Alice moved to St. Margaret Mary's School in West Irondequoit as principal. In December of 1997 she was selected to receive the 1998 "Distinguished Principal Award" from the National Catholic Educational Association.   Each year this award is given to Catholic school educators who manifest in their daily interactions with students and other colleagues their commitment to "teach as Jesus did."[5]   Sister Mary Alice developed a teaching kit for elementary school teachers to share the story of Catherine McAuley and the Sisters of Mercy.

Sister Katherine Ann Rappl, a former science teacher at Notre Dame High School in Elmira, guided the faculty and students at St. Rita's School for over twenty-two years.   An article in the Sisters of Mercy newsletter in November 1998 told the story of her ministry at St. Rita's: "Congratulations to Katherine Ann Rappl who was awarded Channel 8's *Apple for the Teacher* award the week of October 20."   Christina Smith, a second grader at St. Rita, nominated her with the following letter:

> Dear Channel 8, My favorite teacher is my school "head of all teachers."   She is my principal, Katherine Ann Rappl.   And I just found out her last name was Rappl because we all call her Sister Katherine Ann.
>
> She is like a good commercial.   When my teacher, Mrs. Peck, is busy, Sister always fills in.   She is the bestest one in the school.   She never yells!   And

always is there to talk or wait on the bench with you. And the bad stories about her stealing Tooth Fairy money is Sister just kidding.

And I hope you pick Sister Katherine Ann because she likes new food and she never gets to go out much because she's always busy with crazy kids. Thank you.

Sister Katherine Ann was featured during the October 23, 1998 evening news in a segment honoring her hard work and efforts at St. Rita School.[6]

The Business Department of Notre Dame High School in Elmira kept Sister Dolores Ann Stein busy for sixteen years. But she responded to the call to administration during a time when principals were very needed in the elementary school system. In choosing St. Ann's School (Hornell), Dolores Ann continued a long tradition of Mercy presence there. Two years after its opening in 1871, St. Ann's School welcomed 436 students. In 1879, when Father James Early was pastor, the sisters were, for the first time, paid a stipend--$200 a year to each sister for her service to the school and parish. From 1899 to 1901, St. Ann's convent was the motherhouse for the southern tier Sisters of Mercy. Dolores Ann was the twentieth Sister of Mercy to serve as principal. In the 1976 anniversary booklet, the parish made the following dedication:

> To the Sisters of Mercy
> who have given to the "Hornellsville Mission"
> a century of labor and love,
> this booklet is gratefully dedicated.

From Sister M. Eileen Fitzgibbons who worked with elementary school children for forty years, to Sister

Karlien Bach who challenged junior high students for over twenty-five years, the Sisters of Mercy have given a "century of labor and love" to the parish elementary schools.

Catholic Secondary Education

Catholic secondary education grew more slowly in the diocese. According to Father Robert McNamara, Bishop McQuaid's scholastic program, which was so strong in elementary education, was not so successful in establishing secondary schools during the bishop's lifetime.[7] However, when Bishop Hickey was consecrated bishop of Rochester, he moved the secondary educational programs into the forefront. In 1921 he requested two Mercy Sisters for the faculty of Rochester Catholic High School. Mother M. Benedict Donovan, superior at the time, received the request with joy; the Sisters of Mercy had not been included in the faculty when the school opened in the early 1900s during Bishop McQuaid's time. In 1925 Rochester Catholic High School became Aquinas Institute; over the years twenty-one Sisters of Mercy served on its faculty, working in collaboration with the Basilian priests, the Sisters of St. Joseph and lay men and women.

Bishop Hickey encouraged elementary schools, where possible, to add a ninth grade to the existing curriculum. From 1904 to 1911 the Sisters of Mercy maintained a ninth grade in St. Mary's School in Corning. In 1912 St. Ann's School in Hornell added a year of high school, which continued successfully until 1950. St. Mary's School of Business opened in 1914 in conjunction with St. Mary's School on South Street—the first mission of the Rochester Mercy Sisters. Sister M. Pauline Mills, the principal, served the school for over thirty years. However, in 1945 she became ill in the middle of the school term and died on Valentine's Day of that year.

41

Gradually, the need for a special business school declined and the school closed in 1950 despite the creativity and enthusiasm of Sister Carolyn Lattinville (M. William) and Sister M. Christopher Williams, both of whom taught there from the early 1940s until its closure.

Bishop John Francis O'Hern is credited with opening two high schools outside Monroe County. Holy Family, a four year high school housed in the Holy Family school in Auburn, began at the suggestion of Bishop O'Hern. In 1930 he observed empty classrooms in the elementary school building and recommended that a high school be opened. The first principal was a Sister of Mercy, Sister M. Martha Lavey, who also taught classes along with Father Donald M. Cleary, a diocesan priest. The following year a tenth grade was added to the school, and Sister M. Julia Ryan and Father Leo Hastings joined the faculty. Another diocesan priest, Father William E. Davie, became principal in 1932. Seventeen Sisters of Mercy taught there over the years; Sister Jane Hasbrouck (M. Cyprian) who was on the faculty in the early fifties, described the school years at Holy Family as she remembered them:

> It was an ideal place to teach, despite the limitations of space and resources. The size of the school made it possible for the whole faculty to know each student, and there was an easy relationship between teachers and students. A unique parish school, there was a lot of school spirit and morale, and students stayed in touch over the years. Today we would say that we formed a very close school community.[8]

Holy Family High School was gradually replaced by the new Mount Carmel High School. Holy Family High continued under the guidance of Sister M. Julia Ryan until 1957 when the last class graduated. In the commemorative booklet *Holy Family High School 1930-1957*, alumni expressed their feelings in these words,

> the spiritual and intellectual formation of the Holy Family High School students was in the able and dedicated hands of the Sisters of Mercy. These women worked tirelessly without recognition or recompense to educate us and to establish the spirit of Holy Family that we carry with us. We thank them![9]

Holy Family fostered several vocations to the religious life and priesthood. Fifteen graduates became Sisters of Mercy of Rochester. Sister Mary Jaeckle (Mary Aquin) of the class of 1936, the first to enter the community from Holy Family High School, celebrated sixty-five years as a Sister of Mercy in 2002. She remembers in a special way Sister M. Hilary Carroll, a "fine blend of the teacher and the religious." Sister Mary Jaeckle described Holy Family High School as a place of great spirit and camaraderie.

Catholic Secondary Education in Elmira

Like Holy Family High School in Auburn, Elmira Catholic High School grew from one year of high school level education that opened at St. Peter and Paul's School in 1930. Two years later the high school moved to St. Patrick's School in order to accommodate all its students in a four-year program. In 1933 Sisters M. Carmella Coene, M. Constance Casey, and Georgina Lannan, SSJ, joined the faculty. Reverend Francis Reilly, a diocesan priest, was the first principal. On the occasion of the dedication of the expanded Elmira Catholic High School, Bishop John F. O'Hern spoke to a large gathering of people at St. Patrick's Church in Elmira:

43

Our Catholic people of Elmira want this high school. They better than others know the cost of sacrifice. It may have a humble origin, so did the Teacher of Galilee, also his Church. Citizens of the present and of the future will give unending thanks for educating our high school boys and girls in the wisdom of Christ and his Church.[10]

In a telephone interview in June 2001 Sister M. Carmella reflected on the early years at Elmira Catholic High School where she taught the first graduating class of 1934; she taught math and science and knew every student:

Those were happy days. We were very close-knit, few in number. We had very good students who came to school to learn. Our school was unusual; it was a small place and we had very little to work with. With no official sports program, we concentrated on academics and turned out extraordinary men and women who gave to the community.[11]

Elmira Catholic High School thrived for twenty-five years. It boasted many outstanding alumnae/alumni, including members of the priesthood, women religious, civic leaders, and professional business men and women. Eleven of the seventeen women who entered religious life became Sisters of Mercy of Rochester, including Marie Kruckow (Mary Matthew) and Mary Rita Sullivan (Mary Damian), valedictorian and salutatorian of the class of 1935, respectively.

Twenty years would pass before the Rochester diocese again began planning for more secondary schools to educate the growing number of Catholic students at that level. The diocese launched a drive in the early fifties to build four new high schools. In 1952 the "Bishop Kearney"

Jubilee High School Fund Campaign" raised five million dollars to build the new McQuaid Jesuit High School in Rochester, St. Agnes High School in Rochester, Mount Carmel High School in Auburn, and Notre Dame High School in Elmira. Mount Carmel, staffed by the Carmelite Fathers and the Sisters of St. Joseph, replaced Holy Family High in Auburn, and Elmira Catholic High School became Notre Dame High School under the guidance of the Sisters of Mercy.

Notre Dame High School

Notre Dame High School in Elmira opened its doors in September 1955 with thirteen Sisters of Mercy eagerly waiting to greet the first students, the parents and friends who came for the dedication and blessing by Bishop James E. Kearney. On September 24, after the crucifix was blessed by the bishop and hung in the foyer, the people processed with him into the new auditorium for the celebration of the Mass of the Feast of Our Lady of Mercy. Notre Dame students, under the direction of diocesan liturgist Reverend Benedict A. Ehmann, provided the liturgical music program.

In a special supplement to the *Catholic Courier-Journal* on September 22, 1955, the sisters expressed their thanks and appreciation to "their many friends who have shown such keen interest in the progress of Notre Dame High School from its first conception to the opening of its doors on September 7 of this year." The sisters were especially grateful to Mr. Leo Considine, contractor, for his untiring work; to Mr. Cornelius J. Milliken and the staff of the *Elmira Star-Gazette* for their long range and thorough news coverage; to Notre Dame's many benefactors, and to Elmira's loyal clergy for their continued support. Sister M. Cecelia Redmond, principal at St. Patrick's school, had "procured the fine location of Notre Dame on the outskirts of the city of Elmira." Launching Notre Dame High School was a major venture for the Sisters of Mercy at that time, as they were already teaching more than ten thousand students in elementary and secondary schools in the diocese.[12]

(left to right) Sisters Mary Edwina Butler, M. Beatrice Curran, M. Joachim Pearson, M. Carmella Coene and M. Edmond Gauthier

The thirteen pioneer Sisters of Mercy at Notre Dame included Sister M. Raphael Spillane, principal; M. Alberta Kuhn, vice-principal; M. Edwina Butler, M. Hilary Carroll, M. Carmella Coene, M. Beatrice Curran, M. Edmond Gauthier, M. Jane Frances Hauser, M. Patrick Kennedy, M. Jeanne McNiff, M. Joachim Pearson, Mary Anne Steinmetz, and M. Christopher Williams. Reverend Joseph F. Hogan, chaplain, also served as spiritual director and instructor in religion, and was available for private conferences. Some sister pioneers shared their memories of those early days:

Pioneering requires energy, imagination and

enthusiasm. Establishing continuity in a four year scholastic program was a challenge in itself. Fortunately our faculty was experienced and enthusiastic, so the early days were full of unexpected events that became traditions.

Sister M. Edwina Butler, RSM

It was a privilege to pioneer at Notre Dame, especially after having experienced the limited space at Elmira Catholic High School. Our joy in the new school was shared by the Elmira community who appreciated the potential for new opportunities to be offered to their young people.

Sister M. Carmella Coene, RSM[13]

Mary Carmella taught at the former Elmira Catholic High School from 1933 to 1940, and then for ten years at Mercy High School in Rochester. After three years at Holy Family High in Auburn and two years teaching in Hornell and Corning, she returned to Elmira in 1955 to teach science and math at Notre Dame High School. On September 7, 2004, Notre Dame broke ground to begin construction of a new science wing to be named after her: The Sister Mary Carmella Coene Science Wing. The wing includes new earth science, biology and chemistry classrooms and laboratories and a new math and physics classroom. The $4.2 million capital improvement plan also provided health and safety upgrades throughout the school in addition to the science wing.

In January 2000 Sister M. Walter Hickey, principal of Notre Dame since 1975, was the recipient of the Twin Tiers "Outstanding Educator" award. This award is administered by the *Elmira*

Star-Gazette. Recipients are selected by a community panel from nominations submitted by students, parents and other educators. In 2005 Notre Dame celebrated fifty years of service to the people of Elmira and the southern tier of New York State. Mary Walter Hickey served as principal for thirty of those years, an outstanding educator for both students and faculty members alike.

Cardinal Mooney High School

In September 1960 the Diocese of Rochester launched another drive to build two new high schools in the city, one in Irondequoit and one in Greece. Two years later, Bishop Kearney dedicated the Irondequoit high school named for him and staffed by the Irish Christian Brothers and the School Sisters of Notre Dame. The new Greece school, named for a former bishop of Rochester, Edward Cardinal Mooney of Detroit, was dedicated by Bishop Lawrence B. Casey who had been secretary to Cardinal Mooney during his time in Rochester. The Sisters of Mercy joined the Brothers of Holy Cross to staff this school. Sisters of Mercy who were on the first faculty included Sisters M. George Burns, M. Edwina Butler, Gertrude Erb (M. Gerard), M. Edmond Gauthier, Joanne Lappetito (M. Michael), and Patricia Switzer (Joseph Mary).

On the opening day in September 1962, 198 boys came to Cardinal Mooney, followed by 214 young women the next day. Waiting to greet the girls was Sister Mary Edwina, the vice-principal responsible for the women's wing of the building. One year later the enrollment had swelled to 336 boys and 398 young women. Cardinal Mooney High School would eventually welcome over 1300 in the student body. By 1972 the transition was made from co-institutional, separate instruction of boys and girls, to co-educational. Sisters Maureen Flood, Barbara Weyand

and Kathryn Wahl served as vice-principals during these years. Before Cardinal Mooney closed its doors in 1989 because of serious financial difficulties, more than sixty Sisters of Mercy had walked its halls and left the spirit of Mercy with the students and their families. From the ranks of its women graduates, seven entered the Sisters of Mercy.

Sister M. Eymard Hyland, the Sister of Mercy who had the longest tenure at Cardinal Mooney High School (1967-1989), recalls:

> There was a wonderful rapport at Cardinal Mooney among the students, faculty and families. The enthusiasm of the Brothers of Holy Cross and the spirit of the Sisters of Mercy blended into a Mooney spirit which we referred to as the "M & M's" (Mercy/Mooney), making us more of a community than a school. Mooney became a hub for many happy hours, now memories, which made its closing all the harder. But as someone said during those difficult days in 1989, 'As long as even one Mooney student lives, that Mooney spirit lives on.'[14]

The Education of Sister-Teachers

The preparation and education of sisters for the important ministry of teaching became an increasing priority for the Sisters of Mercy in the late 1940s. The rapid growth of the school system in the diocese was an incentive for the congregation to intensify its efforts in the preparation of sister teachers. In the early days, sisters began teaching immediately after their years of novitiate and spent summers and Saturdays completing their degrees.

In 1936, teacher training courses at the Mercy motherhouse were approved by the State Education Department of New York with the understanding that the sisters would meet the requirements for a three year normal school diploma in another institution. In a letter from the State Education Department dated January 2, 1936, and addressed to Sister M. John Rourke, principal of Mercy Normal School, she was advised:

> that the Sisters complete a third year in the Nazareth Normal School [Rochester, New York, staffed by the Sisters of St. Joseph] or another institution offering an approved three year curriculum for the preparation of sister teachers, such as Teachers College, Fordham University, New York City; Mount St. Joseph's Normal School, Buffalo; or other recognized institutions. This arrangement seemed to be satisfactory to the authorities.[15]

In June 1940 Mother M. Liguori received a letter from the State Education Department notifying her that after July 1, 1941, all elementary teachers eligible for certification to teach in the public schools would be required to have four years of approved preparation in elementary education.[16]

In the 1940s the new members of the Sisters of Mercy who were preparing to be teachers attended either Nazareth College or Nazareth Normal School. However, in 1951 a teacher education program was created and inaugurated under the leadership of Sister Mary dePazzi Connor at the Mercy motherhouse with the permission and under the supervision of the New York State Education Department. Its primary purpose was the education and formation of the young Sisters of Mercy who would be future teachers.

Three years later, a provisional charter was granted which recognized the education program as an official college of New York State. The charter was granted with the understanding between the state and the Sisters of

Mercy that a new building would be erected within five years to house the college. So, in May 1954 Catherine McAuley College became a long awaited reality for the Mercy community.

Mother M. Magdalene Schenck (left) and Sister M. dePazzi Connor assist Bishop James E. Kearney at the groundbreaking ceremony for the college wing on September 24, 1957.

On Mercy Day in 1957, the year of the sisters' 100th anniversary in Rochester, Mother M. Magdalene invited the people and priests of the diocese to a groundbreaking ceremony for the new Catherine McAuley College. Bishop Kearney celebrated a pontifical Mass and then turned the first shovelful of earth for the multi-purpose building that would serve the community into the twenty-first century. The building was formally dedicated on November 8, 1959, five years from the granting of the provisional charter. Two floors were reserved for the college program and two floors for a residence for sisters, the novitiate occupying one of these floors. The new building also included a special services wing which housed a reading clinic, speech laboratories, and a testing and guidance center. The generosity of the people of the Rochester diocese made the McAuley building possible; they donated specifically to the reading laboratory, the college library and the sisters' residence on the second and third floors. A tribute to these donors hangs in the first floor of the building, with the names of all who contributed to this project.

An absolute charter was granted in 1959, empowering the college to grant the Associate in Applied Science degree, and a year later the Associate in Arts degree. The State Education Department also gave permission to open the college to women religious of other orders and to lay students on a part-time basis. Professors from Catherine McAuley College also offered college credit courses in science and psychology at St. James Mercy Hospital School of Nursing in Hornell, New York.

In 1967 a major change was made with respect to curriculum. Students would attend the college for only two years and the associate degree was conferred at the end of that period. There were a number of reasons for this decision: (1) a relatively small number of sisters were in the first three years of religious life; (2) the third-year students had sufficient credits to transfer to a four-year college rather than take additional course work at Catherine McAuley College; and (3) the low enrollment brought long-range financial concerns as well as a lack of full-time faculty members. One year later in 1968, with the unanimous consent of its Board of Trustees, and after extensive discussion with Dr. Robert Kirkwood, Executive Director, Commission on High Education, Middle States Association, Catherine McAuley College closed its doors to full-time operation.

Many Sisters of Mercy made the college a vital source of learning, but three are remembered in a special way: Sister M. dePazzi Connor, dean from 1951 to1966; Sister Dorothy Schlueter (M. Peter), a faculty member from 1954 to 1968; and Sister Mary Sullivan (M. Petrus), a faculty member from 1963 to 1967 and president of the college from 1965 to 1968. At the last graduation ceremony on June 4, 1968, Sister Mary Sullivan gave tribute to Sister M. dePazzi:

> To Sister Mary dePazzi, our dean from 1951 to 1966, in every sense the foundress of Catherine McAuley College, we offer our greatest expression of admiration and gratefulness. More than any other single person in the history of this college, Sister M. dePazzi has been its life-force, its movement and its imagination. For all intents and purposes, Sister M. dePazzi was the president of the college, the center of responsibility for it and the bearer of its burdens for the first fourteen years of its existence. The symbols of her dogged work in administration and in teaching, of her intense zeal for the growth of the minds of the community, and her truly charismatic enthusiasm are to be found in every corner of the visible and invisible life of this college.
>
> The decision to close Catherine McAuley College is based on reasons entirely extrinsic to the undeniable and enduring value of Sister M. dePazzi's primary aims and accomplishments. Instead, it is true to say that what is terminated in 1968 is not her work of education and formation but simply one structure, one means of doing that work.
>
> Sister Mary Sullivan, June 4, 1968[17]

After her service at Catherine McAuley College, Sister Dorothy Schlueter was the first woman religious in New York State to become a certified clinical psychologist. She used her education and skills for the Diocese of Rochester as the tribunal clinical psychologist, analyzing petitions for marriage annulment. She also served as a panel psychologist for the New York State Bureau of Disability Determination. She taught psychology at St. John Fisher College, Nazareth College and the University of Rochester and was also a psychologist on the staff of Rochester General Hospital.

Sister Mary Sullivan served on the faculty of Marymount College in Tarrytown, New York and taught at Malcolm-King Harlem Community Extension College. In 1969 she joined the faculty of the College of Liberal Arts at Rochester Institute of Technology. She was appointed dean of this college (1977-1987) and later served as chair of the Academic Senate and the Language and Literature Department.

Reading Laboratory

Sister M. dePazzi also founded the reading laboratory, part of the special services wing of the college. In 1951 it was started as an adjunct of the teacher education program of the Sisters of Mercy. From that time until 1972, thousands of school children were helped to become skilled readers and better students. A testing program and a speech clinic were also included in the services. Mrs. Helen Wheeler, Reading Coordinator for the Rochester Board of Education, visited the laboratory and wrote the following note to Sister M. dePazzi:

> Our general feeling is that here there exists a wonderful situation where children are being rehabilitated in very healthy surroundings. Your

combined leadership, enthusiasm, foresight and thoughtful planning have made this program the success that it is.[18]

After Sister Marilyn Williams completed her Master's in Education degree at Syracuse University, she was appointed to the Reading Laboratory. She believes:

> In an era when there were limited remedial services in both the public and private schools, Catherine McAuley Reading Lab provided helpful diagnostic services, small remedial reading classes and speech therapy, all of which gave children confidence and skills for the road to successful learning.[19]

When the reading laboratory celebrated its twentieth anniversary, Mother M. Bride Claire, major superior of the Rochester community, thanked the dozens of sisters who sacrificed Saturdays and summers to help students succeed in school. She also expressed her gratitude to Sister M. dePazzi for inculcating in the community enthusiasm for the professional teaching of reading. Over the years, the need for this program decreased, and in 1972 the laboratory closed its doors after twenty-one years of valuable services.

The Sister Formation Movement

The Sister Formation movement was responsible for changes in religious life before the advent of the Second Vatican Council in 1962. At an international meeting of religious superiors in 1950, Pope Pius XII urged mother superiors of teaching orders to concentrate on forming every sister into a "dynamic religious: psychologically mature, intellectually disciplined, broadly cultured and professionally competent—in short, a completely integrated personality working for Christ and his Church."[20]

During the next ten years this message influenced the thinking of major superiors, formation personnel, and women religious who were responsible for college education in the United States. Originally, the Sister Formation Conference functioned under the auspices of the National Catholic Education Association. In 1953 interested administrators established the group as a separate organization which would have as its goal "the formation of its women religious in all aspects: spiritual, intellectual and professional."

"Sister Formation grew from just professional certification to a concept of total education supportive of the religious vocation."[21] Eventually the Sister Formation Conference became a committee under the auspices of the Conference of Major Superiors which had been formed in 1959 at the suggestion of the Vatican.

Catherine McAuley College was one response of the Rochester Sisters of Mercy to the challenge of the Sister Formation movement. Its purpose was to educate sister-students in the spirit of their congregation and to provide them with excellent preparation for teaching.

The year 1961 marked the beginning of the Rochester community's active participation in various Sister Formation projects. They responded to the request of the Conference of Major Superiors of Women to assist them in educating young sisters from countries beyond the United States. In 1961 two sisters from Brazil were accepted by the Rochester Sisters of Mercy; they were not able to complete the planned program and returned home within a year. In 1962 two sisters arrived from India: Sister Edith and Sister Selka, both members of the Sisters of the Imitation of Christ. They graduated from Nazareth College in 1967 with four year degrees. In 1964 Sister Therese Mary Ellickal and Sister Attracta Furtado came from South India and successfully completed the program.

A series of noted speakers lectured at gatherings of

sisters on problems of the modern world, renewal and adaptation, scripture, faith, obedience and freedom in order to keep the community informed. A liturgical weekend, an in-service course on scripture, attendance at the Lake Region Sister Formation conferences were some of the spiritual benefits and opportunities for enrichment available for members of the community.

The Sister Formation movement touched the lives of the young women in formation as well as the professed sisters, offering opportunities for personal and professional preparation for the challenges that would come during the Second Vatican Council. In an interview, Sister M. Edwardine Weaver reflected:

> The Sister Formation movement had a major impact on my life by providing me the opportunity to attend the University of Dayton where it broadened my understanding of religious life and the institutional Church. It also provided me with educational tools that would impact my future ministry.[22]

Sister Edwardine served as the superintendent of the Rochester diocesan school system for five years (1981-1986) and studied at the University of Rochester's Warner Graduate School of Education and Human Development. She later served in a dual capacity as the Director of the Catholic School Leadership Program and Director of the Office of Professional Development at the University of Rochester.

The Sister Formation Conference changed its name to the Religious Formation Conference in 1976 when men religious became part of the movement. The group celebrated fifty years of existence in 2004.

CHAPTER FOUR

MEETING THE CHALLENGE OF CHANGE

As the Rochester Sisters of Mercy approached the beginning of the Second Vatican Council, they stood in a promising place in their history, and they welcomed the call to a new and closer relationship with other Sisters of Mercy to promote Catherine McAuley's ideals.

The McAuley Conference

> It is not what Mother McAuley did that should be your guide, but what she would do if she were living now.
>
> Joseph Gallen, SJ, Canon Lawyer

Father Gallen spoke these words in 1955 in Merion (Philadelphia) at a gathering of the major superiors of the seventeen independent congregations of the Sisters of Mercy in the United States. This gathering, later formalized as the McAuley Conference, planted a seed that grew into a new and vibrant relationship among all Sisters of Mercy in the United States within a period of thirty years.

The inspiration for this 1955 Conference came from Sister M. Lawrence Hallagan, a Sister of Mercy of Cedar Rapids, Iowa, who proposed to her own council in August 1954 that she would try "to meet with the Mothers General of the Sisters of Mercy outside the Union, with the hope that they might be able to work together, not for union, but for more unity in thinking and acting."[1]

Sister M. Lawrence was referring to those groups of Mercy Sisters who in 1929 had voted not to join with the thirty-nine motherhouses across the United States when they petitioned Rome to become the Sisters of Mercy of the Union. In 1954 when Sister M. Lawrence first proposed this concept of the seventeen congregations meeting around shared interests, there were 10,386 Sisters of Mercy in the United States: 5,535 in the Union which included nine provinces, and 4,851 in the seventeen independent groups.

At the Institute of Spirituality in Dallas, Pennsylvania, Sister M. Lawrence presented the idea of the conference to a group of Sisters of Mercy and to Father Joseph Gallen, SJ, the director of the Institute. Mother M. Camilla, superior of the Rochester congregation at that time, "enthusiastically supported the project." On September 7, 1954, she and four other representatives sent a letter to the other mothers general asking their opinion on the "feasibility of such a plan."[2]

Mother M. Camilla reported in mid-September that all the superiors were interested in such a gathering, and the Merion (Philadelphia) Sisters of Mercy offered to host the first meeting at Mater Misericordia Convent. Father Joseph Gallen, who had endorsed the idea, was invited to be the main speaker and consultant. It was at this meeting that he challenged the superiors to ask themselves, "What would

Catherine McAuley be doing if she were alive now?"

At the second meeting in the fall of 1955 in Buffalo, New York, the gathering was officially named the McAuley Conference—a title suggested by Mother Gertrude Mary of the Merion community. The goal of the conference was "to find strength in association with persons motivated by the spirit and mission of the same foundress, though separated geographically and governmentally."[3] That this goal was prophetic is evident in the words of Mother M. Patrick McCallion:

> At the very first meeting in Merion it was a pleasure and a delight to know that there were others who shared the same work and problems. The experience was really heart-lifting. At this meeting a common bond of unity was formed which had not existed before, even among the communities of the east . . . .[4]

After the initial gathering, seven more meetings took place from 1955 to 1965, including one educational conference in Pittsburgh in 1957. During these years, three Rochester superiors participated in the McAuley Conference: Mothers M. Camilla McGuire, M. Magdalene Schenck, and M. Bride Claire. Sisters M. Perpetua McHale and M. dePazzi Connor also attended two of the meetings in connection with their work with the sisters in formation.

At the third conference held in West Hartford, Connecticut in 1956, the most controversial issue on the agenda was a proposal to invite the nine provincials of the Sisters of Mercy of the Union to future meetings. After a lengthy discussion, the superiors agreed to invite two representatives from the Sisters of Mercy of the Union: Mother M. Maurice Tobin, Mother General, and her assistant Mother M. Bernardine Purcell. These two women from Bethesda, Maryland, where the Union's Generalate (motherhouse) was located, attended the fourth McAuley Conference held in Cedar Rapids, Iowa in 1957. Sister M. Lawrence Hallagan had missed the West Hartford discussion and was unaware of the decision to invite only the two superiors. With true Midwest courtesy, she invited four neighboring Union provincials to the meeting in Cedar Rapids.[5] The McAuley Conference thus took a new direction.

The Conference continued to meet until 1965. It raised issues and discussed topics that all congregations were dealing with—the formation and education of young religious, the advantages of psychological testing before admitting candidates, the canonization of Catherine McAuley, canon law with respect to religious life, the apostolate, the formation of local superiors, spiritual growth, and the modification of the habit.

The Second Vatican Council, 1962-1965

The Second Vatican Council, which opened in 1962, encouraged religious communities to return to their roots, and to study the charism of their foundress. The Decree on the *Adaptation and Renewal of Religious Life (Perfectae Caritatis)* was promulgated by the Vatican Council in 1965. In it Pope Paul VI and the Council Fathers encouraged the formation of federations of religious congregations who claimed the same foundress. The McAuley Conference delegates were not ready for total union, but they were ready for a federation. The most important change in its structure would be the inclusion of the nine provincials of the Sisters of Mercy of the Union as members with equal voice in the proceedings. At the last business meeting of the Conference, the following resolution was approved by all those present:

BE IT RESOLVED: That in accordance with the

wishes of the Church and expressed through the propositions on religious life of the Second Vatican Council, definite steps be taken toward a World Federation of the Sisters of Mercy; that as one such step this Mother McAuley Conference be formed into a Federation of the Sisters of Mercy of the Americas; that in such federation the autonomy of each Congregation be preserved.[6]

As Sister M. Augustine Roth of Cedar Rapids writes in her history of the McAuley Conference:

On May 15, 1965 the McAuley Conference gave way to the Federation of the Sisters of Mercy of the Americas—the grain of wheat had produced the plant. Ideas had changed since 1955; the tensions between union and independent congregations had eased; the term "federation" no longer connoted a loss of autonomy; "unity", too suggestive of "union" a decade before was in favor in 1965; but the idea of sharing—that basic purpose of the McAuley Conference—did not change. And as the Federation continues, it has as its foundation the Mother McAuley Conference of Sisters of Mercy, who, sharing ideas and sharing in spirit, had indeed been a group of communities that were one in Christ through Mercy.[7]

The McAuley Conference had provided fertile ground for planting the seeds of the Second Vatican Council among the Sisters of Mercy. The sharing and cooperative efforts that had occurred in the Conference pointed out ways to grow and change in the direction the Council was moving. The Rochester community stepped up to the challenge.

In the Council document on the renewal of religious life, all religious were challenged to "adjust their rules and

62

customs to fit the demands of the apostolate to which they are dedicated."[8]

> The adaptation and renewal of the religious life includes both the constant return to the sources of all Christian life and to the original spirit of the institutes and their adaptation to the changed conditions of our times.[9]

Other directives ordered the various institutes to re-examine their governance; re-edit their directories, custom books, books of prayer and ceremonies; suppress obsolete laws; and adapt to the decrees of the Council and its subsequent synod.   Renewal of spirit should "take precedence over even active ministry."[10]

The Sisters of Mercy in Rochester and throughout the United States followed the call of the Vatican Council to adapt and renew religious life. Mother M. Bride Claire was superior of the Rochester congregation from 1961 to 1970 during the years of the Council and the period of renewal that followed. Born in Ireland, Bride Claire had a great love of Catherine McAuley and the Sisters of Mercy. She had served for nine years on the leadership council before being elected as the major superior; thus she came to that role as an experienced woman who was truly loved by the sisters. She moved ahead in the spirit of renewal and made sure the community was moving with her. As she often reminded the sisters, "We have moved with caution and deliberation in our renewal changes to avoid confusion and misunderstanding that often comes when haste is the tempo."[11]

In retrospect, the members of the community did try "to move with caution and deliberation," but misunderstandings surfaced which caused pain for many sisters. This period of history which challenged all women religious, may well be understood only by those who experienced it. Some sisters felt the congregation moved too quickly, while others saw it moving too slowly in adapting to the "changed conditions of our times." Not all welcomed the liturgical renewal and the creativity in community prayer. Local communities struggled to have their daily schedule meet the needs of sisters serving in a variety of ministries. Women accustomed to periods of silence in their day found it difficult to engage in what seemed like endless discussion, only to arrive at a decision that had once been easily made by the superior. These years of change were difficult ones, but as Mother M. Bride had said at the beginning of the renewal: "Each of us will not always agree with the other—we will disagree and that will be good."[12]

Chapter 1967-1969

The initial work of renewing religious life was carried out in a series of meetings called chapters. A chapter is the highest governing body of a congregation while the chapter is in session; the chapter's responsibility, vested in the designated delegates, is to legislate general policy to be implemented at all levels of community life. Pope Paul VI had reminded religious communities that:

> Chapters and councils should faithfully discharge the part in rulings entrusted to them and each should in its own way express that concern for the good of the entire community which all its members share.[13]

Regular chapters had always been held in Rochester for the purpose of making policy as well as for electing the major superior and council, but after the Second Vatican Council, chapters became a vital part of the renewal process and all sisters were invited to be active participants.

On the opening day of the chapter which convened

in September 1967, Mother M. Bride stated: "This chapter will close when we finish the work that we set out to do."[14] The sisters smiled at this remark, but Mother M. Bride was correct, because it was two years before the chapter ended in 1969.

The chapter (1967-1969) adopted a resolution that each sister

> study more deeply the meaning of the vows . . . . that she may live that consecration more eminently and thereby effect within herself a deeper holiness of life which will render more fruitful her apostolic works.[15]

Among other decisions, the chapter empowered the formation team to plan the individual formation of each sister in regard to time, place and duration of formation. It called for a congregation-wide effort to live more simply, to give clearly visible corporate witness to the values of poverty of spirit and simplicity of living. Sisters could, if they wished, return to their baptismal name because, as Vatican II documents reminded them, it is through baptism that we are first called to ministry in the church. Collaboration with the laity in works of mercy became an important goal. Women religious were now encouraged to reach out beyond their former limits and to respond as members of the world community, no longer set apart from the rest of humankind.

At the close of the chapter in 1969, Mother M. Bride wrote to the membership:

> We recognize that the work of renewal has been and will continue to be a difficult time for us, but I firmly believe that the Spirit moves among us. We have caught a new hope, and in the confidence born of our trust in God, we begin a new life with

freshness of vision, vigor of action, courage and enthusiasm.[16]

These words were a source of encouragement and renewed hope for many sisters, but the congregation had experienced many changes: a new habit, a new way of choosing community and ministry, and the departure of many good and holy women who had chosen another direction for their lives. Between 1970 and 1980, 120 women left the Rochester Sisters of Mercy. These women were deeply loved and their leaving was mourned by the whole community of Mercy.

Sister Mary Sullivan reflected on the 1967-69 Chapter twenty years later at a congregational meeting:

> In the Chapter of 1967-69 we struggled with such concepts as human life, the human person, human freedom, woman, conscience, friendship, and pluralism. I remember everyone's pain as we struggled to see whether we should begin to heed more explicitly these human values, or should set them aside as unrelated or alien to our theology of religious life.

The Rochester Sisters of Mercy answered that dilemma when on August 14, 1971, they approved the following Prologue for their *Interim Constitutions*:

> It is now time for us to reaffirm the worth of this ongoing process of measuring ourselves against the Spirit of Christ as expressed in the Gospel and in the life of Catherine McAuley. As a religious community and as individuals, we must not only continue to adapt to the changing times, but in this especially fragmented era we must dare to be

prophetic and to be active participants in effecting meaningful change in all areas of human life. Even as we continue to value the rich symbols and insights of the past, we must continue under the influence of the Holy Spirit and the guidance of the Church to be open to the new, the evolving, and the creative.

A New Look for the Sisters of Mercy

One of the most visible changes in the lives of the Sisters of Mercy after the Second Vatican Council was the adoption of a modified habit. Since 1831 the sisters had basically kept the style of the habit designed by Catherine McAuley, with only slight modifications over the years: a long black pleated dress with a leather belt called a cincture and a large black rosary with an ebony cross inlaid with ivory. A plain wooden crucifix with metal corpus was worn in the belt. A starched muslin headpiece with a broad hemmed collar was covered with black French veiling, and a stiff white bib descended in front to within two inches of the belt.[17] A street veil was added when sisters traveled outside the convent. They also wore large outer sleeves which could be hooked up or removed when their work or recreation required greater flexibility.

Over the years, few changes in habit had been made by most religious orders of women, including the Sisters of Mercy, though simplifying the religious garb was considered as early as 1952. At a meeting of Mothers General in Rome that year, Pope Pius XII had said religious habits should be simple—less cumbersome and more modern, in order to make it easier for sisters to accomplish their many duties.

On September 8, 1958, at a meeting of the McAuley Conference in Cedar Rapids, Iowa, minor changes of habit had been mentioned, such as eliminating the street veil and large outer sleeves, and shortening the cincture (belt). All the Mercy sisters present agreed that they would keep each other informed of any habit changes, because they wished to keep a common external image. In 1963 at North Plainfield, New Jersey, the superior of the Merion Sisters of Mercy, Mother M. Bernard, was asked to contact professional designers and request drawings for possible modification of the Mercy habit.[18]

Sybil Connolly, internationally known Irish designer, accepted the task of creating a new habit for the Sisters of Mercy in America.[19] She had agreed to redesign and modernize the habits of six other religious communities of women. She always approached her assignments responsibly. Thus, in 1963 she prepared herself for her Mercy task by reading Catherine McAuley's life story and visiting the chapel and the foundress's grave at the first Mercy convent on Baggot Street in Dublin.

Ms. Connolly felt that "the style must suit all figures, ages, and be practical for such varied activities as teaching and nursing." She designed three styles, one of which was adopted by many Sisters of Mercy congregations in the United States. It featured a one piece black dress with straight lines, a belt at the waist, and a rolled white collar. A white linen cap headdress with a black waist-length veil completed the habit, which was mid-calf in length.[20]

When the vote was taken to adopt the new habit, 365 Sisters of Mercy of Rochester voted yes, 39 voted no, and 3 ballots were invalid. With the encouragement and example of Mother M. Bride, every sister in the Rochester community began wearing the modified habit on December 28, 1965.

Sister M. Florence Sullivan, principal of Our Lady of Mercy High School, spoke to the student body early in December 1965 to prepare them for the sisters' "new look" when they returned to school after the Christmas holidays.

She described the reasons for the change:

> In these modern times, sisters need to wear clothing
> which is more suited to their ministry and living
> situations.

> The habit which the Rochester Sisters of Mercy will
> be wearing marks a radical change in our attire. As
> we put on our new habit and discard the old one,
> which we love, we are expressing our loyalty and
> our obedience to the Holy Father's wishes.

> Our new attire—entirely different—is still our holy
> habit—it carries the blessing of our original one
> received on our reception day. To us it is a
> sacramental—still dedicating us to the service of
> God.[21]

In her closing remarks to the students, she gave them a
preview of the modified habit, as a sign of her care and
concern for them:

> So you will enjoy your Christmas holidays better
> and so you will appreciate a little more what
> December 28 means to all of us, and because we
> love you, as a Christmas gift to you, I have asked
> Sister M. Aquin to show you how she will look
> when school reopens on January 3.[22]

In other schools where Sisters of Mercy taught, the
sisters also prepared their students ahead of time for the
change. At Notre Dame High School in Elmira, Sister M.
Declan Donovan, principal, talked about the symbolism of
the old habit and the prayers each sister said as she dressed
each day. For the benefit of the students, she placed a
mannequin dressed in the habit in the front hall of the

school. "It was a big change," she said, "and we tried to make it easier for them."[23]

Changes in the habit...

| Mother M. Magdalene Schenck (1945) | Mother M. Bride Claire (1965) | Sister Judith Heberle (1975) |

The changes in clothing continued, and a group of sisters experimented during the summer of 1968 with contemporary clothing: a suit, a two-piece dress or modified habit of black, gray or blue. Two other sisters working in a summer inner city project wore dark blue washable nurses' uniforms. All continued to wear the short black veil. In the evaluation of these experiments, the sisters reacted favorably; they felt that the process had been extremely helpful to them. Individuals and local communities of sisters reflected that looking contemporary seemed appropriate to the effectiveness of their ministry, and they would like to explore this opportunity.

By the end of the twentieth century, nearly all the sisters in the Rochester community were wearing contemporary clothes or a simple black or blue dress. Some still chose to wear a short black veil with a white headband. All sisters wore the Mercy cross as a distinguishing feature: a cross within a cross, which can be worn either on a chain or as a pin. The *Constitutions* describes the present habit:

> In keeping with our Mercy tradition, we wear a silver ring as a sign of consecration. Our religious dress witnesses to simplicity of life in accord with that consecration. We recognize the Mercy Cross as a special symbol of our Institute (#32).

In "The Prophetic Life and Work of Catherine McAuley and the First Sisters of Mercy," Sister Mary Sullivan writes: "The silver ring is a personal and communal identification; it is a mutual pledge between the wearer and the God to whom she put out her hand and to whose word she opened her mouth."[24]

Housing and Community Living

Wearing a new habit was a significant change for sisters as well as for their families, friends and the general public. However, the change sisters faced in housing choices and community living probably had a deeper and more long lasting effect on the lives of women religious.

In pre-Vatican II days, most sisters lived where they worked—in parish, high school or hospital convents or at the motherhouse. The mother superior assigned sisters to particular convents when the annual appointments for their ministries were published each August. The 1954 *Constitutions* states, "The Mother General has the right to transfer the Sisters from one house to another and to assign the offices and employments of the Sisters" (#265).

One newly professed sister described a situation that was typical in the late 1940s:

> There were thirteen of us, ranging in age from twenty to eighty, living in the three-story parish

convent adjacent to the church and across the street from the school. Ten of us taught in the school; two were retired and one sister was our cook. We ate together, recreated together, worked together and worshipped together at daily Mass and at regular times of prayer.[25]

From the earliest days, sisters had lived where they ministered, so they usually lived with the same sisters they worked with all day. If, on a given day, a sister-teacher was unhappy over a directive from her principal, she still sat side by side with her at evening recreation. "The life style of sisters at this time was quasi-monastic, emphasizing institutional living and separation from the world."[26]

In 1965 the Rochester Sisters of Mercy resided in twenty-eight parish convents in addition to convents connected with institutions such as the high schools or the hospitals. Some of these convents were lacking in adequate space and modern equipment, as one sister describes her convent home in the forties:

> The convent was old and in need of repair, but the parish was not financially able to remedy the situation. So we did the best we could, with leaky faucets, worn carpets and drafty rooms. There was a huge attic which we used for storage, but we tried to keep the door closed because bats made their home there.[27]

In the fifties and sixties, when the Catholic schools were flourishing and the sisters made up the majority of the staff, there was a recognized need for larger convents to provide housing for sister-teachers. Many parishes in the diocese of Rochester built new well-equipped convents to meet this need. Some parishes added new sections to already existing convents. Cardinal Mooney High School had a convent on the third floor above the new high school, and Notre Dame Convent in Elmira housed the sisters on the faculty of the high school in a beautiful new building erected in 1966 with generous donations from the parishes of Elmira, Elmira Heights, Horseheads and Waverly. It was a time of growth when many young women were entering religious life. In 1966 the Rochester Sisters of Mercy peaked with 481 members in the community.

In that same year, the Second Vatican Council stated, in the *Decree on the Adaptation and Renewal of Religious Life (Perfectae Caritatis)*:

> The manner of living, praying and working should be suitably adapted everywhere, but especially in mission territories, to the modern physical and psychological circumstances of the members and also, as required by the nature of each institute, to the necessities of the apostolate, the demands of culture, and social and economic circumstances.[28]

During the late sixties, women religious discussed their "manner of living, praying and working." The Rochester Mercys believed that community life must exist for something beyond itself; it must strengthen and enable each sister in her ministry. In the chapter of 1967, Sister Mary Sullivan recommended that the work of the chapter needed to consider "creative, imaginative experimentation with modes of living and working. The chapter will draw up and/or approve descriptions of such experimentation and encourage their implementation."[29]

Before the close of the chapter, delegates voted affirmatively that a sister could request the option of choosing the community in which she would live during 1969-70. This choice would reflect two major responsibilities:

1. their responsibility to embrace a style of religious community living that will both support and give growth to their religious commitment, and

2. their responsibility to be sensitive and generous toward the needs and problems of the human communities of which they are a part: the Church itself, the civic community, the parish communities, the local religious communities, and the whole Congregation itself.[30]

In their 1971 *Interim Constitutions*, support was given to the concept that

> each Sister has the freedom and responsibility to choose the particular local community that will help her and them become fruitful in Gospel presence and service for those to whom they are sent; and that she make this choice carefully recognizing and weighing her responsibility to all the members of the Congregation.[31]

Women religious began to consider the option of living away from their place of work and sharing life with fewer sisters than was possible in the larger institutional living situations. Between 1967 and 1974, eight groups of sisters requested and received approval to move from parish convents to small rented houses. In 1975, three sisters ministering at St. James Mercy Hospital in Hornell asked to move into a house owned by the hospital. Previously they had lived on a floor of the convent attached to the hospital. In their proposal, they said:

> As a group we have felt the need for a more quiet, relaxed, private environment which has not been possible within the second floor of the hospital

building. We also feel the need for a greater sharing of ideals and hopes among ourselves as Sisters.[32]

An interesting development resulted from sisters choosing their own community living situation. Other groups of women religious in the diocese were also looking at alternatives to their living situations; as a result, sisters from different congregations began to live together, some in rented houses, some in existing parish convents. Communities also examined the pros and cons of renting or purchasing houses. The Rochester Sisters of Mercy, with some few exceptions, continued to rent; however in 1982 a task force on housing concluded its study with this message:

> It is possible to become distracted from the main issues by a debate on rental vs. purchase of property. More important is the deeper consideration of why I choose to be in a certain place, whom this living situation allows me to reach, and what values the house itself affirms to those who pass by or enter it.[33]

By the 1980s the future of the parish convent was a cause of concern for both the diocese and the women religious. Martin J. Tracy, president of the Chemung County General Education Board, sent a letter dated May 21, 1981, to the superiors of the Sisters of Mercy and the Sisters of St. Joseph. He informed these superiors that in the interest of reducing costs in the Catholic school system of Chemung County, the board was beginning a study of the cost of housing the seventeen sisters ministering in the schools. It was suggested that representatives of each religious congregation might meet with the sisters concerned to advise them of the situation.[34] In other areas of the Rochester diocese, parishes were concerned about the empty rooms in their convents as sister-teacher personnel decreased and sisters made choices to live in other convents.

In 1983 the Sisters of Mercy were living in twenty-two parish convents: two of them housed a ministry of the sisters; six were intercongregational houses; fourteen provided community living for sisters who ministered in the host parish or in another parish. By 1993 that number had changed from twenty-two to sixteen. By 2003 only ten parish convents were homes for Sisters of Mercy. Parishes had begun to look at different utilization of the convent space; both the parishes and the women religious agreed that there needed to be a sufficient number of sisters living in a parish convent to justify the cost. Parish buildings were subsequently put to use for both creative and practical purposes. Former convents now function as low income housing, halfway houses, foster care homes, prayer centers, family residences, pre-schools, rectories, and parish administration centers.

In November 1983 Sister Jean Marie Kearse, major superior from 1981 to 1989, reflected on how the lives of women religious had changed: "It is a constant challenge to be honest with ourselves as to how we are different today. We must listen to all the voices which speak to us and call us to deepen the gift with which we have been entrusted." Jean Marie closed her remarks with these words:

> I believe—we are different from yesterday. I feel that our God would recognize and embrace us as his daughters—because we are growing in our resemblance to Jesus, His Son.[35]

Creating Social Awareness

The Second Vatican Council also called all

religious to a greater interest and involvement in justice issues. Religious congregations were encouraged to:

> promote among their members an adequate knowledge of the social conditions of the times they live in and of the needs of the Church. In such a way, judging current events wisely in the light of faith and burning with apostolic zeal, they may be able to assist men more effectively.[36]

Women religious responded to this challenge with an "apostolic zeal." In Rochester a significant group of sisters were anxious to extend the vision of the congregation to the needs of the world. Mother M. Bride had shared the comments of a speaker at a Conference of Major Superiors who called women religious to promote courageous initiatives in areas of social justice. "What can you do corporately in regard to social moral issues?" was the question the speaker asked.

At the October 1968 session of the 1967-69 Chapter, the delegates nominated a steering committee of three women, Sisters M. Beatrice Curran, M. Florence Sullivan and Dorothy Keefe, to establish a permanent social justice commission. The chapter members approved the following statements which were eventually included in their 1971 *Interim Constitutions.*

> To be socially just and merciful is a special moral duty of our congregation which names itself "of Mercy."

> We shall give ourselves to frequent and studious reading of the Vatican II *Pastoral Constitution on the Church in the Modern World* as the official summary interpretation of our social justice obligations at this time. We shall try to act upon

and make sacrifices for the fulfillment of the duties and hopes of the Church as she has earnestly expressed them in this document.

Affirmations, Volume II, 1969

In response to the call for involvement in social justice obligations, a commission was formed as recommended by the chapter. Present at the first meeting on November 24, 1968 were: Sisters M. Beatrice Curran, Dorothy Keefe, M. Claude Loeb, Grace Miller, Mary Sullivan, M. Florence Sullivan, and M. Edwardine Weaver. One of their first tasks was to describe the purpose of the commission. The following statement was approved and became part of the bylaws:

Conscious of the needs of contemporary society and the "signs of the times" for religious women, the Social Justice Commission shall be established to create an informed social awareness by guiding intelligent study and effective action in this area. As a result of the Commission's activity, the attitudes of the individual and the Congregation should reflect a desire to be the Christian presence at the crisis centers of human and social change.

The commission, under the direction of its first chairperson, Sister Mary Beatrice Curran, was hopeful that its first steps would involve the congregation in twentieth century renewal of Catherine McAuley's concern for social justice. The following persons were also invited to be members: Reverend P. David Finks, diocesan Vicar for Urban Ministry; Larry Kirwan, Rochester attorney; Monsignor Charles V. Boyle, priest of the Rochester diocese; and Robert McLaughlin, philosophy professor at St. John Fisher College.[37] Only Monsignor Boyle declined the invitation.

The commission immediately launched its agenda. During the first six months, the members met eight times, sponsored three study groups, and provided a film discussion group. They put time and energy into an effort to relieve the housing shortage for low to middle income people, hoping that property behind the motherhouse could be sold for this purpose. The Finance Committee of the Sisters of Mercy had already determined the congregation's need to sell this land in order to meet some financial obligations. However, the sale could not be realized at this time, despite the zeal of the commission members to move the issue forward.

The Social Justice Commission also held workshops for school administrators on the school's role in attitudinal changes on justice and peace and the need to create more programs for "culturally deprived" students. Their study groups covered such topics as migrant workers, welfare, education, housing, taxes, unemployment, healthcare, and local government. The education of sisters in many issues of justice was a top priority for the commission. For example, in the 1970s they supported and encouraged sister educators and others to speak in favor of the reorganization of the Rochester public schools, which would create greater racial diversity in the classrooms.

A careful reading of the minutes of this group shows their extraordinary understanding of the issues of the day and their vision for a more just world. Their agendas cover a variety of topics: Responsible Investments, The Struggle of the United Farm workers, the 1971 Attica Rebellion, Right to Life Issues, Elections, World Hunger, and the role the Central Intelligence Agency (CIA) played in Chile during Salvador Allende's presidency.

In the 1975 Chapter the delegates evaluated the role of the committees and commissions that functioned in the congregation. As a result of this evaluation, the Social Justice Commission was renamed the Mercy and Justice

Committee. Persons other than Sisters of Mercy no longer served on the committee, and two of its nine members were appointed by the superior and her council. The congregation felt the need for an educative group in light of the 1975 Chapter theme, "Justice through Mercy."[38] In January 1976 the Mercy and Justice Committee met for the first time, guided by the following direction:

> The purpose of the Mercy and Justice Committee shall be to reflect on and implement the appropriate Affirmations enunciated in the *Interim Constitutions* 1975. Conscious of the needs of contemporary society and the "signs of the times" for religious women, the Mercy and Justice Committee shall be established to help create an informed social awareness by guiding intelligent study and effective action in this area.[39]

This committee served the congregation for over twenty years. Its purpose clearly echoed the words of Vatican II: "to promote among their members an adequate knowledge of the social conditions of the times they live in."[40]

In the spring of 1986 Sister Jean Marie Kearse, major superior, announced the appointment of Sister Anne Curtis as part-time justice coordinator. In her letter to the congregation, Jean Marie hoped the flow of ideas between the justice coordinator and the Mercy and Justice Committee would "add a new dimension to our desire to address justice issues effectively and creatively."[41] Anne Curtis was active in this role until 1987 when she began missionary work in Chile. Sister Sheila Miller served in this coordinating role from 1988 to 1991, when Anne Curtis returned from Chile. Except for one year (1995-1996) when she was an intern at Network—a Catholic social action organization based in Washington, D.C.—Anne facilitated the work of justice in the Rochester community until 1999 when she began to work full-time for Network.

The Mercy and Justice Committee had been established, according to its bylaws, "to help create an informed social awareness by guiding intelligent study and effective action."[42] One of the means they used to accomplish this goal was the creation and implementation of corporate stances. The committee identified the following values for approving a public stance:

1. The congregation can adopt a public stance regarding a matter of public concern in order to create positive pressure toward a more humane, just and merciful society.

2. This stance must be consistent with gospel values, based on the social teachings of the church, and concerned with an issue that extends beyond our regional community and affects a significant number of people.

3. Each sister is called to participate in formulating this stance by examining and studying the issues involved, weighing the value of the stance and making a decision about it.

Using these values to guide them, the Rochester Mercys have adopted three corporate stances since 1982. Before a decision is made to adopt a stance, there is a process of corporate reflection, which includes education, discussion among the members, and prayer. The congregation reaffirms each stance on a yearly basis after studying the need for any revisions.

The following chart illustrates the history of the Corporate Stances:

	Corporate Stance Title	Date of Ratification
A.	**Resolution on Disarmament**	Ratified 1982
	Revised as Stance on Peace	Reaffirmed 1995
	Revised as Stance on Peace and Non-Violence	Reaffirmed 2004
B.	**Stance Opposing the Death Penalty**	Ratified 1990
	Revised 2003	Reaffirmed 2003
	Revised 2004	Reaffirmed 2004
C.	**Stance on Refugees**	Ratified 1987
	Revised as Stance on Immigration	Reaffirmed 2003
	Revised 2004	Reaffirmed 2004

Through the years, the Justice Coordinators working with the Mercy and Justice Committee also promoted voter registration, recycling, issues around child care, welfare reform, the closing of the School of the Americas, Third World debt reduction, and other social justice concerns. They continued to offer opportunities for education and discussion on significant justice issues.

One of their methods was encouraging sisters to enter into commercial product boycotts with the specific goal of ending unjust policies or practices on the part of the company. The Mercy and Justice Committee called for the boycott of one of the highest corporate taxpayers in South Africa, a major contributor to the government that allowed apartheid to flourish. Another boycotted company was one of the three top manufacturers of nuclear weapons products. Not all members of the Sisters of Mercy approved these boycotts; some questioned the wisdom of a move that affected persons employed by a company but not responsible for its policies. The Mercy and Justice Committee, however, continued to encourage the membership with well researched educational materials. As Sister Sheila Miller wrote to the community in 1989, "As with any boycott, joining is not without its inconveniences. We urge you to consider this as a practical, concrete way you can refuse to cooperate with those who continue to make discrimination and oppression a way of life."[43]

Over time the issues changed, but the Sisters of Mercy were continually called to remain faithful to their 1975 statement on justice:

> To be socially just and merciful is a special duty of our congregation which names itself "of Mercy." This responsibility calls for discernment, decision-making and action within a framework of justice through mercy.[44]

CHAPTER FIVE

NEW MINISTRIES

I n the sixties and seventies new concerns surfaced for
ministry. These concerns reflected changes in
society, challenges from the Second Vatican Council,
and the struggle of sisters to discover new ways to respond
to the emerging needs of the day and to define their role of
service in the mission of the American church. In
Rochester, the sisters' ministry began to reflect a
preferential option for the economically poor, an
acknowledgment of the diverse gifts of women religious,
and a strong desire to re-examine how sisters lived the
corporal and spiritual works of mercy.

Ministry in the Inner City

Sister Mary Sullivan (M. Petrus), president of
Catherine McAuley College, wrote to Bishop James E.
Kearney in August of 1965 to ask his blessing on a new
ministry of the Sisters of Mercy—to work with the poor in
an inner city parish: St. Bridget's in Rochester. In the

summer of 1964 this area had been the scene of "Race Riots" which were precipitated by rampant poverty and economic injustices in the areas of housing, education and employment for people of color.

Sister M. Concepta Walsh welcomes some friends to the Joseph Avenue Center.

Sister Mary Sullivan proposed this idea as a means to involve the sister-students at Catherine McAuley College in the apostolic activities of the Sisters of Mercy, especially among the economically disadvantaged. The ministry would also include volunteer opportunities for professed sisters already engaged in full-time ministry who would like to contribute one hour a week to social work. Mary then did the groundwork, making initial contacts and arrangements for a storefront at 372 Joseph Avenue. A call for volunteers was included in the initial announcement sent out to the congregation in early September 1965 and with this announcement, the Joseph Avenue Center began.

Sister M. Concepta Walsh was appointed full-time to the Joseph Avenue ministry and was put in charge of "all connected with it." The ministry actually opened in November 1965 as an after-school program with volunteers helping children in simple activities such as drawing, music and singing. In mid-November, Sister M. Concepta asked Sister Dorothy Loeb (M. Claude), a volunteer, to facilitate visiting the homes of the children. Many sisters offered to work in the ministry after their own school day was finished. Desmond Stone wrote in the *Democrat and Chronicle* in 1966:

> To Sister M. Concepta and her companions, the world is as small and big as the uplifted face of a child. And you cannot watch these members of the Sisters of Mercy go about their work without realizing that love can indeed be a many-splendored thing.[1]

Although this storefront ministry closed in 1973, sisters lived on Joseph Avenue until 1983, in a house sold to them by the Rochester diocese for the sum of $1.00. During these years, the sisters continued to be present to the people of the area.

Joseph Avenue Academy was an outgrowth of the Joseph Avenue Center. The time spent tutoring the young students convinced the sisters of the need for more regular assistance in reading and math skills. Sister M. Concepta and Sister Barbara DiFiore welcomed ten students to the academy in September 1970. Sister Concepta remembers that the parents were very happy and excited about the fact that their children could be brought up to grade level in math and reading and then be admitted to the neighboring Catholic schools: St. Michael's and Holy Redeemer. Sister Concepta also remembers the wonderful support of the School Sisters of Notre Dame who were the principals of these two schools—Sister Marie Therese Alaimo and Sister John Bosco Boss. Unfortunately, the lack of personnel and finances prevented the growth of the school and it closed after only two years.

St. Michael's Woodshop

Sister Patricia Flynn (M. Blaise) arrived on Joseph Avenue in the fall of 1967, and she immediately set to work planning more activities for boys in the neighborhood. Before 1967 Sister Carol Fox, an after-school volunteer, had realized that the girls were offered more opportunities than the boys. She started a small workshop for boys and taught them how to make shoeshine boxes. Sister Pat Flynn picked up this idea and expanded it. She organized classes in woodworking which were held at the Joseph Avenue house. Eventually she was in need of more room, so she moved out into a vacant building in the area. The woodworking project captured the interest of a number of people who saw its potential. The Sears, Roebuck Corporation supplied equipment for the project, and Eastman Kodak Company donated lumber and the services of two instructors who came twice a week to help the students. Kodak was faithful to this commitment for thirty years. The Sisters of Mercy also remember with gratitude Father Paul Schnacky, a Rochester diocesan priest serving in the inner city, who came daily to the woodshop during its beginning years.

Eventually Sister Pat moved her classes into the parish property of St. Michael's Church: first into a bowling alley and then into the then vacant St. Michael's School. Because of her long association with the parish, she named her ministry St. Michael's Woodshop. Under her direction, the woodshop has been in operation for more than thirty-seven years, located later on St. Paul Street and still serving the youth of the inner city of Rochester.

Inner City Ministries Grow

Throughout the 1960s many other Sisters of Mercy became involved in inner-city ministry. Sisters Dorothy Keefe and Suzanne Klingler worked full-time in Project Head Start, which began as an anti-poverty program initiated and funded by the federal government to help disadvantaged children prepare for kindergarten. Seven Sisters of Mercy as well as School Sisters of Notre Dame and Religious of the Sacred Heart worked summers as teachers and supervisors of inner city centers. Some Sisters of Mercy who were part of this program lived in a house on Adams Street in the city's third ward—within walking distance of Immaculate Conception Church. The large Victorian house was rented for an annual fee of $1.00, as it was scheduled to be demolished as part of an urban renewal project. Project Head Start was located in over thirty schools throughout the city and had a strong parent education component, especially during the summer.

During the summers of 1968 and 1969, Sisters Kathleen Milliken and Eileen Popkoski joined several local clergy of various denominations and other volunteers in the Elmira Ecumenical Service Project. They worked with adults and children on the eastside of the city of Elmira to provide educational and recreational experiences, as well as interdenominational prayer services for all who wished to come.

The House of Mercy

One of the sisters who was involved through the early years in inner city ministry, especially in Project Head Start, was Sister Grace Miller. Later, her great concern for the needs of people in poverty encouraged her to open a House of Mercy in 1985 located at first on Central Park in Rochester, and then at 725 Hudson Avenue, in a building which the Rochester Sisters of Mercy purchased and renovated for that ministry. In a letter to the community written on September 25, 1985, Sister Grace explained the mission of the House of Mercy:

> The purpose of this center is to reach out to those in need, as well as having a place for them to "drop in." Our hope is to respond to the expressed needs of the people by using existing resources or setting up our own, if such resources do not already exist and if it is feasible for them to do so.[2]

The center provided food, clothing and other resources as well as educational assistance in reading and skills needed for daily living. The staff willingly "walked" with people through the social service system.

In 1996 two weeks before Christmas on a cold, snowy night, city officials carried out a surprise inspection of the House of Mercy. They found thirty-five homeless people sleeping on cots, couches and floor mattresses. No one needed to tell the House of Mercy staff and the Sisters of Mercy that this was a violation of a city ordinance; they had no certificate or license to be operating a shelter.

However, the homeless were there and in need. Sister Grace said, "Even some policemen brought us people on really cold, terrible nights."

There was no easy solution to this situation and people lined up on both sides of the controversy. Sister Ann Miller, president of the Mercy community, and Sister Grace met with Mayor William Johnson and city officials to consider an appropriate direction for the House of Mercy.

In the January 24, 1997, *Democrat and Chronicle*, the following story appeared under the byline of Doug Mandelaro, staff writer:

> The House of Mercy "lifted our consciousness" about the plight of hard-to-serve homeless people and will operate unhindered as an emergency shelter, Mayor William A. Johnson Jr. said yesterday.
>
> In turn, the shelter's operator, Sister Grace Miller, and her order, the Sisters of Mercy, agreed to a seven-step plan limiting the facility to a maximum of 19 homeless people.
>
> The sisters also agreed to follow a precise timetable to bring the facility up to state shelter standards and city regulations.[3]

Sister Grace and her staff continued to provide community for the homeless. In 2001, Sister Sheila Stevenson, then president of the Sisters of Mercy of Rochester, and the other members of the leadership team, agreed to separately incorporate the House of Mercy because of the nature of the ministry and the possible liability issues for the religious community. The House of Mercy, with the faithful assistance of Sister Gloria Ruocco and Rita Lewis, continues to minister as a corporation with its own Board of Trustees, and enjoys support from many donors and volunteers.

Rural Ministry

Sister Judith Heberle, elected superior of the congregation in 1970, had for many years been aware of the needs of people in rural areas of the Rochester diocese. With supportive assistance from the diocesan Office of Human Development, Father Neil Miller and Sister Mary Kruckow, Sister Judith chose Tioga County in the southeast section of the diocese as a site to begin rural ministry. Sisters Kathleen Flaherty and Carol Wulforst were the first Mercy sisters to minister in the area. The five parishes of Tioga County enthusiastically endorsed the idea in 1978 and agreed to support the program financially. The Sisters of Mercy also contributed a small yearly subsidy until 1991 when the five parishes of St. Margaret Mary in Apalachin, St. John the Evangelist in Newark Valley, St. Francis in Catatonk, St. Patrick in Owego, and St. James in Waverly decided to incorporate the ministry under a Board of Directors named by the five parishes. The Sisters of Mercy continued to provide personnel but not funding.

As outreach workers accountable to the parishes, the sisters undertook a many faceted ministry: visiting the rural poor, doing hospital follow-up visits in the area, setting up emergency food and clothing centers, taking a census of the needy, matching resources with the needs of the people, and working with human development committees in the parishes. Ten Sisters of Mercy have served in this ministry over the years, including Mercy sisters from other states. When Sister Lisette O'Brien, a Rochester Mercy, retired from the position of director in 2002, Sister Phyllis McGuire, a Sister of Mercy from New Jersey, was selected by the board of the ministry to serve in this position.

In 1988 a Geneseo student who volunteered during his vacation time to help the Tioga County Rural Ministry wrote this remembrance: "It was hard to see the poverty and despair so close to my own home and so close to material wealth. Many students will go back to houses far away, but I go by this area often. I won't forget this . . . ."[4] Sister Judith Heberle, in speaking about this ministry, said "Perhaps this venture will inspire other areas to plan something similar."[5]

One of the sisters who welcomed Sister Judith's challenge was Sister Margaret Louise Snider, who founded Steuben County Rural Ministry in 1980. Two years later she was joined by Sister M. Conleth Kennedy, who would become the second director of the ministry. Sister Margaret Louise Snider once described the mission of this ministry in these words:

> Steuben County Rural Ministry was started for the purpose of serving the emergency material needs of the people in rural Steuben County; providing a Christian presence to the poor, the sick, the lonely, the mourning—the whole suffering community. Sister Conleth Kennedy and I provide food, clothing, transportation, household furnishings, fuel oil—almost any necessity requested by a person or family.
>
> We visit the homes of the people, delivering items, visiting the sick, elderly and infirm, and very often just making friendly visits, getting to know them so that we do become friends. Through the generosity of a realtor, we are fortunate to have a storefront at a very strategic Main Street corner in Canisteo where people can deliver their contributions of food, clothing, etc. or just stop in to talk. Others

come in to pick up food, children's clothing, winter coats, boots, hats and mittens.[6]

The people of the area were generous and accepting of the work of the sisters. Sister Margaret Louise recalls how she started with $87.00, which soon grew through the help of the Ladies of the Society of Italy. The Catholic churches of St. Joachim, Canisteo and St. Mary's, Rexville joined all the Canisteo churches in a genuine ecumenical response to the growing needs of the ministry. Area businesses offered the sisters free pantry space and freezer space for storage. Sister Susan Cain, the third director of the program, finds the same generosity and support from the people of Steuben County as she continues, twenty-five years later, to provide a "Christian presence to the poor, the sick and the lonely."

In 1995 Sister Margaret Mary Mattle also responded to the call to rural ministry and began to serve in the Wayland-Dansville area of Steuben County. She created a ministry of transportation—one of the greatest needs of the people in that area. Before she moved from the ministry in 2002, she successfully transferred all her programs into the hands of the lay people who had worked with her and who knew how to bring their own gifts to the ministry, to continue in the spirit of Mercy.

Ministry in the Southern States

From 1978 to 1982, Sister Phyllis Bernardo was employed by the Edmundite Fathers in Selma to work among the poor in rural Wilcox County, Alabama. Sister Dorothy Loeb ministered in Vredenburgh, Alabama from January 1980 until June 1986. Sister Dorothy was able to bring much needed legal services and community development programs into the area.

Sister Phyllis moved on to Indianola, Mississippi in

1982, and under the auspices of the Diocese of Jackson, ministered in two churches: one to serve white Catholics and one to serve African-American Catholics. Sister M. Concepta Walsh soon joined her and they ministered there and in other needy rural areas for twenty years.

Spirituality Ministry

> For years it has been my desire that we have our own cloister. After prayer and spiritual advice, I propose that a cloister be formed within our own community for sisters who may feel called to the contemplative life on a permanent basis and for those sisters who would wish to spend a short period in the cloister.
>
> Sister M. Cornelia O'Brien, April 7, 1968

These words of Sister M. Cornelia O'Brien launched an experiment that would take three years of study, prayer and the involvement of many sisters before it became a reality in September 1971 at St. Mary's Convent in Corning, New York. Simultaneous with the discussion of this proposal, the Sisters of Mercy were given a large, beautiful house overlooking Seneca Lake in Geneva, New York. The house, called High Acres, was a gift from the Dryer family of Geneva. Mother M. Bride said she considered it a miracle that on the very day the proposal for the house of prayer was being discussed in chapter, Mr. Dryer came to offer High Acres as a gift to the Sisters of Mercy.

For several months the congregation discussed the use of High Acres as a possible house of prayer—a place "whose specific purpose is to foster deep prayer in the life of its members."[7] The final decision was to make High Acres available for community-wide purposes rather than for a contemplative community. Meanwhile the sisters interested in the earlier proposal began to search for another appropriate space. They were hopeful that the vacant St. Patrick convent in Victor would be a possible site as it seemed an "ideal spot." When Sister Judith Heberle spoke to Bishop Joseph Hogan about the possibility of using it, he told her with a mingling of regret and humor, "Sister, I'm moving in there." With equal good humor, the disappointed sisters responded, "At least we have hierarchical taste."[8]

Two years after Sister M. Cornelia had made her initial proposal, the leadership of the congregation approved the following statement of purpose:

> That a House of Prayer be established on an experimental basis and that a core community of sisters be chosen who will live there full-time, creating a more contemplative life than is possible in our other communities.[9]

In September of 1971 the core group consisting of Sisters Cornelia O'Brien, Kathleen Bayer and Lucy Walawender moved into St. Mary's Convent in Corning, which had been vacated by the sisters because of a school consolidation. At the end of the first year, Sister Mary Anne Steinmetz joined the core group when Sister Kathleen Bayer was called to another ministry.

In 1972 Father Francis J. Marino, a priest from the Northeast Province of the Society of Mary (Marist Fathers), joined the community. His presence provided the sisters with a spiritual director as well as a new direction for the House of Prayer. In a letter dated March 12, 1974, Sister Cornelia O'Brien described that focus:

> Our prayer house experience is founded on the Jesus Prayer tradition and extends further into a total liturgical spirituality. Our community living is

designed towards a full integration of the human person. The thrust of our House is contemplative-apostolic, and its members are engaged in a variety of apostolates to bring their blessings to others.[10]

During its five years of ministry, the House of Prayer provided priests, religious and lay people opportunities for spiritual growth through prayer and silence. However, in June 1976 the congregation's leaders, in collaboration with the staff of St. Mary's House of Prayer, made a decision to rethink the House of Prayer in Corning. Sister Judith's communication to the congregation included the following information:

We have discerned for some time now, that a change in direction would be advantageous for our sisters as well as for the congregation. 1976-77 will be considered an interim year for each sister at St. Mary's . . . .

She requested:

- that the Task Force on Prayer Development or another Task Force study the direction of a House of Prayer Center for our congregation;
- that, hopefully, a definite program will be implemented by September of 1977.

Sister Judith closed her letter with these words: "We are grateful for the spiritual riches that the congregation has received through St. Mary's House of Prayer."[11]

Sister Judith's hope for the implementation of a prayer program by 1977 was almost realized. In June 1978 she shared this news:

I am happy to tell you officially that this September

we, as a congregation, will open a center of spirituality for our own use and for those we serve. It has grown out of the realization, expressed in our 1975 Chapter, that true renewal depends on the continual deepening of our faith and prayerfulness. We are calling it simply, "Mercy Prayer Center."[12]

Holy Cross Convent was chosen as the site for the new Prayer Center, with the enthusiastic support of the pastor, Father John O'Malley, the parish council, and Sister M. Eugene Pearson, who would continue to live in the convent and be active in the parish and school.

The sisters responsible for the Prayer Center were Sisters Mary Mercy Basler, M. Maureen Flood, Margaret Mary Mattle, and Virginia Wilson. Sisters Marie Joseph Crowley, a member of the leadership council, and Therese Richardson, principal of St. Andrew School, were members of the support community who shared life with the sisters. Sister Judith reminded the sisters in the congregation:

We have all been called to make our decisions in the light of our responsibility to justice; the sisters intend to shape their life and ministry around this concern for justice and reconciliation among all people. They have yet to work out the ways they will do this on a daily basis, and they ask for your support and encouragement in their efforts.[13]

These words birthed a ministry that was to grow and develop beyond anyone's expectations. Twenty-five years later it serves and is served by sisters and laypeople who desire to deepen and share their spirituality.

In 1986 the Sisters of Mercy, looking for more spacious quarters for their prayer ministry, purchased a large house at 65 Highland Avenue in Rochester. This house, which is now home to the Mercy Prayer Center, had a long-standing history. A gentleman farmer built it in the early 1860s as his retirement home; he left it to his son and from then on the house went through many transfers. The original building took on a special religious character when it was purchased by the Precious Blood Fathers as a minor seminary. Subsequently, members of a Jewish community lived in the house for a time, but circumstances caused them to look in a new direction. The home, once again on the market, was purchased by Will and Adele Gundlach who used it as a haven for people in need and called it the House of God's Goodness. After Adele died, her husband decided to sell the property, and the Sisters of Mercy became the grateful owners.

Today, Sister Jody Kearney, director of the Center since 1993, believes, in the words of the mission statement:

> The Mercy Prayer Center is a ministry of spirituality which offers a hospitable place for holistic growth and healing and for the formation of Christian leaders. Centered in an awareness of God's compassionate love and the spirit of Catherine McAuley, we strive through collaboration and mutuality to invite all to discern, celebrate and respond to God's ongoing call in our lives.[14]

In 1992 Sister Betty Hughes offered her skills as a spiritual director to the Elmira area. The purpose of Misericordia Spiritual Ministry was to provide opportunities for individuals to reflect on their relationship to God and others, and on their faith in relationship to scripture, the church, and their lived experienced. She provided services at the Sisters of Mercy Notre Dame Convent. There people participated in faith-sharing groups, directed retreats, peer supervision for experienced spiritual directors, and days of reflection. This ministry served the people of Elmira for eight years.

Ministry to Women and Children

In January 1968 the sisters at Holy Family Convent in Auburn, New York began a unique experience. Under the leadership of Sister Betty Hughes, they opened the convent as an emergency foster home for children. They agreed to accept boys up to age seven and girls of any age who were referred by the Auburn Welfare Department. The sisters defined "emergency" as a situation in which a case worker needs a place to shelter a child for one night or a maximum time of one week.

In April of that year, a social worker was asked to evaluate the experience, because he had placed six teenage girls ranging in age from thirteen to seventeen years in the convent at Holy Family. In his evaluation, he wrote:

> In the final analysis, it is our fervent hope that the sisters, and those responsible for the continuation of this very real and concrete experiment in Christian Action will feel it to be as warm, and meaningful, and necessary as the children and we who have benefited from it.
>
> Donald A. Lawler, Intake Worker
> Children's Division, April 26, 1968[15]

Another intake worker remembers that the sisters accepted three small children (ages 1, 3 and 4) with only one hour's notice. The children stayed five days, which meant that the sisters had to hire a babysitter while they taught school. In June 1968 after six months working in this new ministry, the sisters agreed that teaching school full-time and providing emergency shelter had some limitations that needed more study. In the fall of 1968 they discontinued this ministry, but it was not many years before the idea captured the imagination of another Sister of Mercy.

In 1973 Sister Gaye Moorhead sent a letter to Sister

M. Judith and the Council, along with a proposal requesting that the Sisters of Mercy provide a residence for hard-to-place foster children who would be cared for by Sisters of Mercy and laywomen. Sister Gaye wrote:

> This proposal grew from research undertaken between October 1971 and January 1973, for the purpose of learning about existing care for physically and mentally handicapped foster children.
>
> I spoke with case workers and supervisors of foster care departments of Wayne County and Monroe County Social Services, with representatives of organizations and homes serving the handicapped child, and with interested individuals. I also visited child care facilities in New York and Michigan and read extensively about rules and guidelines governing foster care. Although this research in no way exhausted the list of possible contacts, visits, and courses of study, it nonetheless established conclusively the need for more foster care facilities and confirmed the desire of local public and private groups to cooperate fully in an undertaking proposed to partially fulfill this need.[16]

The proposal met a significant need and also served the mission of the Sisters of Mercy, since one of their earliest works was the care of homeless children. However, what made the proposal unique was that Sister Gaye Moorhead researched and wrote it during her first two years in religious life. Gaye's concern for foster children had developed during her time as a VISTA volunteer when she experienced firsthand some of the difficulties these children faced in daily life.

When Sister Judith Heberle sent the proposal to the

elected group of sisters who served as an Advisory Board to the superior and council on important issues, they considered the pros and cons of the proposal and then, with some hesitation, voted nine in favor, seven opposed. Sister Judith, reading the proposal, wrote in the margin of the paper as a memo to herself: "Encourage this kind of initiative."[17]

The home, called Andrews Center after its first place of residence, St. Andrew's Convent in Rochester, has flourished. Children have grown and blossomed there for over thirty years, beginning in 1974 when Sister Gaye and Sister Rachel Parlavecchio were the first foster mothers, followed by Sisters Mary Frances Wegman and Kathleen Kolmer in 1977.

Over the years more than 170 children have been loved and nurtured by the sisters. The present co-directors, Sister Kathleen Kolmer and Sister Rita Habecker, SSND, have together given forty-seven years of service to these children. Andrews Center is now located in one section of St. James Convent on Whittington Road in Rochester. It has provided, as Sister Gaye Moorhead predicted, "one small response to a pressing need."

Mercy Residential Services

In the summer of 1977 Sisters Dorothy Loeb, Gratia L'Esperance and Deacon Dan O'Shea worked with the Board of St. Joseph's House of Hospitality in Rochester, exploring the need for a shelter for women and children. A growing number of women in the city found themselves in abusive family situations and sought shelter wherever they could, both for themselves and their children. Dorothy Loeb suggested that some women and children could be housed in one or more of the large convents that had extra rooms. However, the first house to be offered was not a convent but an empty rectory—St. Bridget's in Rochester.

St. Bridget's was renamed Bethany House. The spirit of the house was inspired by the Catholic Worker movement, as was St. Joseph's House of Hospitality. With a group of young volunteers, Sister Dorothy prepared the house for its new ministry. During the Christmas holidays, three women and their children received shelter. They were cared for by Sister Dorothy and Charlotte Parks, a former employee of St. Bridget's, who called it their "dry run." When these two women completed their work at Bethany in early 1978, Sister Kate Vaeth became the first full-time staff member. She was joined by Jean Jesserer, a Nazareth College student, and later by Linda Scibilia, a laywoman from Syracuse. Both women received $10 a week for their service and lived in voluntary simplicity.

In 1980 as this work grew, another need became apparent—housing for pregnant teenage girls who for various reasons could not remain with their families. Father Tony Valente, pastor of St. Michael's Parish in Rochester, offered the vacant convent in his parish. Over 200 volunteers from churches and civic groups renovated the convent; all the household items, paint and equipment were donated. The remodeled convent was founded as a Catholic Worker House of Hospitality and named Melita House—Place of Refuge.

In 1981 the Catholic worker volunteers assumed full staff responsibilities; however, a year later they notified Sister Jean Marie Kearse, the major superior, that they could no longer work and live at Melita House. They were looking for another group to assume responsibility for the ministry. The Sisters of Mercy accepted that responsibility and became sponsors of this ministry. Sisters Jane Schur, Patricia Kenny and Therese Richardson were appointed as full-time staff members with Sister Jane serving as director.

The next phase of this ministry was the founding of Catherine McAuley Housing. This service grew out of a proposal on homelessness presented at the 1989 Chapter.

A task force was formed to research the plight of the homeless in the city of Rochester. The task force concluded that single women and their children were most at risk. In response to this research, the congregation decided to provide housing and personal support to single mothers coming from Melita House after the birth of their children. In January 1991 Sister Janet Korn was asked to work with the task force on implementation of the project. After investigating many small apartment buildings in Rochester, the Sisters of Mercy purchased a five-unit townhouse in May 1992 and renamed it Catherine McAuley Housing. Under Sister Janet's direction, a social worker was hired and the first four young families came to live in this supportive structure.

In 1997 a two-apartment house was added to the property of Catherine McAuley Housing. This house, a gift to the Sisters of Mercy from the family of Sister Gertrude Erb, was named Judith House in honor of Sister Judith Heberle, who had been active in the housing ministry and who had died of cancer in July 1996.

Eventually, Melita House and Catherine McAuley Housing merged into one ministry called Mercy Residential Services. Melita House then moved to the former Holy Rosary Convent on Oriole Street in Rochester; the larger building allowed the staff to provide more services to pregnant girls and housing to single mothers under eighteen. A lay woman, Susan Aiello, now directs the program. Bethany House, begun as a shelter for homeless women, has continued to function in the spirit of the Catholic Worker movement, under the direction of Donna Ecker, an associate of the Sisters of Mercy.

Serving Persons with Special Needs

In 1983 Sister Anne Maloy was the Director of Social Work Services at Lakeside Memorial Hospital in

Brockport, New York. She saw firsthand that many older adults and their caregivers who came to the emergency room during a time of crisis were unprepared for the needs of the aging and had little knowledge of how to access follow-up services. Responding to this observation, she secured the support of the Sisters of Mercy to start a new ministry—Mercy Center with the Aging. Sister Anne, with the assistance of Sister Gratia L'Esperance, envisioned the ministry as a means of providing caregivers of older adults with educational information about the needs of their aging loved ones, as well as information about how to access services available in the community.

Over the past twenty years, Mercy Center with the Aging has served more than 25,000 people. Widely recognized as a source of strength and empowerment for the caregivers of older adults in the community, the Center offers legal and financial information and knowledge about available community services. It provides caregivers with ways to improve their skills and reduce stress by nurturing their spirituality. Sisters Anne and Gratia developed educational programs for faith communities, businesses, school districts, and major healthcare systems in Rochester.

In 2004 Mercy Center with the Aging was recognized as the official Caregiver Resource for Monroe County through the Monroe County Office of Aging. The Center moved from Our Lady of Lourdes parish convent in Brighton to Monroe Community Hospital and was affiliated with the Greater Rochester Alzheimer's Association. It was a year of transitions. Sister Anne Maloy retired, having served twenty-one years as director. Ms. Sharon Boyd, vice president of the Alzheimer's Association, was contracted to serve part-time as oversight manager. She was familiar with the mission of the Mercy Center, having served on its faculty and collaborated on a number of events over the years. Sister Gratia L'Esperance, former assistant director of the Center, serves on its board and volunteers her services to the ministry.

In another field of healthcare, Sister Wanda Hess, a speech and language pathologist, took a big step in 1983 to respond to the needs of a large migrant population and hundreds of senior citizens. State University of New York at Brockport had closed its speech and hearing clinics that year, causing a vacuum in this field in the Rochester area. Sister Wanda, with the approval of the Sisters of Mercy, opened a non-profit speech and hearing clinic in Rochester. The Northwest Hearing and Speech Clinic, as it was called, served individuals suffering the effects of strokes, language problems, voice difficulties, learning disabilities and hearing impairments. Special programs were created to teach English as a second language, and sign language to service some of the large deaf population in the area. The clinic served hundreds of people before it closed in 1994.

Meanwhile, in another part of Rochester, Sister M. Dismas Foster explained her ministry in three words: "I do furniture." She used our Lady of Mount Carmel's parish truck and a two-car garage on parish property, and the furniture business was born in 1986. As Sister M. Dismas described it at that time, "By word of mouth and church bulletins, people that have extra furniture find out I need it; by word of mouth, people that have nothing find out I can help them—and then I put the two together."

Sister M. Dismas found mothers and children living in places for two to three months without a stove or refrigerator; other families slept on the floor without a single piece of furniture in their house. With the help of people in Rochester parishes, she changed people's lives. She also ran a clothing store at the Mt. Carmel school building, with the assistance of Sister M. Regis Straughn and volunteers from St. Thomas the Apostle parish in West Irondequoit. The furniture ministry has continued under the auspices of Our Lady of Mount Carmel Parish and is now coordinated by Sister Julia Norton, pastoral associate.

In the southern part of the diocese the same practical creativity flourished. For example, Mercy Care Center at 405 Linden Place in Elmira, New York, is a daycare program for elderly persons. Established in the summer of 1985, it was the inspiration of Sisters M. Rose Schum and M. Howard Cowan, both registered nurses, who had spent many years of service in the infirmary of the Sisters of Mercy in Rochester. This longtime team began to share ideas and dreams about caring for the elderly. In December 1984 they took up residence in Elmira in the former St. Cecilia's Convent and spent four months transforming their house into a cheerful, homey and safe environment for elderly clients-to-be. They scraped and painted walls and gathered furniture from thrift shops and generous donors. They transformed three rooms upstairs for people who need some daytime rest. An additional room is used as a chapel—a place of quiet and prayer.

The philosophy of Sisters Rose and Mary Howard is that all people, regardless of age or impairment, have a basic need for sociability and stimulation. Affirming the quality of life for their guests and providing support, understanding and relief for families is the mission of Mercy Care Center. One Elmira resident whose mother had been a regular visitor to Mercy Care Center for the past two years reflected: "The sisters make the patients feel very comfortable . . . they provide love and support for families who need a break."[18] After twenty years, the sisters still see each client as unique and enjoyable.

Mercy Outreach Center

This center was first established in 1977 by Corpus Christi Church, as a one room "Drop-in Center" for persons in the neighborhood. Four years later, in 1981, a specific unmet need became evident: health care accessibility. The Center then began to focus its energies on providing primary health care for the uninsured through the efforts of the parish and with the assistance of the greater Rochester community.

For almost a quarter of a century this ministry was successful in its outreach to people who needed healthcare. However, when the parish underwent a period of significant internal change, the administration began to look for an appropriate group to take responsibility for this needed and viable healthcare ministry. They invited the Sisters of Mercy to accept this responsibility.

Sister Sheila Stevenson and the leadership council welcomed the opportunity to be part of this work of mercy. Sister Kathleen Ann Kolb, a registered nurse and the former director of Lourdes Hall infirmary, became the director. The Center was separately incorporated, and in 2001 the name was changed to Mercy Outreach Center, Inc.

Over the past 27 years, the original one-room drop-in center has become a treatment facility with four clinical consultation rooms, a lab area, a dental office, a dental hygiene office, two counseling rooms, a massage/reiki room, two large meeting spaces, a waiting room and a reception office. The Center, located at 142 Webster Avenue in Rochester, offers space, equipment and supplies free of charge for use by medical and dental professionals who, in turn, provide free services. The majority of its clients are working but unable to afford the cost of health insurance. Networking with other service providers has been key to helping people access services beyond what is provided at the Mercy Outreach Center. In June 2004, Sister Kathleen Ann left the ministry to serve on the leadership council of the Sisters of Mercy. The Board of Mercy Outreach Center chose Penny Gardner, already a staff member, as director. She and her staff continue the mission of providing accessible healthcare to those in need.

Ministries of the Diocese of Rochester

In addition to the hundreds of sisters who taught generations of children in the Catholic school system, the diocese has benefited from the gifts of many Sisters of Mercy, who with members of other religious congregations, have served in pastoral and administrative positions in the Diocese of Rochester.

Working in the Diocesan Pastoral office (Chancery), Sisters of Mercy have served as director of Faith Formation, Religious Education, Special Pastoral Ministries; as superintendent of schools, associate superintendent, coordinator of services in Youth Ministry, Adult Education, Human Development, Liturgy, Urban Ministry, Social Justice Awareness; as executive director of the Pastoral Council, assistant director of the Permanent Diaconate Program, administrator of the Bishop's Office and vice-chancellor of the Diocese, as well as on many diocesan committees, task forces, boards, and councils.

Moreover, in the years after Vatican II, the role of faith formation in the parish for people of all ages became a priority. The Rochester Diocese turned its attention to the growing need for professional religious education personnel in parishes. In 1972 Bishop Joseph L. Hogan wrote:

> Years of searching, years of sincere dedicated volunteer effort, years of an unspoken feeling of dissatisfaction with quality, have proven to be a healthy source for a new development in parish religious education efforts. In our diocese and all over the country, a new phenomenon has established itself: the Religious Education Coordinator.[19]

The diocese then established a goal of hiring full-time,

paid, qualified persons to coordinate religious education in every parish by 1974.

In 1966 Sisters Nancy Brady and Mary Jo Langie became the first full-time members of this ministry from the Sisters of Mercy. Six years later there were fourteen Sisters of Mercy serving as religious educators. Several continued during the seventies and eighties, but by 1992 only a few Mercy sisters remained in this ministry, which is now staffed mostly by highly competent lay men and women.

Vatican Council II also brought other changes to the ministries of parishes: a renewed sense of social justice issues, more involvement of the laity in parish councils and committees, a new direction in religious education and sacramental preparation. Parish staffs grew larger and the need for parish personnel increased. To respond to all these new needs, religious and members of the laity began to function in some parishes in the role of pastoral associate. Women religious were among the first to serve in this capacity, and Sisters Barbara Moore, Susan Altpeter, Carol Fox and Mary Jo Langie were among the first Mercy sisters to be recognized in this role. In 1977 nineteen Sisters of Mercy worked in parishes as pastoral associates; twenty years later there were thirty-six Mercy sisters who were or had been active in this ministry.

In 1975 Mount Carmel parish experienced the first team pastorate in the history of the Rochester diocese. Sister M. Regis Straughn and Sister Carol Fox were appointed "co-pastors" with Father Laurence Tracy. On September 4, 1975, Bishop Joseph L. Hogan wrote the following letter to Sister Carol Fox:

> I have approved the concept of the pastoral administration of a parish being equally shared by clergy, religious and lay people. Our Lady of Mount Carmel Parish recommends itself as a

starting point for the practical implementation of the concept in the Diocese. As with any other new approach to ministry, the arrangement I have approved for Mt. Carmel is experimental and subject to ongoing evaluation. The process followed in determining the appointment of personnel to the pastoral administration at Mt. Carmel will basically be the guide in determining similar arrangements in other parishes.

I am pleased to appoint you now to the pastoral administration of Our Lady of Mt. Carmel Church, Rochester, New York to function in a co-pastoral relationship with Sister Regis Straughn, R.S.M. and the Reverend Laurence C. Tracy. For canonical and legal requirements Father Tracy is designated Pastor of record.

With a blessing, I am sincerely yours in Christ,
Most Reverend Joseph L. Hogan, D.D.
Bishop of Rochester[20]

In 1976 Sister Julia Norton was entrusted with the care of the Hispanic Community at St. Patrick's, Rochester "until a qualified priest would be ready to accept this role."[21] Ten years later, in the fall of 1985, Sister Rita Heberle was appointed temporary administrator of Immaculate Heart of Mary Church in Painted Post while the pastor was on sabbatical leave. At the same time, Sister Julia Norton served as the temporary administrator at Our Lady of Mount Carmel Parish while its pastor was on sabbatical leave. Sister Kay Schwenzer filled this role at St. Michael's parish.

Based on these experiences and on similar responsibilities held by other women religious, the diocese introduced in 1994 a new role of service, the pastoral administrator. This individual is a canonically appointed lay person, religious or deacon, who is directly responsible for assuring the daily spiritual and temporal welfare of a parish. The pastoral administrator directs the entire parish in consultation with the parish council and other appropriate advisory groups. The liturgical needs of the people are served by a priest whom the bishop appoints as the Sacramental Minister.

In 1994 Sister Mary Wintish was installed by Bishop Matthew Clark as the pastoral administrator at All Saints parish in Lansing, New York. Sister Barbara Stinard was appointed as temporary pastoral administrator of Holy Cross parish in Dryden, New York. In 2002 she was appointed to St. Christopher's in Chili in the same role. When the pastor of Our Lady Queen of Peace parish in Brighton was appointed vicar general of the diocese, the bishop invited Sister Jacqulyn Reichart to serve as a temporary pastoral administrator of the parish, a role she filled for six years.

The Parish Visitor is another role that provides excellent service to parish people. The job description for this ministry differs from parish to parish, but the woman religious or lay person who serves in this capacity visits the homebound and those recently hospitalized. The focus of this work is often the elderly of the parish. Sister Elaine Kolesnik, parish visitor at St. John the Evangelist (Humboldt Street, Rochester), served over five hundred senior parishioners annually during her nineteen years in this ministry. Sister Rita Biel, in service to the people of Holy Cross parish (Rochester) since 1986, visited over 200 people monthly in the eighteen nursing homes in the parish. More than twenty Rochester sisters have served in this ministry.

Mercy sisters have also contributed to both faith formation and pastoral ministry as chaplains or campus ministers at colleges and universities in the Rochester diocese. Sister Patricia MacDonald was the first member of the Rochester community to become a university chaplain, serving at Cornell University from 1967 to 1971. Sister Kathleen Milliken was a campus minister at the Newman Oratory of the State University of New York at Brockport (1972-1982); Sister Kathleen Mary O'Connell ministered at the State College of New York at Geneseo (1973-1984); Sister Marlene Vigna was campus minister at Rochester Institute of Technology (1987-1997); Sisters Patricia Beairsto and Virginia Taylor ministered at Monroe Community College; Sister Virginia was also a campus minister at Ithaca College; and Sisters Kathleen Wayne and Jacqulyn Reichart served in campus ministry at the University of Rochester.

Over the years, many laywomen and women religious have moved into new and challenging work in the Rochester diocese, a fact which reflects the commitment of the diocese to the role of women in the Church.

Summer Camps

"If the Sisters of Mercy won't come, we'll have to close the camp," was the phone message in late spring, 1943. Mother M. Liguori McHale responded positively— and thus began the long association of the sisters with Camp Stella Maris, a summer camp for boys and girls sponsored by the Diocese of Rochester. Founded in 1926 by two seminarians, Stella Maris became a diocesan ministry in 1930, with increasing numbers of campers served by seminarians as counselors and domestic staff.[22]

Mother Liguori asked for volunteers from the sisters, because the seminarians who usually staffed the food service and nursing needs of the camp were now in an accelerated course of studies because of World War II, and would not be available until August. Five sisters answered the call to serve in this very new and different ministry. Over the years from 1943 to 1967, 189 Sisters of Mercy gave their summers to the camp as cooks, nurses, sacristans and housekeepers. In 1967 Mother M. Bride decided that the sisters needed more time for their own educational growth and development, and informed the diocese that they would no longer be available for the camp.

However, sisters were called upon once again in 1971 to minister with the lay staff at Stella Maris, working in arts and crafts and as the camp nurse. Three sisters eventually served as camp director: Sisters Joanne Lappetito, Arlene Semesky and Jody Kearney. Sisters of Mercy also acted as counselors, instructors in arts and crafts, and as physical education director.

During this same period of time, other sisters were busy at two summer camps owned by the Sisters of Mercy: Camp Maplewood, directed by Sister Mary Lou Seitz, opened on the campus of Notre Dame High School in Elmira in the summer of 1969. Camp Silver Birch, named by Sister M. Finn Bar Bartley because of the silver birches on the motherhouse property, opened in July 1970 with Sister Mary Ann Binsack as director; her idea for the camp on the grounds of Mercy High School in Rochester was based on her experience as a counselor at Camp Maplewood the previous summer. Both camps had similar activities: swimming, nature study, crafts, games, hikes, sports and special events such as scavenger hunts or treasure hunts. Camp Maplewood added trips to Harris Hill, and Sullivan's Monument, roller skating, and group tennis lessons. Sister Marilyn Williams, who was director at Camp Silver Birch from 1989 to 1998, recalls that "Each July was a special time for us because of the enthusiastic staff and campers."[23]

For twenty-nine years, these camps provided an atmosphere of friendship, care, love and laughter where children could grow and share the fun of childhood summers. When the camps closed permanently, the counselors and the children said Goodbye with sad hearts but many happy memories.

Ministry of Prayer

Catherine McAuley instructed the sisters that "the spiritual and corporal works of Mercy constitute the business of our lives." At a certain time in each sister's life, she acknowledges that she is being called more to the spiritual works of Mercy. Retirement years, which differ for every person, give sisters the opportunity to live the words of the *Constitutions*: "through the special ministry of prayer and patient suffering we witness to union with the crucified Christ, encouraging those engaged in other works of mercy and interceding for the whole church," (*Constitutions #4*).

The Rochester Sisters of Mercy, in their retirement years, fulfill this ministry of prayer for those engaged "in other works of mercy." Their prayer embraces diocesan leaders, men and women in public office, those on death row, people in nursing homes and hospitals, health professionals, those discerning vocations to the religious life and priesthood, and those suffering from homelessness, racial prejudice, violence and war. On the feast of Our Lady of Mercy (September 24), the sisters are commissioned to this ministry of prayer by the members of the leadership team.

Other Ministries

Beside the ministries described in this chapter, and the institutional ministries described in other chapters, individual Sisters of Mercy in the Rochester community have been asked to serve in a broad spectrum of other ministries: as author, attorney, jail minister, home health aide liaison, pastoral counselor, college teacher, massage therapist, home-hospital teacher, tutor, lobbyist, interfaith minister of preaching, secretary/receptionist, parish organist, social worker, caretaker, cook. Each year they, like the others, are formally commissioned to these ministries.

In the words of their *Constitutions*, the Sisters of Mercy are reminded that "by collaborating with others in works of mercy, we continually learn from them how to be more merciful" (#6). Catherine McAuley was particularly adept at encouraging and inviting people in all walks of life to collaborate with her in the works of mercy. This same spirit has continued through the years, and the vow of service today includes collaborative work with associates, board members, co-ministers, other co-workers, and volunteers. They have indeed learned from one another how to be more merciful.

CHAPTER SIX

THE CALL OF LATIN AMERICA

I n 1963 a young Irish priest named Kevin O'Boyle was ministering in a parish of sixty thousand people in a poor area of Santiago, Chile. He offered Mass on street corners because he had no parish church or chapel. There were no clinics for health care and only one school available for the children of all these families. Father Kevin's dream was "to see sisters nursing and teaching in our parish."[1]

In that same year thousands of miles away in Rochester, New York, a young Irish superior named Mary Bride Claire was discerning the call of Pope John XXIII to send men and women religious to minister in Latin America. In the late 1950s and early 1960s the need for religious personnel in Latin America was often on the agenda of all the annual meetings held for major superiors. In 1961 Pope John XXIII issued an appeal to the superiors in the United States to share their abundance of both goods and personnel with their less fortunate brothers and sisters to the south. At the 1964 meeting of Major Superiors of

Women, Father John Considine, a Maryknoll priest, spoke pleadingly of the needs of the Church in Latin America and the responsibility of religious in the United States to share "out of their abundance," especially personnel. A two-week workshop for major superiors interested in sending sisters to the missions was held at the Center of Intercultural Formation in Cuernavaca, Mexico in late December 1964. Mother M. Bride Claire attended this workshop, so she could pray with and talk to others who were knowledgeable of the Latin American reality. The superiors were encouraged to visit the missionary area personally, so they would understand what they were asking their sisters to do. Father Segundo Galilea, a presenter at the workshop, recommended Santiago, Chile to Mother M. Bride because he knew of the need for religious there. His descriptions of the poor of Chile affected her very deeply, and after the Cuernavaca workshop ended, she returned home to Rochester full of enthusiasm. She describes in her own words the welcome she received:

> That evening as I arrived home from Cuernavaca, the Sisters were leaving the chapel at the close of Benediction of the Blessed Sacrament. I had a captive audience as I related some of the dire needs I had become aware of during the workshop. The sisters were very interested and enthusiastic and assured me that they would pray that some of our sisters would choose to spend some time working for the needy people in Latin America, because they said, "It will bring blessings on our Congregation."[2]

One month later, in February 1965, Father Kevin O'Boyle, the Irish priest ministering in Santiago, Chile wrote a letter to Mother M. Bride:

> Dear Mother Bride,
> I have just got back from my vacation, and while

visiting some priest friends in Mateira, Brazil, I met the Sisters of St. Joseph from Rochester. I mentioned our parish here in Santiago de Chile, and also mentioned our great need of sisters. Sister Rose Alma gave me your address and said you are anxious to send some sisters to South America.

Two nights ago I met an Irish Divine Word father from Waterford, Ireland and he said he had met you in Cuernavaca. So here I am at my typewriter making my first contact with you and your community.

He described the poverty in his parish and the great need they had for sisters. He closed his letter with an appeal that Mother M. Bride never forgot for the rest of her life:

If you would like to come to Chile we will receive you. The work is difficult, the area is tough, the challenge is great, and so this makes it more interesting and rewarding.[3]

Mother M. Bride had already been encouraged by Father Segundo Galilea to go to Santiago to see conditions for herself, so within the month she was on her way to visit Chile. In a letter written February 27, 1965, from Santiago, she shared this news with the waiting sisters at home:

Perhaps you are wondering what I'm doing here. Well, let me say, there haven't been many spare moments. Every order of priests in Santiago seemed to have heard of my arrival here and I've been spending whole days with each of them— Maryknollers, Holy Cross, Columbans and Precious Blood. I am going back to see the Columban situation again. Perhaps it's the Holy Spirit guiding me—I know you are praying the novena with great fervor—but I'm anxious to find out more about the proposal they have to offer. Or maybe it's Father Kevin O'Boyle's winning ways. He is only 29 and you should see the job he's been given to do. Such faith and trust and courage are truly edifying. They have six parishes and they cater only to the poor. They are really apostolic. No, I have not made a decision. This will need a lot of prayer and thought.[4]

But the "winning ways" of Kevin O'Boyle won out in the end, especially when, in reply to Mother Bride's question, "What can you offer my sisters?" he responded "Absolutely nothing." Her reply "I'll take it" marked the commitment of the Sisters of Mercy of Rochester to this new and challenging ministry.[5] The people of San Luis parish in Santiago soon heard the joyous news that four Sisters of Mercy from Rochester would arrive in December 1965 after attending language school in Cuernavaca, Mexico.

The entire membership of the Sisters of Mercy participated in a novena to St. Joseph as Mother M. Bride and the sisters on the leadership council prayed and reflected over the names of sisters who had volunteered for Chile—a total of sixty. From these sixty names, four were chosen to be the first Sisters of Mercy in Chile. On March 25, 1965, the announcement came in a letter sent to all convents. In it Mother M. Bride shared the names of the women who would "Carry the Mercy Spirit from Rochester to Santiago":

Sister Mary Terrance (Jean DeVoldre)
Sister Mary Canisius (Margaret Spellecy)
Sister Mary Joan (Janet Korn)
Sister Mary dePorres (Mary Jane Nelson)

On August 21, 1965, the Sacred Heart Cathedral of the Diocese of Rochester was packed to capacity as families and friends said farewell in a departure ceremony presided over by Bishop James E. Kearney and Auxiliary Bishop Lawrence B. Casey. For the first time in the history of the congregation, novices appeared in public wearing their white veils. One hundred twenty-seven sisters sang in the sisters' choir. On August 23rd, the four sisters left for intensive study of Spanish in Cuernavaca, Mexico; from there, they would fly directly to Chile.

The Mission Begins

Dear Mother Bride,
Foundation Day has arrived in Chile! We landed in Chile around 1:30 on December 24th. We were so surprised when Father Kevin, Father Hugh, Sister Ann Walter and Mother Teresa met us right outside the airplane. They got a special permission to go out there—they had never received this permission before. The rest of the Maryknollers from San Alberto and many Columbans were up on the observation deck. It really was a grand welcome!

How we love the Columbans already! Father Kevin is all you said he was and more. After the welcome at the airport we went to San Andres and had lunch with a good group of Columbans. We almost felt as if we were walking into Ireland itself! Then came the big thrill of going to San Luis—we are so happy with the parish and the convent is just lovely. It should be finished by the end of January but then it could be longer, too. Now all you have said has come to life for us. The Church is part-way up and so is Father's rectory. (He has been pushing the convent instead of these). Midnight Mass—was celebrated in the Church—open-air style—and we attended this.

Letter from Missionaries
December 27, 1965[6]

By March 1966 the sisters had moved into the new convent provided for them by the Columban priests. The San Luis parish team was formed with the four Rochester Mercys, the Columban Fathers, Kevin O'Boyle and Michael Walsh, and an English priest, Joseph Carty, who was an associate of the Columbans. They divided the area of almost 60,000 people into three sectors, to do catechetical work, to meet the individual needs of people and to identify the issues that needed their special attention. For the four sisters, the language continued to be the most difficult adjustment. In letters home, they mourned, "It's like being a child again trying to communicate." Father O'Boyle promised them it would get easier with the years. Janet Korn describes the missionary's day in a letter written from Santiago:

> Each morning we meet with a few committed parishioners for a concelebrated mass. This is followed by a shared meditation in which we search the Gospels to help us in knowing and filling ourselves with Christ whom we preach. Besides these times of prayer together, our priest-sister team meets once a week to discuss the organizational end of our work. By this team effort we hope to show the people the strength that can be derived from Christian community living and the responsibility each man has for his brother.
>
> Besides personal home visits by the catechist or team member we have a series of meetings designed for the social and spiritual development of the

parents during the four years that the child is enrolled in religion classes. We hope that eventually these people will work themselves into places of leadership in the social, political and cultural community, bringing with them their Christian principles.[7]

Sisters Janet Caufield and Jane Kenrick joined the missionary sisters in December 1966 bringing new gifts to the Rochester group. They worked in the parish of San Andres with four Columban priests. Three of these priests were from Ireland: Hugh McGonagle, Pat McConville and Tim Connelly, and one was from New Zealand, Sean O'Connor. Their ministry matched the efforts of the San Luis sisters and priests in training catechists, meeting with parents, visiting homes, working with youth, and beginning discussion groups around faith issues. Sister Janet Caufield used her musical ability to help with liturgical celebrations.

Sisters Maureen O'Byrne and Barbara McGrath accepted the challenge of Chile in 1967. The Columban priests invited Maureen and Barbara to serve with them at Santa Catalina, an urban area of tightly packed high-rise apartments. The parish was divided into four sectors, and each of the four priests ministered in one sector, while Maureen and Barbara worked in all four sectors. Barbara concentrated her efforts on the youth; Maureen, besides her other efforts, began a small employment agency for poor women of the parish. During their time in Chile, they lived in one of the high-rise apartments within the parish of Santa Catalina, provided for them by the Columbans. In 1969 Maureen left Chile. Barbara continued at Santa Catalina but lived with the sisters at San Luis. In July 1976 Barbara returned to Rochester. The other Sisters of Mercy continued to serve in the parishes of San Luis and San Andres.

Sister Marilyn Gerstner arrived in 1968 and settled

in San Luis. In 1971 the group welcomed Sisters Doris Hamilton and Margaret Mungovan. Doris served in San Luis parish; Margaret went to San Andres to minister with Janet Caufield and Jane Kenrick. In 1973 the Columbans made the decision to withdraw from San Andres parish. They felt parish leaders could continue the work and that they were needed in poorer areas. The three sisters working at San Andres returned to San Luis. Their presence there was welcomed and needed because three of the original missionary sisters had left Chile: Sisters Jean DeVoldre, Mary Jane Nelson and Margaret Spellecy. Jean had been elected a delegate to the 1967 Chapter in Rochester. When she returned to the motherhouse in the summer of 1967, she decided not to continue as a Sister of Mercy. Mary Jane Nelson also chose a new life direction when she came back to the states in 1969. Margaret (Peggy) Spellecy left Santiago and the Mercy community in 1972 to marry Michael Walsh, the Columban priest who ministered with the sisters in San Luis parish. Thus, in 1973 Janet Korn, Marilyn Gerstner and Doris Hamilton were the only sisters serving with the Columban priests in San Luis.

From the beginning of the Latin American mission, the Rochester sisters invested themselves in the future of the Catholic church of Chile. They look back on those early years remembering, as Sister Jane Kenrick does, "a dynamic, developing church, open to change," and committed to two great challenges—forming communities of Christian leaders and accompanying the poor in their struggle for a better life.[8] The Church changed as it became open to the problems of the world. According to Sister Janet Korn, sisters moved into housing settlements called *poblaciones* in order to live with the poor, not just minister to them.

In a letter addressed to Sister M. Florence Sullivan, the archivist of the Rochester congregation, Janet laughingly wrote: "We have tried at least 101 different projects to create and find jobs, build community, and improve the standard of living. Many of these were short-lived, serving a purpose for a time; others failed due to many different reasons that you have to see to believe."[9]

In 1974 Sister Jane Kenrick opened a laundry cooperative. The poor of the *poblaciones* would wash and iron sheets, pillowcases and tablecloths brought to them by the wealthy women of the *barrio alto*. Many of the women of the *poblaciones* had husbands who were killed, imprisoned or without work as a result of the political situation in Chile. The money used to start this project was a gift from the bishops of Australia to the Columban priests.

Sister Marilyn Gertsner organized a self-help sewing class where the women made clothes for their families as well as for wealthy foreign women living in Santiago. All the sisters were involved in soup kitchens, a project initiated by the Diocese of Santiago to help those suffering from hunger. There were six soup kitchens in San Luis parish alone. This program was partly financed by the World Hunger Fund of the Rochester Sisters of Mercy.

Sister Janet Korn raised rabbits, or, as she says, "tried to." The first rabbits were stolen, the second group "got sick and died." Janet also involved herself in a new project—a sewing cooperative. In a small wooden shack, a group of women set up a business to make pants. They received the previously cut pants from the manufacturers and sewed them together. When the manufacturers went out of business, the women borrowed capital and invested it in material from which they made and sold pants for school children, as well as clothes for a boutique in the downtown area.

In 1984 a beauty school was organized by a professional beautician with help from Sister Margaret

Mungovan. Their goal was also to help people who were suffering from widespread unemployment; purchase of needed materials was difficult for the women, so Margaret appealed to the Diocese of Rochester for assistance. The beauty school project was one of three chosen by Operation Breadbox to receive support from Rochester parishes through the Office of Social Ministry. When the project closed in 1988, Margaret gave Father John Firpo, the director of Social Ministry, a detailed accounting of the financial transactions and the disposition of equipment.

Salvador Allende and the Coup

The Sisters of Mercy had been in Chile five years when a major event changed the direction of the country: the election of Salvador Allende, the first democratically elected socialist president in the western world. Allende's new government faced serious economic problems. As a result, the government decided to redistribute wealth and land in Chile. The copper industry was nationalized, as were the banks. However, Allende led a polarized society and the United States, through the Central Intelligence Agency, was doing everything in its power to eliminate his government and its policies.

On September 11, 1973, General Augusto Pinochet, commander-in-chief of the Chilean army, staged a military coup to overthrow the constitutionally elected Popular Unity government of Salvador Allende, who had hoped that peace and prosperity would come through socialism. President Allende died in La Moneda, the presidential palace, and his ministers and collaborators were arrested and sent to prison. Many of them were later killed, simply "disappeared" or went into exile.

Under General Pinochet, who declared himself president, seventeen years of dictatorship began which did not end until March 11, 1990. Pinochet closed the Chilean

Parliament, suspended the constitutions, banned all political and trade union activity and imposed strict controls over the media. According to official documents, before the end of this regime, 3,197 people died or "disappeared" as the result of human rights violations. The true number may never be known. Church leaders who defended individual rights, and doctors who treated injured victims also suffered persecution. Priests and sisters denounced the injustices of this time, and tried to help the persecuted. They worked with the families of the disappeared and several of them risked their lives by hiding people who were seeking asylum.

In October 1975 a Holy Cross priest asked Dr. Sheila Cassidy, a thirty-seven year old medical doctor from England, to treat a wounded man, a member of the Revolutionary Leftist Movement who was being sheltered at San Andres convent, now occupied by another group of women religious. Because of this action, Dr. Cassidy was targeted by General Pinochet's secret police. In November, while she was caring for an ill patient at the Columban priests' Center House in Santiago, the police shot their way into the house, killing the housekeeper. Sheila was taken away, questioned, tortured and put in solitary confinement. On December 29, 1975, she was finally released and expelled from the country. Sheila Cassidy was a good friend of the sisters, and Janet Korn remembers waiting for news of her with a "heart full of fear."

Cardinal Raul Silva, head of the Santiago archdiocese, fought the repression of the Pinochet government and worked with the poor. In cooperation with Protestant churches and a Jewish rabbi, he organized the Ecumenical Committee for Peace which set up economic self-help enterprises: farm co-ops, health clinics and soup kitchens for the poor. Under pressure from the government, this Peace Committee was dissolved in 1975. Cardinal Silva immediately created an archdiocesan department called the Vicariate of Solidarity, which he housed next to the Santiago Cathedral so it was protected by church status. The Vicariate provided legal, medical, and social services to thousands of people and became a center for human rights groups. Thus the Catholic Church was a beacon of hope in a very dark time, a strong force calling people to stand up to the dictatorship. The violence and repression of this period continued into the 1980s, and each Mercy missionary learned to deal with the reality in her own way.

In 1974 on the first anniversary of the September 11th Coup, the military searched the houses in a twelve-block area that included the convent at San Luis. Every man was taken out of his house and forced to lie face down in a field behind the church. Jane Kenrick and Janet Caufield remember how terrified they were because Father Peter Deckman, a Rochester priest serving in Bolivia, had come for some quiet time and was asleep in the convent. When the soldiers surrounded the bed with their guns ready, they could not wake him. Jane explained that he had come "exhausted." The soldiers commanded, "Wake him." Jane and Janet did, but they never forgot the look on Peter Deckman's face when he woke to those guns pointed at him. The soldiers told him to remain in the house until the search was ended. He did!

Throughout the Pinochet years, the sisters participated in activities protesting the torture and repression. Sister Anne Curtis, who arrived in Chile in 1987, remembers, "We stood alongside courageous Chileans in saying No to the dictatorship, and we experienced the harsh action of the police—tear gas, water cannons and detention."

In a July 1985 letter to Sister Elaine Kolesnik, Margaret Mungovan wrote,

My friend is free on bail, accused of doing harm to

the government by comments she made in one of her film critiques which appeared in a Jesuit magazine here. If her case isn't dismissed, she faces reprisal. What she said is the absolute truth, but it costs to tell the truth about what's really happening in Chile.[10]

"It cannot be underestimated," recalls Anne Curtis, "how we struggled through these years to build community, respond to overwhelming poverty amid a violent dictatorship and adjust to living in another culture as well as learn to be in community with a wide diversity of cultures." In addition, there was the sorrow of coming face to face with the truth of the United States' role in the downfall of Salvadore Allende and the rise of the Pinochet dictatorship.

New Women—New Life

For five years, from 1971 to 1976, no new Rochester sisters came to Chile, and six of the eleven women who came from 1965 to 1971 had for various personal reasons returned to Rochester. Jane Kenrick recalls a night when the group gathered together to look at their future: "It seemed very black because we did not feel that there were more sisters interested in coming to Chile. We tried to decide whether it would be better to leave or to stay until we could no longer go on."[11] They chose to stay because they had faith in their call to Chile and their belief in the mission of the Sisters of Mercy to the people. As a result of their discussion, Sister Margaret Mungovan wrote an "appeal letter to those sisters considering a change in work." Her words were a challenge to all those who read the letter. It told the story of what Chile meant to the sisters ministering there:

128

Are you free to settle about seven thousand miles from home for a limited time or even indefinitely? Would you accept the frustration and pain of learning to speak a new language? Could you put up with being ineffective for at least a whole year? Would bicycle or foot power suffice for locomotion in the parish area? Could you bring an extra supply of patience to wait for meetings to begin where the people either don't wear watches or ignore them? Would you wrap yourself in several layers of sweaters and a jacket or poncho and not mind wearing constantly muddied boots during three or four months of winter?

Do you long to work among people who will immediately accept and love you and assure you of their need of you? Would you like to bring the Gospel message to many whose religion has consisted in receiving Baptism, making their First (and only) Confession and Communion, taking part in Palm Sunday and Good Friday services, devotion to Our Lady without having a real encounter with her Son? Would it thrill you to witness the slow but real changes that take place in the lives of adults who participate in classes to learn to prepare their children for First Communion or in other types of formation? Can you believe that you would experience the power of Jesus Who makes the impossible possible and gives comfort and strength in moments of loneliness and discouragement? Are you aware that there is much more to communication than the spoken word, and that it is possible to form lasting friendships while the language still limps?

Would working without pressure free you to be

more creative? Would you enjoy setting up your own schedule, leaving it flexible enough to make a sudden change of plans on a given day? Would you feel comfortable living where times to relax are seen not as a luxury, but as a necessity and where one day a week is totally free for whatever one wishes to do? Does the possibility of living in one of the finest climates, in a city surrounded by the second-highest mountains in the world appeal to you? And would your heart leap at the sight of the winter snows on those mountains sparkling in the sun?

If you can answer most of these questions affirmatively, then Chile is calling you. Our congregation will complete eleven years here at the end of 1976. The Chileans can see this as a fine example of fidelity to commitment. Will you be the ones to help extend this commitment into the second decade?

The Chilean community never claimed "the appeal letter did it," but not long after it more people began to ask about serving in Chile. They received a letter from Sister Kay Schwenzer (Rochester), asking if it would be possible for her to be part of the community of Mercy in Chile. From Australia came an inquiry from Anna Gleeson, a Sister of Mercy interested in missionary work. It was the beginning of new life. Since that time, new sisters have arrived, not only from Rochester, but also from New Zealand, Ireland and other parts of the United States. Kay Schwenzer came to Santiago for two months in 1976 before attending language school. She returned in 1977 prepared for full-time ministry. That same year Anna Gleeson arrived from Australia.

Janet Korn and Kay Schwenzer investigated areas

where they might serve, but before a decision was made, Jesús Rodríguez Iglesias, a Spanish priest serving in Santiago, wrote to the Sisters of Mercy in Rochester requesting women religious for his parish: "Without a doubt, there must be sisters there, who with great joy, would like to come to this country and consecrate themselves to the 'evangelization of the poor.'"[12] Janet Korn from San Luis and Kay Schwenzer, newly arrived, responded to his plea, and in January 1978 they were welcomed to Santa Ana by the people of the *población*. Santa Ana was part of the parish of Nuestra Senora del Carmen. Sister Janet Wahl came to Santa Ana in March 1978, and Sister Margaret Mary Wintish arrived in 1979. Sister Margaret Mary had spent two months at San Luis before going to language school in Cochabamba, Bolivia. At Christmas time in Cochabamba, she injured her ankle in a fall, which necessitated her return to the United States. In 1979 she went back to Santiago to minister at Santa Ana; however, her injury forced her to return to Rochester permanently in March 1980.

Janet Wahl arrived in Chile after completing language school in Cochabamba. Previous to her study in Cochabamba, she had served as assistant to the Rochester superior, Sister Judith Heberle, from 1973 to 1977. In October 1974 she and Janet Korn had attended a meeting at the Inter-Church Center in New York City regarding the covert actions of the CIA in Chile. Janet Wahl, along with fourteen other Protestant and Roman Catholic missioners in Chile, sent an "Open Letter" to President Gerald Ford protesting the role of the United States government in the 1973 coup: President Ford had publicly defended the CIA's actions as "in the best interest of the people in Chile." The Chilean missionaries challenged him with their truth: "CIA funds were allocated to bribe the Chilean congress, to support national strikes and foment the civil disorder which precipitated the coup."[13]

In 1976 Janet Wahl brought to the attention of the Central Administration of the Rochester Sisters of Mercy the Project for Juridical Assistance to Political Detainees Imprisoned by the Military Government in Chile. This project provided financial support to lawyers who took on the defense of political prisoners as well as aid to the detainees and their families. The Central Administration (the elected advisors to the superior general and council) approved participation in this project, so the Sisters of Mercy contributed from their own financial resources, and Sister Judith Heberle wrote to corporations and individuals requesting donations. The money earmarked for this cause was sent to the Vicariate of Solidarity in Santiago for appropriate disbursement.

During her last years in Chile, Sister Marilyn Gerstner struggled to get help from the United States to obtain the release of political prisoners. She motivated Janet Wahl to adopt the same cause. Together they wrote endless letters of petition to the United States Embassy in Santiago, to members of the U.S. Congress, churches and religious congregations, in an attempt to have released from Chilean prisons detainees who had not been charged with any specific crime.

Back in Rochester, Sister Phyllis Bernardo worked by telephone with Marilyn Gerstner on the parole of two particular Chileans, Augustin Crotez del Campo and Juan Esteban Lagos Castillo. Phyllis spent hours on the phone with people in Washington D.C. In 1976 both these men and Juan's family were released. They came to Rochester under the sponsorship of the Sisters of Mercy, with assistance from the Spanish Apostolate of the diocese as well as Catholic parishes in the Rochester diocese.

The Chilean Formation Program Begins

Beginning around 1980 we began to talk about a

formation program for young women interested in being Sisters of Mercy. Will we ever forget those discussions! We went round and round in circles, and if ever there was a time when we were absolutely confused and in conflict, it was then.[14]

These words were spoken by Sister Anna Gleeson—the Australian Sister of Mercy who had been in Chile three years working with the Rochester Mercys.

The decision to look into a possible formation program was painful because in the late 1960s a young Chilean woman had lived with the Sisters of Mercy in order to discern her call to religious life. This experience had ended unhappily, so some sisters were wary of trying again. Yet they asked each other, "What is God saying to us? Who will be responsible? Will it change our lifestyle and manner of ministering? How many years will we be in Chile?[15]"

Sister Kay Schwenzer, the first director of the novitiate in Chile, writes of the development of the formation program:

> In July 1979 three sisters (Janet Caufield, Anna Gleeson, Jane Kenrick) participated in a meeting with the Sisters of Mercy in Argentina; some of the Argentinean sisters raised the question of starting basic formation in Chile. Later, through the Sisters of Mercy Latin American/Caribbean Conferences in Jamaica in 1980 and in Honduras in 1981, we discovered that this was a growing question among the Sisters of Mercy throughout Latin America.

The sisters soon discovered increased vocational interest and searching among the youth. Sister Jane Kenrick began a mixed vocational interest group in San Luis parish in 1980, and Sister Kay Schwenzer began a group in her parish, Nuesta Senora del Carmen, in 1981. Several young women expressed more specific interest in the congregation, so Jane maintained closer contact with them.

For over a year the sisters in Chile had regular weekly reflection sessions, and much of the time was spent on this topic of formation. Kay Schwenzer recalled: "We have had hopes, doubts, fears, bursts of enthusiasm and conviction, and times of feeling incapable, but it seems that through it all someone keeps pushing us onward."[16] In June 1980 Graciela Lagos, a young Chilean from San Luis parish who had known the sisters since 1965, became a postulant with the Sisters of Mercy in Argentina. In April 1981 she began her novitiate formation. The Mercy community decided to take the risk into the unknown. They offered Graciela Lagos the opportunity of finishing her novitiate in Chile and continuing as a Sister of Mercy in Chile. Graciela lived with Kay and Janet Wahl at Santa Ana and participated, as did later novices, in the formation program offered in Santiago by the Chilean Conference of Men and Women Religious.

Sister Maria Inés
Olguin Caro

Sister Lia Nora
González Sandoval

Soledad Cantillana Calderón entered the community in 1984, and was the first Chilean to profess vows as a Sister of Mercy. Lía González Sandoval, who had worked with the sisters at Santa Ana, and María Elena Prado Normabueno entered in 1986. María Inés Olguin Caro arrived in 1987. Although Ana María Parada Escobar, who entered in 1993, did not complete her first year, she brought the richness of her culture to the group. Almost ten years passed before two other young women joined the Mercy community: Lilian Silva Aparcio and Valeria Vicencio Catalán. Eventually Graciela Lagos, the first novice, and María Elena Prado chose to journey in a new direction. Looking back on the time of formation, Kay Schwenzer reflects: "We made mistakes with these Chilean women because of a lack of good understanding of their values and culture, but through it all we grew."

The presence of the Chilean women brought new hope for the future. The mission of the Rochester sisters would continue with these sisters who came with such a passion to serve the poor of their country. As Anna Gleeson remembers, "They challenged us to move out of ourselves, to inculturate far more deeply than we'd been able to do or were capable of doing before."[17]

In 1987 Lía González, who had been received into the community less than a year, shared with the sisters her "signs of hope" for the future:

> Now let's take a look at the signs of hope that I see. First of all—formation in Chile. I feel bold enough to begin with formation, at the same time being fully aware of the mutual risk on the part of the congregation as well as the Chileans.
>
> The sisters had to open their homes and hearts to the Chilean women/people. It is one thing to work among the people but there still exists the privacy of

the house that one may need as a foreigner with her own culture. But formation in Chile meant opening yourselves totally to another culture because they are two distant relatives. I feel the risk of losing one's own identity not only applies to North Americans, but applies as well to the Chileans.

As Chileans, we enter a reality distinct from what we are used to. We enter a different social class and it would be very easy to accept the economic standards of another culture and even invent needs that we wouldn't have otherwise. It would be easy to fall into patterns which wouldn't allow us to question the call of Jesus—to live simply.

But in all this lies a great hope. In spite of all the differences our great hope rests in God. God's love is far greater than national borders and cultures.[18]

Third World Experience

Lía's words, "God's love is far greater than national borders and cultures," were a truth made real for the Rochester sisters when the congregation began the "Third World Experience." This program gave one or two professed sisters the opportunity to spend one month with the sisters in Santiago to experience a Third World culture and to give support and encouragement to the Rochester women ministering there. When Sisters Anne Marie Lennon and Jane Schur were preparing for their visit in 1981, the Sisters in Chile wrote these words to them: "We hope that by exposure to our everyday Chilean reality, you may be touched and evangelized by this reality and by the Chilean people."

One of the important results of these visits was

sharing the experience back home. The Rochester sisters felt much more connected to the Chilean people when they heard about them firsthand from more sisters who had spent time in the actual situation. The sisters had an increased awareness of the challenge of working far from home in a different culture and language.

Several sisters came home feeling the call to missionary work and returned to Chile later to serve the people they had met during their month's experience. Sisters Joanne Deck and Anne Marie Mathis had their Third World experience in 1983 and returned full-time in 1985, after their missionary preparation in Birmingham, England and their language study in Cochabamba, Bolivia. Sisters Anne Curtis and Carol Wulforst were sensitized by the Chilean reality in July 1985. They went back to Chile in 1987.

Other Rochester sisters visited Chile and none returned home untouched by the visit. Sisters Rosemary Sherman and Barbara DiFiore experienced a church community similar to the early Church in the people's concern for one another and their willingness to share responsibility in the parish. Sisters Joanne Bringley and Maureen Servas realized "it was the poor who can teach us what it really means to be rich."[19] Perhaps Lía González said it best:

The Third World experience is a sign of hope. It is not simply a matter of thinking that the Sisters are going to come to Chile and then desire to return here to work, but it may be that they come to receive the message from the poor and to take this back to their own country.[20]

New Ministry, New Possibilities

On June 15, 1985, Sisters Joanne Deck and Anne Marie Mathis arrived in Chile after three months of language study in Cochabamba. Just six months later, in December, the Mercy sisters celebrated the twentieth anniversary of their Chile foundation. Joanne and Anne Marie joined Kay Schwenzer and Margaret Mungovan at Santa Ana. They remained there until January 1986 when Joanne, Anne Marie and Kay moved to the commune of La Pintana in the Southern Zone. This decision, made after visiting several different areas, opened up new possibilities for ministry where the presence of the Church had been minimal. The sisters worked with a Maryknoll priest, Father Robert Coyne, a Maryknoll brother and other groups of women religious in a poor, crowded area, the poorest of all the municipalities of Santiago. There were only seven public phones, and the sisters walked ten minutes to make a phone call. The unemployment rate was very high, and people were under stress in their living situations. If they had their light and water cut off, they connected the electricity themselves illegally. There was no lack of needs to meet in this area. Since Kay Schwenzer was also the novice director; the novices joined this community as they were received into the Sisters of Mercy—a challenge for Kay as she balanced pastoral responsibilities with novitiate responsibilities. Eventually four novices ministered in this area with Kay and Anne Marie: Soledad Cantillana, Lía González, María Inés Olguin and María Elena Prado. In March 1987 Joanne Deck decided to return to San Luis parish.

In the late eighties and nineties, when Sisters Anne Curtis (1987), Carol Wulforst (1987), Margaret Mary Mattle (1991), and Theresa Rutty (1996) came to Chile, the ministry scene was very different. Most new missionaries chose their ministry after they arrived, discerning the needs of the people and their own skills. Anne Curtis lived and worked in Jesus the Carpenter parish in the Huamachuco area of Santiago, a parish served by the Maryknoll priests. One of the priests, Charlie Mulligan, was a Maryknoll associate who belonged to the Diocese of Rochester, New York. The Maryknoll priests eventually moved from this parish and Chilean priests accepted responsibility for the area.

Anne Curtis also worked with the Australian Sisters of Mercy, especially Sister Jackie Ford, to create a Casa de la Mujer (Women's House). The house was a dream of the women of the *población*. One woman described it:

> We dream of something we believe will be difficult but not impossible — a house —"*una casa.*" A woman's house in the *población* for the *pobladoras* (women of the shanty towns of Chile), "our" house. A place where we'd be able to receive any woman in need and offer a space where women can come to grow.[21]

In addition to providing a place for the women to meet and share their pains and struggles, to attend workshops (on topics like violence, human relations, sexuality), the house also furnished a site for a doctor, a social worker and a psychologist to offer services for the poor of the neighborhood.

Other Australian Sisters of Mercy who worked in this area were Anna Gleeson, Patricia McDermott and Veronica Ekerick. Joan Doyle, who came in 1995 on a temporary basis before going to Peru, also served in Huamachuco. Sisters Jackie Ford and Patricia McDermott moved with her to Peru to open a new ministry. Sister Margaret Milne, a Mercy from New Zealand who arrived in Chile in 1992, now ministers as the only Sister of Mercy at Huamachuco. She provides basic nursing care and advocacy within the health system. She also works with Capacitar—an international group working toward the empowerment and spiritual development of women in Third World countries.

Sisters Louise Dantzig (Brooklyn) and Ann Kennelly (New Zealand) also created a house for women, Ruca Catalina McAuley (House of Catherine McAuley), in Santiago. Together they successfully sought donations from groups to provide the space and the services needed. In 2002 this house was enlarged and renovated through the generosity of friends of the Rochester Sisters of Mercy. Its focus was to help women see themselves as persons of dignity and self-worth. The House now contains additional space for short-term housing for the homeless and people in the city who need medical care, as well as room in which to give health care to the uninsured.

Sister Carol Wulforst brought her gifts of compassion and gentleness to the parish of Nuestra Senora de las Americas; she lived at both San Luis and Santa Monica convents. Before the Sisters of Mercy lived at Santa Monica, a house belonging to the Santiago archdiocese, it was home for Maryknoll priests serving in Santiago. In 1989 it became the novitiate house for the Sisters of Mercy, where Sisters Jane Kenrick, Ann Kennelly (New Zealand), Lía González and María Inés Olguin lived, Jane serving then as the director of novices.

A New Governing Structure

In 1987 the seventeen sisters in the Chilean community gathered at a retreat house in Santiago for a week of prayer and reflection to examine the past history of their mission to the people of Chile. They called this experience "Graced History" because it was a way of looking at their personal and communal history from a faith perspective. Sisters Janet Korn and Margaret Mattle led the group through the process. They shared their "light history" and their "dark history" and their hopes for the future. Every sister present for this assembly was profoundly moved and knew that the mission of the Sisters of Mercy would be deeply affected by the graces of this time.

One of the results of this gathering was the desire to form a new structure of government. The community in Chile had changed significantly over twenty-three years. It was evident something new was needed to enable the mission of Mercy in Latin America to move forward. The group no longer embraced only sisters from Rochester; there were women from Australia, New Zealand, and other parts of the United States. In addition, Chilean sisters were in formation and other women were in association. All these facts were blessings and signs of growth, but the community realized that these changes required new developments and a process to make good decisions. Sister Jean Marie Kearse, the Rochester superior at the time, worked with the group to finalize the government structure, which they defined in the following way:

> The form of government of the Sisters of Mercy of Rochester in Chile is a Regional Government that facilitates and animates their life and mission, encourages the fullest participation of the Sisters in the decisions which affect their lives, and enables all to respond with greater freedom and energy to the needs of the poor and of the times.[22]

The final structure called for an elected coordinator with two elected council members and three commissions: Communication, Formation, and Mission. Sister Anne Curtis explained to the Rochester sisters:

> This is a thumbnail sketch of the government structure. We are entering into it with trust, as there is much still to be worked out and lived through. It has been an exciting and scary time—it was energizing to be together . . . we are full of hope.[23]

141

After a number of years, the three commissions no longer served a worthwhile purpose so they were eliminated, but three elected leaders are still part of the present government structure. In 2002 three Chilean sisters for the first time were elected to this leadership group: Lía González, Soledad Cantillana and María Inés Olguin.

First World Experience

Experiences need to go both ways if boundaries are to diminish. The third world experience brought a deeper understanding of Chile to the Rochester sisters; the first world experience made Rochester real to the Chilean sisters. In January 1994 Sisters Soledad Cantillana, Lía González and María Inés Olguin came to Rochester to learn about their Rochester roots. María Inés wanted to know the history of the Rochester congregation and "to feel part of the bigger group." Lía felt that being one of only three Chileans in the congregation was a big responsibility. "I want to grow in Mercy," she said, "but with a Chilean identity." Soledad (Sole) added, "We want to feel at home."[24]

The preparations for their journey began in June 1993. Sister Louise Dantzig (Brooklyn) was the contact person between Chile and the United States. She gathered the three sisters together to discuss their expectations. The results were faxed to the members of the welcoming committee who would coordinate their visit in Rochester: Anne Curtis, Janet Korn and Kay Schwenzer. Their expectations of the Rochester visit, as recorded by Louise Dantzig, were these:

1. Unanimous hope: To visit the places where the sisters work, and very especially, the most rural areas.

2. Visit Niagara Falls (from the Canadian side if possible).

3. Get to know the older sisters, visit those in the infirmary where possible.

4. Expressed a special interest in Melita House, Kay Schwenzer's parish, and any centers of Hispanic peoples.

5. Would like to offer a taste of Chile, a type of *Fonda Chilena* with Chilean music, dance, food etc. They are willing and eager to prepare *calzones rotos*, etc. and bring along some Chilean wine.

6. They would like to meet the families of the Rochester sisters who work in Chile (maybe at this *Fonda*?).

7. Though they are arming themselves with a bit of English, they hope the sisters will speak slowly and be patient with them!!

8. They all hope that their time will include moments of peace and quiet, with some unscheduled, unplanned moments—a time to reflect and absorb, "*a ritmo no tan rapido*" (a slower pace).

9. They're afraid of the cold!! We assured them that there is heat in houses, cars, etc. (unconvinced . . .), will bring boots, etc.[25]

The Chilean sisters were prophetic in their concern about being cold, because 1994/1995 was one of Rochester's coldest, most snow-filled winters. They never let the superior, Sister Ann Miller, forget that she had promised them a mild winter. The warmth of their welcome from the Rochester community made up for the cold outside, and the snow didn't hinder their ministry visits or their visits to the Rochester convents. They even made the trip to Niagara Falls, though the sisters on the welcoming committee went with misgiving.

At the end of their visit, almost the whole community joined them for the farewell—a *Fonda Chilean* complete with Chilean music, dance and food. At the airport, the next day, there were both laughter and tears as the Chilean Sisters of Mercy waved good-bye to their Rochester sisters after their first "First World" experience. Sole's hope had been realized, "We feel at home." Maria Inés added, "We are all one in Mercy."

Moving into the 21st Century

Sister Margaret Mary Mattle, who with Janet Korn had facilitated the Graced History Assembly in 1987, was welcomed back to San Luis in 1991 as a missionary. At first, she worked with Sister Ann Kennelly in a small community within San Luis Parish, which the Columban priests had initiated at the request of the people. Margaret and Ann organized catechesis, helped with liturgies, gathered census data, and more importantly, enabled the people to develop and minister to their own community. Margaret also ministered to the women at Ruca Catalina McAuley, the house for women in Santiago.

Eventually, Margaret Mary Mattle joined Jane Kenrick in Viña del Mar, a city on the Pacific coast. In January 1992, Jane and two Ursuline sisters, Mimi Ballard and Gia Mudd, joined Mauricio Villegus, the pastor of Parroquia San Rafael, to minister in the diocese of Valparaiso. This marked the first time the Rochester Mercys left the diocese of Santiago to minister in another

144

diocese. Margaret Mary Mattle lived with Jane in Viña del Mar, but served as a pastoral associate in Parroquia La Matriz in Valparaiso where she ministered to the very poor and had a special ministry to prostitutes. She worked with Jose Gutierrez, a diocesan priest who had suffered greatly during the Pinochet regime and was deeply loved by the people of the area. After Margaret had been in Chile one year, she shared these thoughts about her ministry:

> It is occurring to me that, even as I open myself to the culture of these people, to their language and their way of life, I will never fully understand them, much less be able to express myself adequately in their language. I will never be as competent here as I might have been in my own culture and language. However, I am convinced that 'competence' is not what they expect from me. They want to share friendship, to feel respected, and to search together for God and the meaning of the life God has given us.[26]

Sister Theresa Rutty, who came to Chile in 1996, worked from 1996 to 2002 in Rungue, a farm area about two hours outside of Santiago. These are Theresa's words as she describes life at Rungue:

> Sisters Lia González and Anne Marie Mathis and I form the little community here. Life is very simple. Each morning we must collect water for the day's use in various containers, buckets, bottles or pitchers. Laundry is done by hand. Cooking is creative with whatever is at hand—usually fresh vegetables and rice combined with a small amount of meat and fruit for dessert. The household tasks, ministry, prayer, joys and sorrows are shared mutually. Amid the shortage of water, abundance

of ants and the daily surprises of a new place we find much joy and laughter. And, we look forward to our two postulants joining us in January (Lilian Silva Aparicio and Valeria Vicencio Catalán).[27]

After six years of service in Rungue, Theresa moved to work with the sisters in Copiapo. She attends to the needs of the elderly in nursing homes and private homes, and specializes in foot care including massage. She also offers spiritual ministry and comfort for the elderly. Copiapo is a twelve-hour bus ride north from Santiago through the desert; it is a desert mining town that has been growing over the years. In 1995 Joanne Deck and Maria Inés Olguin along with Sister Judith Frikker, a Mercy sister from Detroit, left Santiago to minister to the people of Copiapo.

Judith served both as a physician in a city-operated health clinic and as a pastoral minister at La Parroquia Jesus de Nazaret where Joanne and Maria Inés minister.[28] When she returned to her community in Detroit, Maria Inés and Joanne began a new ministry that provides housing and friendship for Chilean girls who come from areas where there are no schools or live at too great a distance to travel to school on a daily basis. The sisters encourage the girls in their studies, so they can obtain a secondary school education that will enable them to study at the university. Education for women is important for the future. Joanne says, "I feel as if I'm watching my own girls grow up."

In 2005 Sisters Lía and Valeria remain with the ministry at Rungue, but Anne Marie Mathis has joined Soledad Cantillana and Lilian Silva in the small community of Pelequén, where they are the first women religious to minister in that area. The sisters work with the youth, and provide religious education and sacramental preparation as well as health care for the poor. Soledad, the second Chilean woman to join the Sisters of Mercy, also serves as parish nurse, providing alternative medicines as well as spiritual ministry.

In 1966 when Sister Jane Kenrick began her ministry in Chile, she never imagined that she would still be there to celebrate forty years; but, as she says, "I can't imagine being anywhere else." In Viña del Mar, Jane has developed a program of pastoral and social care for those affected by HIV/AIDS. She is in the process of developing an HIV/AIDS program for children, services now needed for this growing population. Community, support, prayer, transportation, and medical needs are all a part of the overall program. Of her ministry, Jane says, "I am very fortunate, blessed and enriched by all the wonderful people God has put in my path. The people here hold a true place in my heart. If I left, it would be as if I were leaving my family."

Sister Janet Caufield would echo those same words; she and Jane arrived in Chile together in 1966. Janet still lives in the San Luis house and serves in the same parish area that Father Kevin O'Boyle invited Mother M. Bride to "come and see" in February 1965. The house, now owned by the Rochester Sisters of Mercy, functions as a Center House for the Mercy community, because it is large enough to accommodate visitors and to provide temporary housing for sisters beginning their service in Chile. The parish, once home to the Columbans, is now served by Father Roberto Arjijo, a priest of the Archdiocese of Santiago.

Sister Josephine Twomey, a Mercy sister from Cork, Ireland, joined the community at San Luis in 1991. She and Margaret Mattle had met at language school in Cochabamba. At the present time Josie and Janet Caufield serve in pastoral ministry and religious education in San Luis parish. They work with families in sacramental preparation of their children and provide paraliturgical services in the absence of a priest, a vital service because the parish priest comes only twice a month for Mass in the various chapels of the parish. Janet and Josie have trained lay ministers to help in this service. Forty years ago, there was not one trained volunteer; today there are twenty-two lay volunteer ministers.

In 1965 Father Kevin O'Boyle promised Mother M. Bride that he could offer her sisters "nothing." It was her confident, faith-filled response—"I'll take it"—that planted a seed of hope in the soil of Chile. Over the years that seed has been sustained by the spirit of thirty-one Sisters of Mercy who have come from many lands to link their lives with the people of Chile. Twenty of these women came from Rochester; some stayed for only two or three years; others will tell you they think of remaining forever in Chile, because they have come to see it as home. Eleven Sisters of Mercy came from other countries or other parts of the United States; six sisters came from Australia between 1979 and 1995, two from New Zealand and one each from Ireland, Brooklyn and Detroit. These women were active not only in ministry, but in the community of the Sisters of Mercy, serving as elected leaders and contributing their gifts to the Chilean formation program as companions or directors.

Bishop Matthew H. Clark and Sister Soledad Cantillana Calderón at the 20th anniversary of the Chilean Foundation

All of these women learned what Kay Schwenzer expressed after her years in Chile: "You do not need positive, concrete results to prove that you are a successful missionary. You let go of your own desire for success and are at peace with your gospel presence to these people." "Being with the poor here," adds Janet Caufield, "has been the greatest source of richness in my life."

Rochester Remembers

The people of the Diocese of Rochester have also walked the Chilean journey over these forty years. In 1993 the community of sisters in Chile wrote the following letter to the Rochester diocese:

> Greetings to the people of the Rochester Diocese. Celebrations are in order to honor all of you who have for 25 years faithfully maintained the Sisters of Mercy who minister to the poor and needy in Chile.
>
> Where have you been in Chile, and where are you now? During the sixteen and a half years of dictatorship, you were feeding poor children in "*comedores*." You were walking with the families of those who had been tortured or killed. You were braving tear gas and water wagons while protesting against the flagrant injustices. You were encouraging women whose families had no income or less than minimum to join a laundry cooperative which even to this day functions to a limited degree.
>
> Those long years saw many tragedies in Chile. You were there in the floods that inundated the poor areas every few days. You sent relief. The earthquake of 1985 became a focus for your

generosity. You came to Chile to visit in the person of Bishop Casey first, then Bishop Hogan and those who accompanied him. You have come to us each time Bishop Matthew Clark has paid us a visit.[29]

It was Bishop Fulton Sheen, the successor of Bishop James E. Kearney, who organized the first diocesan mission collection in 1969. This collection was to support the sisters and priests of the diocese working in mission areas of the world. This annual collection continues in the Rochester diocese. In 1976 Bishop Joseph Hogan, the seventh bishop of Rochester, encouraged the people of the diocese to be generous in their missionary contributions by reminding them, "I want the Church of Rochester to be a missionary Church, for I believe this is central to abundant life in Christ."[30]

Many years ago, Bishop Matthew Clark wrote about his visit to the missions, and his words are still remembered: "I have been inspired by our sisters in Brazil (Rochester Sisters of St. Joseph) and in Chile. They are beautiful women in whom all the Diocese of Rochester can justly take pride."[31]

When in 1985 the Rochester congregation commemorated the twentieth anniversary of their missionary presence in Chile, Sister Janet Korn, one of the first to be chosen for the mission, remembered those days with gratitude:

> In 1965 the Chileans were simply "a people we left home to serve." Now twenty years later, these men and women are our friends, our companions; we have found a home with them.[32]

As the Rochester Sisters and Associates of Mercy celebrate forty years of ministry to the people of Chile, the depth of their commitment to and love for the poor of Chile remains unchanged. Lía González, a Chilean Sister of Mercy, shares her beliefs:

> The Sisters of Mercy are a congregation that responds to the signs of the times and they respond out of love for the people. Come what may for the people, the Sisters make the Chileans' pain their own. In spite of the repression, the Sisters are standing among the people as they should be. For that reason I am convinced that we are a congregation that is not going to die because the Spirit of God is present.[33]

The Chilean mission has experienced joy and laughter since its beginning, but it also shares a history of both light and darkness as the missionary sisters continue to struggle with separation from family and friends, language difficulties, adapting to a new culture, the overwhelming poverty, and the challenge of reflecting on and renewing the ministry of the Sisters of Mercy in Chile. Father Kevin O'Boyle's words to Mother M. Bride still call to us:

> If you would like to come to Chile we will receive you. The work is difficult, the area is tough, the challenge is great, and so this makes it more interesting and rewarding.

CHAPTER SEVEN

HEALTHCARE MINISTRY

The history of St. James Mercy Hospital begins with the story of a priest—Father James Early. His story unfolds in the late 1800s when Father Early was a contemporary of Bishop Bernard McQuaid, Rochester's first bishop. In many ways, these two men were alike. They were strong in their beliefs, completely dedicated to the church and future-oriented. In 1865 Bishop Timon appointed Father Early pastor of St. Patrick's Church in Rochester when that city was still part of the Buffalo diocese. Father Early was also Bishop Timon's first choice to be bishop of the new diocese of Rochester. However, when word came from Rome, Bernard McQuaid had been chosen instead of James Early.[1]

When Bishop McQuaid arrived in Rochester in 1868, he named Father Early as vicar general of the new diocese; as time went on, a growing disagreement between the bishop and the vicar general caused Father Early to resign as rector of St. Patrick's Church—which Bishop McQuaid had designated as the diocesan cathedral. Father

152

Early requested that he be allowed to return to Buffalo, and Bishop McQuaid granted his request. Bishop Stephen V. Ryan, who had succeeded Bishop Timon as bishop of Buffalo, welcomed Father Early, whom he considered one of the most generous and talented clergymen of the time.

This action proved to be highly advantageous for the city of Hornell and Steuben County, because in 1879 Father Early was appointed pastor of St. Ann's Church in Hornell. The Sisters of Mercy were teaching in the parish school there, and in 1882 they opened the Academy of Mercy with Father Early as one of the trustees. Serving in that same capacity as trustees were Sisters M. Dolores Clancy and M. Catherine Monaghan, Mercy sisters from the Batavia motherhouse. These women were to play an important role in the founding of St. James Mercy Hospital.

In the 1880s Hornell was an active railroad town, and it was not uncommon that workers were involved in accidents. Father Early, who was described in 1896 by the Honorable Harlo Hakes as "one of the most earnest and unselfish Christian workers in this field," was increasingly concerned about the welfare of the railroad workers. He saw the need for a hospital to care for the sick and injured, and it was his dream to provide one for Hornell.[2]

In 1889 Father Early made a will in which he left property to St. Ann's Church "for the purpose of founding and establishing a hospital in the city of Hornell to be entrusted to the care of the Sisters of Mercy." This property contained a small farm house called the "Water Cure." It was this building that became the first hospital.[3]

In February 1890 Father Early created a corporation for the hospital under the laws of New York State. Among the nine trustees named were two Sisters of Mercy—Sister M. Dolores Clancy and Sister M. Catherine Monaghan, who had served with Father Early as trustees of the Academy of Mercy. On February 13, 1890, Father Early deeded to this newly formed corporation his property on the corner of Canisteo and Van Scoter streets. A condition set forth in the deed was that "The Sisters of Mercy shall have perpetual charge of the hospital and shall have the right to free chapel exercises therein, and at least two of their number shall always be members of the Board of Trustees."[4] Three days later, on February 16, 1890, Father James Early died, having made his dream of a hospital into a reality and, like Catherine McAuley, having provided a home "for poor suffering humanity." In his honor, the hospital was named St. James Mercy.

On the feast of St. Catherine of Siena, April 30, 1890, the first Mass was celebrated in the chapel of the new hospital. The hospital housed two wards, one for men, one for women; they could accommodate approximately fifteen patients. Sister M. Catherine Monaghan was appointed the first CEO (then called the "matron"). In 1901, after Bishop McQuaid had acquired the four southern tier counties from the Buffalo diocese, these sisters were part of the group that remained with the Batavia motherhouse. Sister M. Dolores Clancy at the time was major superior of the Batavia sisters and would become the first superior of the united communities of Buffalo and Batavia. Sister M. Catherine Monaghan left Hornell in 1892, and in 1903 she initiated the founding of Mercy Hospital in Buffalo.

During the early days of the hospital, the work was handicapped by lack of funds and want of equipment. Dr. W.R. Wakerman recalled his experience of the early days:

> When I came to town in the spring of 1894, the Institution was used mostly for the care of persons injured on the railroad and other accident cases. In fact, it was an Emergency Hospital—very few private patients being received at that time, owing to lack of equipment. There was only one private room as I remember, fully furnished, and that was the Adsit Room. Some money had been raised

through the efforts of the Staff, by lawn festivals, baseball games, etc. and a small amount of surgical instruments and supplies were purchased, a cabinet made for them, and a room fitted up for operations.

In the summer of 1898, the trustees greatly increased the capacity of the institution by making much needed additions. A fine, well lighted operating room, modern kitchens, laundry and three spacious wards were built. Since then the patronage of hospital has greatly increased and its capacity has been taxed many times during the past year.

About a year ago (1904) a Women's Board of Managers was organized. They have issued a printed report of their work for the year which shows they have raised a total of $1,319.97.[5]

The Women's Board, now called the Auxiliary, still functions and contributes in many ways to the hospital's success.

In the history of the hospital, two stories have been frequently repeated down through the years that have no basis in fact. The first story claims that Father Early gave the land on which the hospital is built to the city of Hornell so that "the sisters would at all times be sure of a salary and that the institution could be kept in good repair backed by public finances." Father Early's will is very clear that the property was given first to St. Ann's Church, Hornell, then to the group who served as trustees for the new hospital corporation. The city of Hornell was never involved in any of these transactions.

The second source of confusion concerned the ownership of the hospital. In the late 1970s some questions surfaced that prompted the Sisters of Mercy to research the issue of ownership with their own legal counsel. The research undertaken by Father Adam Maida, later the archbishop of Detroit, proved that the Sisters of Mercy did not have ownership of the hospital at any time. However, from 1961 to 1970 they did have legal control of the corporation that owned the hospital because the Board of Trustees consisted entirely of Rochester Sisters of Mercy. A correct statement of the legal structure from 1961 to 1970 would be that the corporation owned the hospital and that the sisters governed the corporation.[6]

Total membership on the Board of Trustees was given to the sisters in 1961 since at that time the sisters began to have a major financial stake in the hospital, either through guaranteeing hospital financial obligations or through direct loans to the hospital. Total membership on the board was appropriate then, because of the sisters' financial investment in the corporation. The Hornell newspaper articles at that time, indicating that the sisters had assumed ownership of the hospital, were incorrect.

Merger Discussion

In June 1974, St. James Mercy and Bethesda Community Hospital met to discuss the possibility of making a greater number of health services available to more people locally by eliminating unnecessary duplication of these services in the two hospitals. Conversation about sharing between the two hospitals goes back to 1971. This goal seemed to have great value, but the idea of merging a Catholic hospital and a non-denominational hospital raised misunderstandings and feelings of distrust.

In the mid-seventies, New York State put pressure on both Boards of Trustees to combine maternity units because of a declining birth rate throughout the state. Sister René McNiff was then administrator of the hospital and seeing the value of this wrote to the Central Administration of the Sisters of Mercy:

What has been said of maternity could be related to many other areas of the hospital. It seemed reasonable to our board, to take a serious look at combining services, possibly even merging. [7]

The hospitals accepted a grant from the Regional Medical Program in 1975 and employed the consulting firm of Block and McGibony from Silver Spring, Maryland to do a study for both hospitals. The study, received a year and a half later, did not meet their expectations. A second study done by the Nixon, Hargrave law firm was beneficial in showing the hospitals how they could merge if they wished to do so.

In January 1982 Sister René shared with the staff at St. James Mercy the news of great progress between the two hospitals:

> The new consolidation is on its way. It was a very important decision for the future of people in the Hornell area and for everyone who is deeply tied to either institution. Without it the level of health care offered locally would have gradually diminished because no one could have continued to afford two expensive sets of duplicated services. The new hospital will be called Bethesda Mercy Health Care Center.

However, after a dozen years of discussion and recommendations, Bethesda Community Hospital was closed by the New York State Health Department in 1985 before any merger was possible. St. James Mercy then purchased the Bethesda property and reopened it as Mercy Care, a skilled nursing facility. In 1998 eighty additional beds were added and the 120 bed nursing facility was renamed McAuley Manor at Mercy Care, in honor of Catherine McAuley, the first Sister of Mercy.

Education for Healthcare

In an effort to provide good medical care for their patients, the hospital decided to educate women to be nurses. In the early 1900s, a registered nurse from Rochester, known to this day as "Miss Moore" came to Hornell to instruct two young sisters in the skills of nursing. These two sisters, Mary deSales Reilly and Mary Aid Leary, graduated from the training school and began their years of service to the hospital.

In 1912 the School of Nursing was officially opened and registered with the New York State Department of Education. In 1915, Sister Mary deSales was appointed Director of the School of Nursing. When a separate building was identified for the nursing school, it was named DeSales Hall in tribute to Sister M. deSales and in appreciation of her twenty-nine years of service to St. James Mercy Hospital. Reorganization and registration of the school with the New York State Department of Education took place in 1939. The school was granted full accreditation by the National League for Nursing in 1958.

By 1996, a three year nursing program was no longer feasible or recommended for nursing graduates. The Board of Trustees therefore accepted the recommendation of the management team to close the school in 1997. Over a thousand nurses had earned their diplomas from this School of Nursing, which had consistently received accreditation from the National League for Nursing. CEO Paul Shephard wrote about the school's closing:

> While it is with deep regret that we acknowledge the end of an era, we feel hopeful that we can continue the spirit of the School of Nursing that

began in 1900 as the "St. James Training School." In formal recognition of the school, its history and heritage, the hospital administration has created the DeSales Scholarship Fund, named after Sister Mary deSales, one of the first graduates and later one of the most dynamic and dedicated directors of the school. The DeSales Scholarship will provide ongoing continuing education for nurses within the St. James Mercy Health System. This will ensure that Sr. deSales' commitment to the hospital and our community will continue by providing educational opportunities to those that have dedicated their talents to a career in nursing.[8]

The hospital also sponsored the School of Radiologic Technology (formerly the School of X-Ray). Founded in 1948 by Dr. William McFarland with the assistance of Sister M. Colette Frank and Sister Miriam Joseph Newman, the school has grown with distinction over the years because of the increased need for registered technologists in today's healthcare world.

Upstate Health Partners

Though the proposed merger with Bethesda Hospital was never realized, there was a constant effort on the part of the administration to improve St. James Mercy's ability to provide excellent service to the rural area of Steuben County. In 1995 the hospital signed an agreement with Strong Memorial Hospital in Rochester and Jones Memorial Hospital in Wellsville (Allegany County) to form a new health network called Upstate Health Partners. Patients no longer had to travel to Rochester for specialized services; the specialists came to Hornell and Wellsville.

Paul Shephard, the first layperson to be CEO of St. James Mercy, praised the network "as a way to ensure a wide range of health services for people in the community."[9]

Issues of Relationship

Research in the 1970s proved that the Sisters of Mercy did not own the hospital, but what relationship did they have to St. James Mercy Hospital? For many years the large number of sisters serving in the hospital created a strong bond of communication and interest within the Rochester community. However, over the years fewer sisters were available for nursing and the number of sisters serving the hospital declined dramatically. In the late 1980s the administration of the hospital and the leadership of the Sisters of Mercy struggled to define their precise relationship.

Did the Sisters of Mercy sponsor the hospital or were they simply collaborators in its works of mercy? The congregation defined sponsorship as "a relationship of support, influence and responsibility for the future of a ministry."[10] Sisters of Mercy still sat on the Board of Trustees, but in a limited number. They did not have a financial obligation to the hospital, approve its mission statement or appoint the CEO. How were they to name their relationship to a ministry that held so many memories for the Mercy sisters?

In the midst of this dialogue, the hospital became part of a new reality which created a new and stronger relationship between the Sisters of Mercy and St. James Mercy. In 1986 ten congregations of women religious, all Sisters of Mercy located on the east coast, came together with their health ministries to form a new entity—Eastern Mercy Health System. The goal of Eastern Mercy was to build a common vision for the future of Catholic health care, to strengthen the role of sponsorship, and to plan strategically for the future. Since the Rochester major superior sat on the Sponsors Council of Eastern Mercy Health System as well as on the board of St. James Mercy Hospital, there was a greater investment of her time and concern for health care.

From 1890 until 1990, there was a Sister of Mercy ministering as president/CEO of the hospital—from Sister Catherine Monaghan in 1890 to Sister René McNiff in 1990. Sister René came to Hornell in 1966 to serve as CEO. By 1968 she had directed the building of a three million dollar West Wing and by 1990 she had completed a 23 million dollar new construction and renovation project. During these twenty plus years she continued to remodel and update every part of the health system. Sister René's list of accomplishments during her thirty-year tenure as CEO is impressive. The depth of her creativity and future-oriented vision allowed St. James Mercy to provide facilities and programs needed for quality healthcare.

In 1997 Eastern Mercy joined Allegany Health System and the Sisters of Providence Health System to form Catholic Health East. The sponsors of these three health systems formed this new system in order to maintain sponsorship of their institutions through the new entity, to continue the healing mission of Jesus, but also to use its collective strength and resources to pioneer new and creative ways to meet community health needs.

In October 2002 the Rochester Sisters of Mercy became officially the canonical Public Juridic Person for St. James Mercy Health System, accepting responsibility for its Catholic identity and the oversight of its mission, values and philosophy through Catholic Health East. In the words of Clarence (Ted) La Liberty, CEO, "Our health system is nurtured by its relationship with Catholic Health East and the Sisters of Mercy of Rochester."[11]

Witnessing to Mercy

Over one hundred years of collaboration among the sisters, medical staff and lay people transformed the hospital from a fifteen-bed unit to St. James Mercy Health System, including an acute care wing, a 120-bed nursing home, a cardiac catheterization lab, rural clinics, a dialysis center, adult and children's daycare, alcohol rehabilitation, psychiatric care for adults and adolescents, and a residence for single mothers and their children.

More than sixty sisters served in the hospital over the course of its one hundred years. In addition, sisters were nurses, x-ray technicians, lab technicians, physical therapists, dietitians, department directors and administrators, as well as professors in the School of Nursing. Father James Early's wish that the hospital would be entrusted to the care of the Sisters of Mercy is lived out in the following history:

- Dr. William Tracy in praising Sister M. deSales, said of her, "You are the most capable surgical nurse I have known. In fact you could finish the operation if necessary."

- Sister M. Aquinas Spellacy served twenty-nine years as the head of the Maternity Department. During that time she helped deliver five thousand babies. At her golden jubilee celebration, the mayor of Hornell, Frances P. Hogan, reported with pride that he was an "Aquinas Baby."[12]

- Sister M. Colette Frank is credited with founding the School of Radiologic Technology, along with Dr. James McFarland and Sister Miriam Joseph Newman. She served as director of the school from 1952 until 1973 when Sister Margaret Ann Lawson assumed this position.

- Sister M. René McNiff as CEO solicited funding to open a rural dental clinic to serve the poor and uninsured. She also obtained the funding to remodel a building into a nine-unit apartment house for single mothers and their children.

- Sister Marian Elizabeth Schantz published the hospital newsletter *Mercy Echoes* for ten years.

- Sister M. Augustine Malley came to the hospital in 1976 and served in the pastoral care department until 1997. She was the first woman to head that department.

- Sister Ann Caufield (Scholastica) served St. James Mercy as a nurse (1951-57), as CEO (1957-66), and finally as a nurse practitioner at the MacDonald Clinic, which provided care for the people in the rural areas of Woodhull, Jasper, Troupsburg and Addison. The clinic opened in March 1974, funded by a grant from the Rochester Regional Medical Program and the Dr. Fayette Macdonald Building Corporation. Dr. MacDonald, a physician, had served the medical needs of the people of this area for thirty-five years. Sister Ann, who was also a registered physician assistant, dedicated herself to this rural population until her retirement in 1993.

- Sister Janet Wahl developed a growing concern for the sick poor as a result of her years in Chile as a missionary. When she returned home to the states, she began studies to qualify as a physician assistant. In Hornell, she worked with the hospital administration to establish the Cameron Valley Health Care Center, a partnership among many groups. The town of Cameron furnished the land site and met additional specific needs. An initial grant came from the Appalachian Regional Commission. Later grants came from the Bethesda Foundation, Inc., and the Sisters of Mercy Funding Resource Corporation for Ministries with the Needy (Silver Spring, MD). The grant assistance recognized the needs of the rural underserved area that would be served by the clinic for primary and preventive health care. Sister Janet opened the Center in July 1989 and served there until 2001.

- Sister Patricia Prinzing was the first sister appointed at St. James Mercy to a new role in Catholic health care. In 1990 she became Vice-President for Mission Services; her responsibilities covered the areas of mission/values, the Mercy charism, ethical issues, advocacy, leadership development and spiritual care.

At this writing no Sisters of Mercy serve in St. James Mercy Health System; however, they continue their support and influence by serving on the board of trustees and board committees and acting as sponsors of the health system by their membership in Catholic Health East. Their presence through the years is personified in the spirit of Sister M. deSales Reilly, who served over sixty years at the hospital. Dr. Arthur Karl told her, "Your wisdom through the years has been an inspiration."[13]

In the end, the history of the hospital proves the truth of its mission statement:

> Faithful to the pioneering spirit of our founder, Father James Early, and rooted in the traditions of the Sisters of Mercy, St. James Mercy Health System responds with innovation and excellence in meeting the diverse health needs of the rural community which it serves, with special concern for the poor, underserved and disadvantaged.

Healthcare Needs of the Sisters

When the new motherhouse on Blossom Road was dedicated in May 1931 the sisters rejoiced that they had a building "well-equipped for the activity of the community." After fifteen years in the crowded conditions of St. John's Park, the new building met all their expectations. They gave thanks for the vision of Mother M. Irene Consedine and the financial skills of Mother M. Liguori McHale, who, working together, had made this building possible.

When the motherhouse was built, the Sisters of Mercy were still a relatively young community, numbering about 178, so their understanding of the space needed for infirm or ill sisters was limited. A section of the second floor was designated for the infirmary. The area included five single rooms for sisters who would be in need of care on a temporary or permanent basis, a bathroom, kitchen, and storage space. The care of the sisters in the infirmary was provided, not by sisters who were trained nurses, but by professed sisters who were willing to give this service to the sick. They were assisted in their care giving by novices in the early years of their religious formation.

Beginning in 1947 sisters who were registered nurses from St. James Mercy Hospital took turns serving in the motherhouse infirmary on a one-year basis. Sisters M. Andre Streb, Dorothy Loeb, Ann Caufield, Cornelia O'Brien, and Kieran Byrne contributed their service and skill. During these years, the infirmary outgrew its five rooms and absorbed other bedrooms on the second floor. Novices continued to provide care under the supervision of the sister-nurse.

Sister M. Rose Schum and Sister M. Howard Cowan, both registered nurses, were assigned to the care of the infirm in 1951. These two sisters served lovingly and generously in the infirmary for almost twenty years, giving of themselves twenty-four hours a day. They recognized the need to acquire more space for the infirmary and to update materials and equipment. In November 1970 they wrote the following letter to Sister Judith Heberle and the leadership council, expressing their concerns and offering a recommendation for improving the situation:

> We strongly urge that the present motherhouse infirmary be transferred to St. James Mercy Hospital. The transfer would alleviate some of the present problems. Hospital trained aides, LPNs and RNs would cover treatments and medications. Housekeeping and kitchen needs would be assumed by the Congregation. There would be immediate access to doctors, adequate laboratory facilities and available inhalation, physical and occupational therapies.

> We suggest that the area to be occupied by the Sisters be apart from the hospital proper. The Sisters who are still ambulatory and independent would enjoy a community room and lunch room, and they would have contact with the Sisters staffing the hospital. While this area would not be part of the hospital proper, neither would it be directly a part of the convent—it would be a home-like area staffed twenty-four hours a day by hospital medical personnel.

> We hope we have made it clear that it is for the good of our Sisters that we have asked for this change.[14]

This letter prompted Sister Judith Heberle to form a task force to study the needs of the infirmary and to examine the possibility of using St. James Mercy Hospital, as suggested by Sisters M. Rose and Howard. In 1975 the

Infirmary Task Force recommended to Sister Judith and the leadership council the need for a modern health care facility. They suggested remodeling some part of the motherhouse to accommodate infirm sisters, who were still housed in the original infirmary built in 1931. The area chosen was the second floor of the Catherine McAuley wing, which at the time was a residence for active sisters. Sister Janet Wahl, assistant to Sister Judith, accepted responsibility for the renovation.

In 1977 the Sisters of Mercy appealed to the people of the Rochester diocese for financial help toward the cost of the new infirmary. With Bishop Joseph L. Hogan's support and encouragement, the sisters launched a funding effort to raise $125,000. Bishop Hogan, who served as honorary chairman of the Infirmary Appeal, asked the faithful of the diocese for their support of the project:

> For 120 years, the Sisters of Mercy have written a glowing chapter in the history of our diocese. Thousands of the faithful, young and old, have benefited from their dedication, devotion, sympathy and prayers. There are few, if any, causes more worthy than the care and comfort of those Sisters who have sacrificed so greatly for others . . . I am pleased to urge support for their appeal.[15]

Bishop Hogan's words proved persuasive. The sisters exceeded their goal of $125,000. In November 1977 the new infirmary, named Lourdes Hall, opened with twenty-one rooms with private bathrooms, a call system by each bed, a dining area, a large kitchen, ample storage areas, laundry facilities and a chapel designed especially for the retired and infirm sisters. Bishop Hogan presided at the first Mass celebrated in the chapel on February 11, 1978, the feast of Our Lady of Lourdes.

The creation of Lourdes Hall was the work of many

sisters. Some served on one or other of the numerous committees, others spoke in parishes throughout the diocese telling the Mercy story and describing the need for a new infirmary. Sister Jane Frances Hauser, a member of the leadership council from 1973 to 1977, ably handled the difficult task of relocating all the occupants of the space designated for the new infirmary.

The professed sisters who resided in McAuley were relocated to rooms in the motherhouse. The major superior and council whose offices were in McAuley were moved into the small wing of the McAuley building which was originally built for a reading laboratory. After the reading laboratory closed it had been used by the guidance department of Mercy High School. The guidance department , in turn, moved from this area to the first floor of the motherhouse. Sisters M. Rose and M. Howard never anticipated all these changes, but they rejoiced as the infirmary became a reality.

By the late 1980s, the healthcare needs of the sisters had again changed considerably. Each year fewer sisters needed twenty-four hour skilled nursing care, but more required services that did not fit the structure of the Lourdes Hall infirmary. Sister Kathleen Ann Kolb, who served as the director of the infirmary from 1984 to 1996, began to explore other models of healthcare that would meet this need and be more cost effective.

In 1995 Sister Ann Miller, president, and the leadership team received a $25,000 grant from the Tri-Conference Retirement Office to be used to hire the services of Health Care Management Associates of Albany, New York to conduct a planning review for the long-term productive use of the motherhouse. The leadership team also wanted to explore licensing the infirmary for possible reimbursement. The operation of the motherhouse and the infirmary was by then a significant and growing cost for the Rochester community. Health Care Associates proposed a number of models, such as: an Adult Home, Enriched Housing Program, Assisted Living Program, or Independent Housing. Unfortunately, these programs were not feasible in the present motherhouse building, given New York State regulations.

After exploration of the various options, a decision was made, on the recommendation of Sister Kathleen Ann, to look at the possibility of a PACE center at the Mercy motherhouse. PACE is the acronym for Program for All-Inclusive Care of the Elderly, and the local program was under the auspices of Via Health of Rochester. Modeled on a program first developed in San Francisco, it is based on a "nursing home without walls" concept. A PACE center in the motherhouse would allow eligible sisters living there to receive healthcare at the same site as their convent home.

In the winter of 1996, Via Health invited Sisters Ann Miller, Pat Prinzing, Kathleen Ann Kolb, and Mary Fran Wegman to visit a PACE center in Milwaukee sponsored by the Franciscan Sisters. Sister Mary Fran, a member of the leadership team and a registered nurse, was given the responsibility to work with Via Health to create the program, which in Rochester was called Independent Living for Seniors (ILS).

During 1996-97 under the direction of LeChase Construction, the infirmary floor was redesigned into an adult day care center, a clinic, a dining area, treatment rooms, offices, and bedrooms with private baths. In addition, four suites with living room, small kitchen, bedroom and bath were designed on the third floor for priests and lay people. The sisters, priests and lay men and women who would live on this floor would be eligible to receive the services of the Independent Living for Seniors program.

The sisters in residence at the motherhouse during this time of transition learned to live out of boxes and share crowded quarters, because those on two floors had to be relocated in order to renovate the needed area. They accepted it with good humor, but they also welcomed the completion of the renovation.

In September 1998 the ILS Center opened its doors to the broader community with approximately sixty lay participants attending the adult day care program. During the day these participants engage in social activities, are provided with meals and snacks, receive personal care, participate in physical and occupational therapy, and receive medical care by the physician or nurse practitioner in the on-site clinic.

Sister M. Eileen Fitzgibbons

Since its beginning, this undertaking has allowed the Sisters of Mercy to reduce their infirmary costs, make better use of space and provide housing and health services to people beyond their religious community. The Independent Living for Seniors program in the McAuley Residence served a total of twenty-three priests, twenty-two lay people and sixty sisters during its first seven years.

Sister Mary Fran Wegman, director of the program, comments:

> In reflecting back over the past years, one cannot help but see the spirit of the Gospel and Catherine McAuley permeating our choice as a community to move in this direction. Our choice has enabled us to use our most valuable resource, our sisters, in welcoming the most frail among us. The community spirit that has been created among the McAuley residents and our communities of sisters at the motherhouse is a wonderful witness to the charism of Mercy. In turn, our lives have been richly blessed by the presence of our residents, their families and friends.[16]

The diocesan priests who are residents, have, in Sister Mary Fran's words, "blessed all by their presence," but their fellow priests have also blessed the program through their generosity. In gratitude for the hospitality offered to the resident priests, the Clergy Relief Society, an organization of the Diocese of Rochester, has given significant contributions on a regular basis. Sister Carolyn Knipper, director of major gifts in the Sisters of Mercy advancement office, worked with Fathers William Graf and Thomas Wheeland to respond to the needs of the McAuley residents. Since 1997 the Rochester priests, through the Clergy Relief Society, have contributed to the purchase of needed equipment. A partial listing of these contributions includes a twelve-passenger wheelchair-accessible van, electric scooters, an ice machine, a gas dryer, a call bell system, and a Room Alert which guarantees a safe environment for people with dementia. These gifts, given so generously, recall Catherine McAuley's desire "to promote the ease and comfort of the sick person."

Sister Mary Fran Wegman and Associates Judy Clark and Kathleen Rimlinger are Community Care Coordinators who advocate for the needs of those persons in the Independent Living for Seniors program.

The Sisters of Mercy who dedicated the five-bed infirmary in 1931 would be surprised at how it has grown in seventy-five years. However, they would not be at all surprised that their community of sisters were still "witnessing to mercy by reverencing the dignity of each person and creating a spirit of hospitality."[17]

CHAPTER EIGHT

DISCOVERING NEW RELATIONSHIPS

T he Sisters of Mercy "have written a glowing chapter in the history of our diocese." Bishop Hogan's words, written in 1976 to open the appeal for a new infirmary, were echoes of past years. Since their arrival at St. Mary's in 1857, the Sisters of Mercy have been deeply blessed by generous friends and benefactors who have shared their material resources so the sisters could minister more effectively to the needy of their time.

The history of the Mercy sisters is closely connected to the generosity of the people of the Rochester diocese. The records in the Mercy archives offer sufficient proof of this.[1]

January 1859:   We, Sisters of Mercy, in our early days had to resort to every legitimate way possible to accumulate sufficient funds to subsist and to balance the yearly budget. The Ladies of

St. Mary's parish were always managing festivals of one type or another for us. Tea parties were held in the afternoon because such events attracted one set of clientele, while ice cream socials attracted another group. At one season of the year, oyster festivals were popular and the Young Ladies and Young Men's associations would schedule one of these for the Sisters' benefit each season.

March 1873:   The Auburn pastor asked his parishioners to 'stage a fair' for the benefit of the sisters.

June 1882:   A group of friends of the sisters organized a silver anniversary celebration—a main feature was a concert, which brought in an amount which helped the sisters meet daily needs.

January 1916:   Bishop Hickey requested a special collection in local churches to help defray the expenses following the South Street fire.

October 1927:   The music teachers in all the convents scheduled as many lessons as their day would accommodate. The only extant letter from Mother Mary Irene

Consedine found in the archives is a plea to the music teachers to increase, if possible, their "music money" returns to the Motherhouse as it would be badly needed to help build Mercy High School.

June 1944:

My dear Mother Magdalene,
I am enclosing a check to the amount of $34,281.16, which amount represents the money collected in the Diocese of Rochester on the occasion of the Jubilee of the Sisters of Mercy.

William F. Bergan
Chancellor

February 1951:

Many of the sisters' families and friends contributed to the building of the new motherhouse chapel, but one of the best remembered gifts was from Lizzie Farrell who had been a girl in the Industrial School at St. Mary's, Rochester. When the school closed in 1905 she continued to live with the sisters and work in the motherhouse laundry. Her gift of $1000 to the chapel was in memory of Sister M. Magdalene Jennings who died in 1918.

September 1955:	The sisters expressed their thanks and appreciation to their many friends who had shown such interest in the progress of Notre Dame High School (Elmira)
November 1959:	The generosity of the people of the Rochester diocese made Catherine McAuley College a reality.

The Mercy Guild

Mother M. Irene, superior in the first quarter of the twentieth century, was aware of the need of the Sisters of Mercy for financial support in order to continue their works of mercy. In 1927 she organized a group of women who were to become lifelong friends of the sisters. She invited ten ladies to St. Mary's Convent on South Street to discuss ways of soliciting financial help. Just five days later, a special meeting was called to discuss the possibility of organizing a permanent group or guild that would perpetuate itself and be a source of revenue for the sisters. The decision was unanimous that they would have a "Mercy Guild" dedicated to St. Theresa, the Little Flower of Jesus.

After receiving the approval of Bishop Hickey and his vicar-general, Monsignor John F. O'Hern (later the bishop of Rochester), the Mercy Guild grew rapidly, with the encouragement and zeal of Mother M. Borgia O'Keefe, bursar of the community. Each member was asked to give one dollar a year, and was to receive in return "many spiritual benefits." Guild members met on the first Wednesday of the month. Major activities included card parties and dinners for the benefit of the new high school.

By June 1928, Guild membership had grown considerably, and a constitution for the Guild was drawn up and accepted. Within the first three years the members formed a board of directors and a working structure of various committees.

During the 1930s the Mercy Guild flourished with Mother M. Liguori, superior of the Sisters of Mercy, as honorary president. In January 1930 Guild members planned bazaars, card parties, luncheons and rummage sales to raise needed funds for the Sisters of Mercy. At an April 2, 1930 meeting, Mother M. Borgia reminded the ladies "not to lose sight of the Mercy Guild as the St. Theresa of the Little Flower Society." The Constitution stated that the purpose of the Guild was to stimulate devotion to the Little Flower as well as to advance the educational projects of the Mercy order.

Despite their busy schedules, the dedicated women of the Mercy Guild also visited the sick and homebound in a real spirit of mercy. Many who gave their time and effort to help the struggling Mercy community were mothers or aunts of the sisters. They continued their efforts for the Sisters of Mercy until 1969 when the Mercy Guild, at the recommendation of the Sisters of Mercy, was reorganized as the Auxiliary of the Sisters of Mercy.[2]

Over the years, more than two thousand women were loyal members of this group. All of their names are recorded in the Tribute Corridor at the Blossom Road motherhouse. It was their dedication and sustained effort that helped the sisters through some difficult financial times.

The History of the Founders Club

On August 30, 1968, Mother M. Bride, then superior general, sent a letter to a small group of friends inviting them to be charter members of a newly organized group to be called "The Founders Club." She indicated in her letter that those who wished to be members were "invited to contribute dues of $100 or more each year," the dues for an associate member would be $50.[3] All members would be invited to a special dinner on May 6, 1969. Sister M. Bride explained in the letter that the funds raised from this new endeavor would help with the expense of educating sister novices at various area colleges. These novices had been attending Catherine McAuley College, which was owned and staffed by the Sisters of Mercy. However, the college had closed in June 1968 (for the reasons explained in Chapter Three), and this change created a financial burden for the Sisters of Mercy community.

At the first annual dinner of the Founders Club in May 1969 the membership list included seventy members and thirty-eight associate members. They gave the Sisters of Mercy a check for $10,000, which Mother M. Bride received with the "great gratitude" of the sisters.

In 1970 after Mother M. Bride resigned because of poor health, Sister Judith Heberle became the superior. In a December 1970 letter to the sisters, Sister Judith stated that "The Founders Club was adopted as a congregational venture in the fall of 1968 as we realized there was a need for a fund raising project."[4]

A Board of Advisors was chosen to direct the activities of the new group. The early members were: Most Reverend Joseph L. Hogan, D.D., Bishop of Rochester, Mrs. Walter B. D. Hickey, Father Daniel Brent, Paul Brescia, Mrs. Harold Coleman, Gerard T. Guerinot, M.D., Henry J. Kearse, Daniel G. Kennedy, Eugene H. Langie, and Father Anthony Valente. Mrs. Walter B.D. Hickey was the first chairperson, followed by Gerard T. Guerinot, M.D. Miss Regina Kennedy was the third chairperson of the Club, and then Dr. Guerinot was chosen again. He directed the group until 2001.[5]

In the fall of 1976 Sister Jean Marie Kearse, an elected member of the leadership council, suggested that all Founders Club members be invited to Christmas Midnight Mass in the motherhouse chapel; this Mass would be offered for their intentions. The tradition of inviting the benefactors to Christmas Mass has continued to the present.

In March 1982 Dr. Guerinot and Sister Nancy Whitley, the liaison to the Founders Club, sent a letter indicating that "dinners and a mail subscription campaign are not sufficient to defray the escalating costs of education." Therefore, the Board of Advisors decided to hold a major fundraiser at the Eastman Theatre; the fundraiser would be two performances by the Leahy Family—a Canadian family of ten children who sang, danced and played musical instruments. The financial goal of the Founders Club was $50,000. They did not meet their goal the first year, but they started a precedent that would benefit the Sisters of Mercy far into the future.

The Leahys were followed in succeeding years by other performers, including Bill Cosby, Rich Little, Judy Collins, Peter, Paul and Mary, The Canadian Brass, The Harlem Boys Choir, Anne Murray, and the Smothers Brothers. In 2002, thirty-four years after their founding in 1968, the program for the Eastman Theater event was dedicated to the men and women of the Founders Club. Sister Sheila Stevenson, president of the Sisters of Mercy spoke of the dedication of the Founders Club members:

> Over 34 years a committed and hardworking group of people who make up the Founders Club of the Sisters of Mercy worked to raise funds: initially, in support of the ongoing educational needs of our sisters, and later for the needs of our ministries. Concerts such as this, at the Eastman Theatre and occasional other venues, have spanned 19 of those 34 years and have become the signature event of the

Sisters of Mercy and Founders Club. Tonight we celebrate the many members, past and present, of the Founders Club; and we dedicate tonight's concert to you. Thank you to each of you who have given your energy, resources and talent to ensure the success of these fundraising endeavors. You have enabled the works of Mercy to continue; you have truly been our partners in ministry. For all that you have done and continue to do we thank you very much. You have touched our hearts and touched the hearts of many people who have been served through our works of Mercy. Thank you all.[6]

Sister Sheila praised Dr. Gerard Guerinot, longtime president of the group, with these words: "Over the years, you have continued Catherine McAuley's legacy and taught us the modern day art of raising funds. Your work has been a positive force in the life and mission of our Mercy community."[7]

Bishop Matthew H. Clark, Sister Sheila Stevenson and Dr. Gerard T. Guerinot

The Fund Development Office

In the fall of 1986 Sister Jean Marie Kearse, president, and her council approved Sister Nancy Whitley's recommendation to establish a fund development office. The purpose of this office was:

- to educate the public to the Mission of Mercy
- to provide an opportunity for the public to share in the service to the poor, sick and ignorant
- to raise funds for the
    ongoing Mission of Mercy,
    education of the sisters as
        preparation for their service,
    foreign missionary work,
    domestic missionary work, and
    the needs of the retired and infirm
        sisters.

Sister Nancy Whitley, vice-president of the Rochester community, had oversight of this office. When her term as a member of the leadership team ended in 1989, she accepted the role full-time. She continued in this position until 1992, when she went to Dublin to minister at the Mercy International Centre. Sister Carolyn Knipper then accepted responsibility for the work of fund development for the Sisters of Mercy. Long-lasting relationships had been formed between the Sisters of Mercy and their loyal friends at the annual suppers and sales where people met year after year to visit with sisters who had taught them or been their friends at school. Sisters M. Bonaventure Hall, Ann Cullen, and M. Dismas Foster were just a few of the sisters who worked to make all this happen. These suppers and sales funded new roofs, new motherhouse windows, a new boiler, a remodeled kitchen, and the chapel roof as well as the sisters' work with the needy. An Office of Mercy Communication and Advancement now oversees all fundraising activities, and the Founders Club has become part of the Mercy Advancement Board, bringing that group of friends into a larger circle of relationships.

In 1987 when Sister Jean Marie Kearse explained the creation of the Fund Development Office, she wrote to the friends and families of the Sisters of Mercy:

> With your assistance perhaps we can be the means by which someone is touched by mercy, thus extending the reach of your hearts and hands. We need each other in this endeavor.[8]

The story of the Sisters of Mercy in the Rochester diocese is also the story of their friends and benefactors who have helped to extend their ministries beyond what they could have done alone.

Collaboration Among Women Religious

Sister Jean Marie's words to benefactors, "we need each other in this endeavor," are also appropriate for the members of the Intercongregational Council, a group of women religious in the Rochester diocese who came together in 1971 "to share ideas and seek a solution to common problems as a means of strengthening the witness of religious, furthering our service in the Diocese and thus extending the Kingdom of God."[9]

In the early years of the diocese, the relationships between the Sisters of St. Joseph and the Sisters of Mercy were sometimes distant, because of Bishop Bernard McQuaid's obvious preference for the Sisters of St. Joseph and his apparent lack of recognition of the Sisters of

Mercy. The Sisters of St. Joseph grew rapidly in number while the Mercys struggled to survive.

Over the years, circumstances changed and new relationships developed between the two religious communities. They grew in appreciation of the ministries of one another and in an understanding of how much they could accomplish together. In January 1971 this new understanding was formalized at a meeting of the leadership of the two orders. The meeting had been arranged by Mother Agnes Cecilia Troy, SSJ and Sister Judith Heberle, RSM, superiors of their respective communities. Each saw the importance of such a gathering for the women religious in the diocese. The purpose as expressed at that meeting was threefold: (1) mutual understanding between the congregations; (2) collaborative efforts around ministry; and (3) better service for the people of the Church of Rochester.

Meetings were held regularly during 1971. From January 1972 to December 1975, "about six rather informal meetings" were held. During the December 1975 meeting, the decision was made to invite the School Sisters of Notre Dame to attend, since they had the next largest group of sisters in the diocese even though they had no motherhouse here.

In 1982 Sister Muriel Curran, SSND, from Baltimore, the first full-time vicar for religious in the diocese, was invited to be part of the group. Her presence as a representative of the bishop helped to move the agenda in new directions and brought a fresh voice to the meetings. Her successor, Sister Dolores Banick, an Immaculate Heart of Mary sister from Scranton, continued this representation until 1991. After Dolores Banick resigned from the position of vicar for religious, there was a period of time when no one served the bishop in this particular role. Different expectations of this position existed among the men and women religious. In 1992-93, the diocesan vicar general, Father John Mulligan, and the chancellor, Father Kevin McKenna, initiated a study of the role of vicar for religious. They interviewed the superiors of all men and women religious in the diocese. The majority opinion was that religious, even though they were grateful for the ministry of the women vicars, felt comfortable dealing directly with the bishop. In consultation with the Intercongregational Council, the diocese made the decision not to continue the role of vicar for religious. The service previously provided by this position would be handled through the diocesan personnel office and the chancellor's office.[10]

The agendas of the Intercongregational Council covered a variety of topics that span over thirty years of meetings. Agendas reflected the significant changes in the lives of women religious as well as their concern for the mission of the church and their role in that mission. The following topics reflect some of the interests of the group:

Sisters Living Needs	Retirement needs
Urban Catholic schools	Social justice issues
Joint personnel planning	Long Range Planning
Study of Southern Tier convents	Shelter for the homeless
Role of the Vicar for Religious	Women's Ordination issues
Relationship to the Diocesan Sisters Council	Congregations' mission work in South America[11]

In addition to this sampling of topics, beginning in 1977 the Council spent time in researching and eventually sponsoring Spirit House, an intercongregational community of women religious that serves as a therapeutic community aimed at healing the whole person. This community helps those experiencing major life difficulties such as depression, midlife issues, and recovery from alcohol or chemical dependency.

The proposal for this new ministry came from Sister Mollie Brown, a Sister of Mercy with considerable education and experience in this field. In March 1985, about four years after its official opening, the Intercongregational Council recommended that Spirit House become separately incorporated. Though the ICC no longer sponsors it, the fact that this excellent program is still functioning at Spirit House is a tribute to the research and planning of the Council and Sister Mollie Brown. Sister Mary Ann Ayers now directs the program.

A second project of the ICC was initiated in 1988 when the Sisters of Mercy and the Sisters of St. Joseph of Rochester cooperated to establish the Tanzanian Sisters Project, which continues into the present. With the support of Nazareth College of Rochester, which provides tuition scholarships, and the many generous donors who contribute to living expenses, the two congregations have enabled ten native Tanzanian Sisters of the Congregation of Our Lady of Usambara to receive a college education. Sister Kathleen Milliken, RSM and Sister Maura Wilson, SSJ have directed and sustained this program since its inception.

Sister Christa Kimashi
and Sister Frieda Kisaka

In March 1979 the Intercongregational Council accepted their biggest challenge—the work of the Sisters Living Needs Committee, which began in 1971 as the "Sisters Maintenance Committee," a group formed by the Priests Council to study the adequacy of the compensation system for women religious in the diocese. The committee was composed entirely of priests (with four sisters listed as consultants). Two years later, the ICC sent a proposal to Bishop Matthew Clark requesting a "support salary" sufficient to allow the congregations to pay for their own transportation and housing, and to contribute to the support of their elderly and infirm members whose earlier stipends had not provided for retirement funding.

In January 1984 Bishop Clark commissioned a group of priests, sisters, and lay men and women to look at this question. This group was called the Women Religious Compensation Committee (WRCC). Sister Muriel Curran, vicar for religious, worked with this committee throughout its existence. In November 1986 the committee recommended the elimination of the current compensation system which consisted of a cash stipend for the ministry of the women religious, with housing and transportation provided in varying ways. The committee's recommendation was the gradual replacement of this method with a system that provided a salary that would permit the congregation to pay all the housing and transportation costs.[12]

This recommendation evoked questions and concerns from parish councils, pastors, and especially women religious themselves. However, the recommendations were phased in over a period of ten years, so that issues could be addressed as they arose. By 1998 all women religious in ministries under the auspices of the diocese were earning salaries commensurate with their education and experience and sufficient to provide them with a support system that met current economic needs.

The work of the Intercongregational Council continues; it recently marked its thirty-fourth year of cooperative planning among women religious in the Rochester diocese. A majority of these years have been in collaboration with Bishop Matthew H. Clark, eighth Bishop of Rochester. Since his arrival in 1979, Bishop Clark has consistently encouraged and supported the ministry of women in this diocese; his efforts have included the publication of a pastoral on women in the Church: *The Fire in the Thornbush.* The closing remarks of the bishop's pastoral challenged the Church of Rochester to consider the future for women in ministry:

> In this spirit I ask all in the Diocese of Rochester to consider prayerfully and thoughtfully the following observations: It is imperative for our present well-being and future growth that we pray about, reflect upon and discuss the participation of women in the life of the Church.
>
> We stand in need of that kind of conversion of heart which will call us away from any attitudes or ways of thinking contrary to the Gospel. As this kind of communal attitudinal change occurs, we will enter creatively into the future and enrich and be enriched by the ministry of women in the Church.[13]

Since 1971 the leadership of the Intercongregational Council has never wavered from its original purpose, which was to promote mutual understanding between the congregations, and to collaborate in ministry in order to provide better service for the people of the Diocese of Rochester. Perhaps the best testimony to its success is the comment of Bishop Matthew Clark: "I enjoy these Intercongregational Council meetings because the sisters are obviously such good friends."[14]

Associate Membership

As the women religious of the Rochester diocese continued their collaboration with one another through the

Intercongregational Council, the Sisters of Mercy also entered into a collaborative relationship with lay men and women in a program called Associate Membership.

The suggestion for a program inviting lay people to share in the life and ministry of the Sisters of Mercy first surfaced at the chapter of 1975. At that time a task force, including Sisters Carol Fox, Julia Norton, Kate Vaeth, and Jean Marie Kearse, was established to study the question of associate membership. In 1977 the outline for an associate program was studied, and in April 1978 a small group of sisters and one interested lay woman, Mary Ellen Fischer, began developing ways for lay women to participate in community, prayer and ministry. When the leadership approved the program in December 1978, Sister Kate Vaeth was appointed as its first director. The chapter held in August 1979 gave final approval, and the first associate, Mary Ellen Fischer, was accepted. Mary Ellen reflected on her life as a Mercy associate, as she looked back after 25 years:

> The twenty-five years of association in Mercy have been a precious gift. I have been affirmed, encouraged, supported, blessed, spiritually nourished and loved by the sisters and associates of Rochester and of the Americas.[15]

At the 1983 chapter the concept of having men in the associate program was presented. Further discussion and consultation with the congregation took place over a number of years, with the majority of sisters favoring the inclusion of men. Sister Jean Marie Kearse, superior, and the leadership team then affirmed this direction.

A southern tier branch of Mercy associates was organized in April 1986 at Notre Dame Convent in Elmira. An active group of women and men now meet regularly, sharing their spirituality and mercy ministry in the Elmira,

Corning, Owego and Ithaca areas.

Associates are women and men from all walks of life who have experienced a personal call to Mercy, and who wish to live this call daily through their prayer and support of Mercy ministries. They respond by entering into a formal relationship with the Sisters of Mercy, to share in the vision, mission and charism of Catherine McAuley and to participate in spiritual, communal and ministerial ways. Some members of the clergy have also chosen to become Mercy associates.

Associates are an extension of the religious community into the broader community of the church and world. Their status is not membership in the congregation in the full sense of the word and does not involve the canonical character of the Institute. For example an associate does not take vows and has no financial responsibility to the community.

Association is in keeping with the Mercy charism; Catherine McAuley not only served those deprived by society, but also enabled others to join her in service. As Sisters Joanna Regan and Isabelle Keiss say in their book, *Tender Courage*, Catherine called others to Mercy by connecting "the rich to the poor, the healthy to the sick, the educated and skilled to the uninstructed, the influential to those of no consequence, the powerful to the weak, to do the work of God on earth."[16]

Candidates for the associate program go through a ten-month period of study, which includes learning about Catherine McAuley, Frances Warde and the history of the Sisters of Mercy in Ireland, the United States and Rochester. They also participate in a program of prayer and discernment as they consider becoming an associate. Each candidate then makes a covenant agreement with the Sisters of Mercy, renews it annually, and promises to further the mission of mercy in some special way. Associates also volunteer in a number of ministries, while continuing to assume their normal responsibilities as family members and in the workplace.

Associates thus carry on Catherine McAuley's vision of reaching out in merciful service to people in need, while sharing in community, prayer, and spiritual development with the sisters.

The Mercy Association Core Team, with ten to twelve members, including at least six associates and four to six sisters, meets twice a year and represents associates in both the northern and southern tiers of New York State. Accountable to the Sisters of Mercy leadership team, the core team has two purposes: to assist in the development and direction of Mercy Association, and to increase community awareness and participation in the program.

Sister Janet Korn was appointed director of the associate program in 1981. Associate Patricia Albrecht assumed this role in 1988, followed by Associate Barbara Giehl in 1991 and Sister Audrey Synnott in 1994. Sister Nancy Whitley and Associate Mary Austin now co-direct the program.

> The associates are a group of wonderfully committed women and men who live out the spiritual and corporal works of Mercy as true followers of Catherine McAuley. They are an inspiration to me and to all our Sisters of Mercy.[17]

These words express Sister Nancy's experience with associate members, who now number 133 lay men and women who "share in various aspects of Mercy life and ministry" (Directory 6.1).

The Associate Program in Chile

In 1983 Sister Margaret Mungovan was committed to building an associate program for the women of Chile.

The Chilean program started with just two women, as the Sisters of Mercy themselves had begun with "two" in 1831. Before their preparation was completed, one Chilean woman dropped out of the program, but two more joined, so in April 1985 three Chilean women made their covenant with the Sisters of Mercy. Sister Margaret Mungovan later described the Chilean associates:

> The associates are all busy women because they have already been 'doing' mercy for many years, in visiting the sick and praying with them, especially with the dying. They console the bereaved by being present and praying at wakes and funerals. They belong to groups of social service, finding clothes and food for needy families, and some of the associates are as needy as those they serve. A particular work of our associates is the making of blankets for those who lack warm covering for winter nights. They use pieces of skirts, trousers, coats or jackets cut into squares which they sew together, adding a filler and a lining. Many a family has rejoiced over such a gift. Some crochet blankets. Others dedicate themselves to making clothes for newborns, especially to help unwed mothers.[18]

The sisters in Chile saw firsthand how the Chilean associates loved and respected Margaret Mungovan. She provided them with opportunities for prayer and celebration. From her they learned about the Sisters of Mercy. Margaret also offered the associates the gift of time and space by planning overnight retreats with them, recognizing that Chilean women in the *poblaciones* have little time or space of their own.

Sister Anne Marie Mathis became the director in 1996. In 2002 Sister Janet Caufield assumed the role for

the eighteen Chilean women who now carry the spirit of
'Catalina" McAuley into their daily lives.

Developing Leadership (1969-Present)

The Second Vatican Council was a call to new and
collaborative relationships within religious communities.
The document on renewal of religious life (*Perfectae
Caritatis*) reminded women religious that "an effective
renewal and adaptation demands the cooperation of all
members." Superiors were encouraged "to take counsel in
an appropriate way and hear the members in those things
which concern the future well being of the whole Institute."

The Institute *Constitutions* (approved in 1991)
affirmed that direction:

> Each regional and local community
> provides participative structures
> to afford its members the opportunity
> to influence the direction of their community and
> to shape its policies and those of the Institute
> in promoting the common good
> and in facilitating the mission.
>
> *Constitutions* #76

"Providing participative structures to give members
the opportunity to influence the direction of their
community" would not have been written into early
editions of the *Constitutions*. Authority and responsibility
appeared to lie wholly with the elected superior and her
council members. The 1954 edition of the *Constitutions*
states: "Supreme internal authority in the Congregation is
exercised ordinarily by the Mother General assisted by her
Council and extraordinarily by the legitimately assembled
General Chapter."

As a result of the Vatican II decree on the renewal

of religious life, the Rochester Sisters of Mercy introduced their first "participative structure" in 1969. The Chapter of 1967-69 created a new group named the Senate. This body consisted of fifteen sisters elected by the professed members of the congregation. It was established for the following purposes:

> To provide a channel of communication in order to implement a collegial sharing of government;
>
> To be advisory and consultative to the Superior General and her Council; and
>
> To prepare for the General Chapter.[19]

These three purposes appear simple and direct, but in 1969 they were revolutionary and opened up a new world for the Rochester congregation. As Sister M. Florence Sullivan writes:

> It was not customary in that period for the superiors themselves to discuss administrative issues with the general membership of the congregation. They made their decisions behind closed doors, after consultation only with their administrative group and advisors.[20]

This new group, the Senate, functioned for a brief two years—until a new participative structure was inaugurated in 1971—but the quality of its projects and the foresight of its membership are impressive. The sisters elected to the Senate identified, in consultation with the superior and council, not only internal issues, but important external issues. For example, they conducted a survey of the diocesan schools staffed by the Sisters of Mercy. This was a period of great stress for schools. Enrollment was low and there were fewer sisters to staff schools.

Consequently, the cost of operating a school was increasing. The purpose of the study was twofold: to work with the principals in recognizing the strengths already present, and to identify needed improvements to ensure that each school was a "center for Christian formation in a high level of academic excellence."[21] The members of the Senate shared their findings and recommendations with the diocesan office of education, Bishop Joseph L. Hogan, and Auxiliary Bishop John McCafferty. They also organized meetings for pastors and Senate members to discuss the schools' future.

The Senate did not limit their concerns to parish elementary schools, but also encouraged the promotion of quality religious education programs that were both adult-centered and child-centered. A proposal was also submitted to the diocese to form a steering committee to study the possibility of a diocesan counseling center for priests and men and women religious. The Senate members believed the role of a vicar for religious embraced other functions besides canonical investigations. The priest vicar at that time had a full-time job exclusive of his services to women and men religious. The Senate also recommended establishment of geographically located Penance Centers where priests with some gift for spiritual direction would be available. At that time, priests traveled to each convent in the diocese every week to hear the confessions of sisters.

In March 1970 the Senate members made recommendations to the superior and council regarding the future of the Catherine McAuley Reading Laboratory; the formation of a house of prayer; the concerns of the sisters staffing Our Lady of Mount Carmel School; and the request of the Joseph Avenue Center to open a school for children with special educational needs. With Mother M. Bride and the council, they also studied the advisability of accepting Chilean candidates into the congregation.

The 1967-69 Chapter had created the Senate as advisory to the superior general and the council. In 1971 the chapter broadened the base of government by forming the Central Administration, a policy-making body consisting of twelve elected sisters and the superior general and council—a total of seventeen women. The function of this governing body was to determine new policies, evaluate existing policies, and approve adequate guidelines for the growth, development, and operation of the congregation, as well as to engage in long-range planning in those areas delegated to it. The group had the right to offer formal deliberative votes in those matters which affected the entire congregation.

The superior and council were members of the Central Administration, while the Senate had acted in an advisory capacity to the congregational leadership. The Central Administration was divided into four boards that covered areas of major concern—the names of the boards indicated their specific area of concern: Personal Development; Temporalities and Gospel Values; Pastoral Concerns; Ecclesial Life and Community. Communication was a high priority for this group, and they assigned representatives to each convent in order to report monthly to the local houses about their agendas. As the years passed, the group reconfigured its method of dealing with areas of concerns and dealt more directly with commissions and committees. The Central Administration existed from 1971 to 1985. Its contribution to the life of the Rochester community was significant and long-lasting.

During Chapter 1985 the delegates discussed a proposal to reshape the Central Administration. The Government Task Force, through study and consultation with Sister Elizabeth McDonough, O.P., a canon lawyer, had identified some problem areas that needed change. Central Administration, which had no canonical status, had exercised a deliberative vote on two issues that only the superior and council could approve. Elizabeth McDonough believed the roles of the superior, councilors and members of the Central Administration were too mixed to function appropriately. The proposed reshaping provided an advisory group for the superior and council, allowed for greater creativity for the group, and moved away from a policy-making mode.[22] In September 1985 the Central Administration became the Advisory Board of the Sisters of Mercy.

The Bylaws of the Advisory Board, written in 1985, explained the following purpose of the board:

> The Advisory Board is responsible to advise the major superior and council, including assisting in developing guidelines and planning, and in involving the broader membership in areas that affect the common good of the Congregation.[23]

Sister Jean Marie Kearse, superior, wrote the following words to the community when the first meeting of the Advisory Board was held on September 28, 1985:

> The giving of advice is a sacred trust. It requires a listening spirit and the willingness to explore multiple avenues of possibility and information-seeking before offering advice. The limit of my experience, expertise and wisdom is quickly met, as is the Council's, and so the broader range of creativity and ability possessed by the members of the Advisory Board augment our ability to serve you well.[24]

From 1985 until 1997 the Advisory Board listened, learned and offered their wisdom on a broad and challenging range of topics. The members were involved in preparation for the separate incorporation of the two congregation-owned high schools, the remodeling of the motherhouse chapel, the purchase of property for Mercy Prayer Center and Catherine McAuley Housing, as well as the sale of thirty-two acres of property to build housing for the elderly on Clover Street behind Mercy High School. They approved hiring the Marriott Company to manage maintenance, environmental services and food preparation in both the motherhouse and Mercy High School.

In preparation for the 1997 chapter, the Advisory Board discussed the governance structure and their own role in this structure. Since its formation in 1985, the Advisory Board had experienced annual changes in a third of its membership. Therefore, the sisters brought a variety of experiences to the board. In the later years, the issues placed on the agenda by the leadership team often called for specific kinds of expertise—expertise not always found in an elected group. In addition, the community recognized the need for the membership to accept more responsibility for the internal working of the regional community in order to free the superior and council to do more "long range and strategic planning as well as the promotion of the charism and its appropriate adaptation and renewal."[25]

In the Chapter of 1997 the Rochester community restructured its governance plan in preparation for entering the 21st century. In their own words, the sisters proclaimed:

> Our deepest relationships in Mercy are manifested in mutual trust and reverence, in truth, in prayer and patience, and in willingness to listen to one another. Therefore, we desire to affirm our life in community by giving witness to it in our modes of governance. As a community of women, we commit ourselves to develop structures of governance and ways of being together in community that seek and promote the fullness of

life and potential of all women.[26]

The term "chapter" had been used since our first *Constitutions* was approved by Rome in 1841; in the *Constitutions* of 1991 it referred to the "authoritative policy-making body of the regional community when in formal session." The new governance plan of 1997 used the term "assembly," so the Institute chapter could be clearly designated in a distinct way. Four committees were formed to do the preparatory and follow-up work of the assembly and to fulfill designated tasks for the regional community and the president and council. These committees are called to serve in the areas of Mission, Community Life and Membership, Lifelong Development, and Stewardship. The chairpersons of these committees, other members elected by all the sisters, and the president of the Rochester regional community form the Assembly Steering Committee to "facilitate the work of the assembly and act as a central advisory group to the president and council."[27] This form of participative government functions effectively to fulfill the desire of the Rochester Sisters of Mercy that all they do in the area of governance be for the sake of the mission.

> We understand Catherine McAuley to have been a woman centered in God and faithful to Jesus and the Gospel. Therefore, we desire that our individual and corporate decision-making be characterized by such centeredness and fidelity.[28]

CHAPTER NINE
A NEW FUTURE (1965-1981)

As the Rochester community struggled after Vatican Council II to articulate their vision and identity and to meet the challenges of the renewal process, they were also involved in the formation of the new Federation of Sisters of Mercy. This was originally called the McAuley Conference and its members grappled with the choices needed to create a new future for the Sisters of Mercy. The members of the McAuley Conference had voted in May 1965:

> That according to the wishes of the Church, definite steps be taken toward a World Federation of the Sisters of Mercy;
>
> That as one such step this Mother McAuley Conference be formed into a Federation of the Sisters of Mercy of the Americas;
>
> That in such federation the autonomy of each Congregation be preserved.

All the leadership councils of the Mercy congregations had voted unanimously in favor of the Federation. The temporary officers of the Federation were: Mother M. Thomas Aquinas Carroll (Pittsburgh), president, Mother M. Regina Cunningham (Bethesda), vice-president; Mother M. Bernard Graham (Merion), secretary; and Mother M. Patrick McCallion (Plainfield), treasurer. They were elected at the May 1965 meeting of the McAuley Conference in Hooksett, New Hampshire.[1] In June 1965 they met for the first time to begin the business of planning a new structure.

The temporary officers consulted with two canon lawyers about the canonical status of the Federation and the need to petition Rome for approval. Each canonist had a different opinion:

> One took the position that the description of the kind of organization we anticipated fitted better that of an association than a federation. Consequently he felt that no authorization from the Holy See was necessary. The second canonist welcomed the whole movement of the Sisters of Mercy toward a federation as a new step in ecclesiastical organizations of religious life. He encouraged applying to the Sacred Congregation of Religious for a definite status as a federation.[2]

The officers decided to draft a letter to be sent to Cardinal Antoniutti of the Sacred Congregation of Religious to petition the blessing of His Holiness Pope Paul VI on this initial step toward the Federation.

On August 12, 1965, Mother M. Thomas Aquinas, president of the Federation, received a letter from the Sacred Congregation of Religious expressing their pleasure about the new federation. Monsignor Joseph Verdelli wrote: "This is preeminently in line with the views of the

Holy See and, as you know, has been the desire of this Sacred Congregation for some time." Mother Thomas Aquinas was encouraged to "draw up a workable set of statutes to govern the Federation, to be submitted to the Sacred Congregation."[3]

Meanwhile Father Edward Heston, C.S.C., a member of the Sacred Congregation of Religious from the United States, was invited to act as the agent for the Federation of the Sisters of Mercy of the Americas. In January 1966 he presented to Pope Paul VI the petition for approval of the status of the Federation of the Sisters of Mercy. Two months later, in March 1966, Father Heston wrote indicating that there might be some delay regarding the approval of the status. He agreed that this was probably only a temporary delay, but he did voice some concern about the habit change of the Sisters of Mercy. He believed that the Sacred Congregation might expect the Federation "to arrive at substantial uniformity as to general cut and color of the habit" among all the Mercy congregations. However, by March 1966 the Rochester Sisters of Mercy had been wearing the Sybil Connolly habit since December 1965. A subsequent letter from Father Bernard Ransing, a temporary replacement for Father Heston, encouraged Mother M. Thomas Aquinas to go ahead with the June 1966 meeting and not wait for approval of the statutes.[4]

At the same time, the Federation officers sent a letter to Mother Mary Gabriel of the Dublin congregation of the Sisters of Mercy in Carysfort Park, Ireland, acquainting her with what had already been done by the Federation and asking whether she would wish to take the initiative in calling together representatives of the Sisters of Mercy from all parts of the world. A reply was received from Mother Gabriel to the effect that "the Archbishop did not think it feasible for the Carysfort sisters at this time to undertake such a program, but that he did approve of her attending the meeting of the Federation in Pittsburgh as an

observer."[5]   Since the original intent of the McAuley
Conference members was to form a "World Federation of
the Sisters of Mercy," they included invitations to their
meetings to Sisters of Mercy throughout the world.

Mother M. Bride Claire, serving as Rochester's
major superior from 1961 to 1970, attended the Federation
meetings from 1965 to 1970, the early years of the
Federation. She served on the By-Laws committee. Sister
Judith Heberle served as assistant to Mother M. Bride. In
1970, when Sister Judith was elected major superior, she
became an active member of the Federation for eleven
years; nine of those years as an officer of the group—
serving as president, vice-president, past president,
secretary and secretary-treasurer.

Sister Judith participated in the sixth annual
Federation meeting held in Ireland and in Rome in 1971.
The Federation had planned this meeting as a pilgrimage
for their members, hoping to reflect in Ireland on the
renewal of religious life and, in the words of Vatican II, to
"refound the Institute in the spirit of Catherine McAuley."
This meeting began in Limerick with a joint session of the
Irish Federation (both the North and South of Ireland) and
the Federation of the Sisters of Mercy of the Americas. An
instant rapport developed between these two groups, as
well as with the observers from South Africa, England and
Australia.

Four regional meetings in Ireland were scheduled
for the following days. The purpose of these was to meet
with many members of each of the Irish congregations.
Dundalk, Galway, Limerick, and Carlow were the
appointed places.   The visiting group of sisters now
scattered in smaller groups to these four cities, joining with
hundreds of Mercy Sisters of Ireland. The same pattern of
meeting prevailed, but discussions following the formal
session took on a slightly different tone since many young
sisters and those not holding major offices in their

communities were now in attendance. In-depth and extensive sharing occurred. Topics of interest centered around lifestyles in community living, prayer, and apostolic works.[6]

The pilgrimage of the Federation members continued on to Rome, where they spoke with members of the Sacred Congregation of Religious and discussed their desire to be more involved in ecclesial policy-making. They hoped for a more supportive rather than paternalistic relationship with the Sacred Congregation. At an audience with Pope Paul VI, Sister Kieran Flynn, president of the Federation, presented the pope with a spiritual gift of Masses and a thousand dollars from the Federation.

For the next ten years the Federation met annually to deal with questions of renewal, *Constitutions*, formation, ecumenism, preservation of Catherine McAuley's spirit and charisms, and the need for a deepened spirituality. In 1970 they had chosen a full-time executive director, Sister Jerome McHale, and had established an office in Pittsburgh. In 1973 the objectives of the Federation were identified: (1) to deepen awareness of the Gospel message as lived and interpreted in the Mercy tradition of Catherine McAuley; and (2) to intensify mutual support and sharing in a climate of union and charity to fulfill more effectively the mission of the Church.[7]

All novices from each Mercy congregation were invited to participate in a formation program called Searching Mercy. This program originated as an opportunity for all Union novices to come together in a three-week learning experience that was designed "to provide opportunities for a deeper understanding of rootedness in community and sharing with one another." The first Rochester novices to attend this Mercy program were Sisters Anne Curtis, Joan Binnie and Nancy Kelly. The program was held in the Union Generalate Building in Bethesda, Maryland. The first director was Sister Jean

Marie Sullivan from the St. Louis, Missouri province.[8]

By 1978 the Federation chose to focus on justice issues. The members expressed in a vote their desire to be "a leadership voice of the Sisters of Mercy of the Americas, addressing issues of justice in Church and society."[9] At its meeting in August 1977 the Leadership Conference of Women Religious invited men and women religious "to examine the relationship of multinational corporations to the plight of the poor."[10] This was one of the forces that moved the Federation members into a strong focus on justice. Sister Judith Heberle returned from all meetings of the Federation and the Leadership Conference of Women Religious filled with enthusiasm for justice concerns and a desire to share these issues with her sisters in Rochester. Since the Second Vatican Council and the publication of their 1971 *Interim Constitutions*, the Rochester sisters embraced the call to "action on behalf of justice."[11] Sister Judith believed the Federation gave strength to our corporate voice, and her zeal was contagious.

In a slide presentation at the 1980 meeting in Holyoke, Massachusetts, Sister Judith traced the Federation's past. She encouraged membership to "thank God for our history . . . for the directions of the Spirit . . . for the inspirations of each other . . . for the heritage that is ours from Catherine McAuley."[12] At this same session, Sister Joanne Lappetito (Rochester) was chosen as executive director, and the Federation office moved to Rochester, New York. The office remained in Rochester during the tenure of Sister Amy Hoey (New Hampshire) who followed Sister Joanne as executive director. It closed in 1989 when the position of executive director was eliminated to prepare for a new governmental structure for the Mercy sisters of the Americas.

This new structure was a major agenda item at the April 1980 meeting of the Federation. The Executive Council of the Federation had discussed this idea among themselves many times. Now they put it forth for the whole group's discussion. As a result of small group sharing, a number of ideas emerged. The members felt there was great potential within the Federation for closer bonds among the Sisters of Mercy, but at the same time they sensed the inadequacy of the present structure to accomplish that goal.

The delegates called for a task force of three persons whose purpose was "to develop processes that included all members of the Federation in discovering alternative structures to the Federation."[13] In May 1980 this task force was named the Mercy Futures Study Committee. It included Sister Madonna Moran (New Hampshire), Sister Mary Ellen Quinn (Omaha), and Sister Judith Heberle (Rochester). The main task of this committee was to bring a recommendation about the future of the Federation to the June 1981 meeting.

June 27, 1981, was a red letter day for the Federation. After discussion and prayer, they passed the following resolution:

> That the Executive Council of the Federation select a task force of persons to develop through a process of education and consultation a new model of relationship for the Sisters of Mercy of the Americas and the necessary governmental structures to implement it.[14]

This government structure would eventually become the Institute of the Sisters of Mercy of the Americas, uniting all Catherine McAuley's congregations in the United States. Ten years later that government structure became a reality.

Mercy Futures (1981-1989)

The Executive Council of the Federation took its

first step toward developing a model for the new government structure by approving a nine-member task force with Sister Doris Gottemoeller (Cincinnati) as the project director. Rochester hosted the first meeting of the Mercy Futures Task Force in November 1981. Their challenge was:

1. To develop a new model of organization and governance for the Sisters of Mercy of the Americas.

2. To develop processes that provide the opportunity for dialogue, input-feedback, and education on the proposed model.[15]

Sister Judith Heberle, a member of this Mercy Futures Task Force, had just completed ten and a half years as major superior of the Rochester sisters. Her hopes and her heart were deeply involved in the future of the Sisters of Mercy of the Americas. At a talk she gave in 1982 to the Rochester community, she shared her convictions:

I believe, sisters, we are at a historic moment in our lives. Our common origins and our common concerns have brought us closer together. I believe that it is indeed a spirit-filled time for us and that as expressed by so many, the time is ripe for us to be creative, to unite all our congregations, to search for the opportunities open to us for putting the gifts among us at the service of the total Church, to unify, strengthen and broaden our vision and to become a strong voice for justice in proclaiming our call to be Sisters of Mercy.[16]

Despite Sister Judith's optimism, a decade of dialoguing, consensus building, planning, meeting, listening and re-defining was needed before 1991 when the new government structure for all Sisters of Mercy in the Americas was approved and implemented. This decade was also a time of growth in relationships, in learning more about individual Mercy communities, in creating new opportunities to bring Mercy to our world. The directors of ministry from all the Mercy groups met to discuss ways to provide the services of Sisters of Mercy to the most impoverished areas of our country. They formed a committee called "New Foundations" who researched several areas for potential service. The Appalachian area of the Richmond, Virginia diocese was the first chosen. One group of sisters went to Pocahontas, Virginia in 1984; another team went to Cedar Bluff, Virginia in 1987. The sisters ministering in these two areas came from Buffalo, Baltimore, Burlingame, Cincinnati, Providence and West Hartford. Sister Livia Ann Ruocco from Rochester served in the area during the summer of 1986. Sisters Noreen Graney and Ann Miller, ministry directors in Rochester, served on the "New Foundations" committee during their time on the leadership council.

A nationwide Teleconference, funded by the Catholic Communications Campaign, linked all Sisters of Mercy by satellite in September 1986. The subject was "Beyond Giving: Mercy Ministry with Women." Three thousand sisters at thirty-two locations in twenty-two states participated in this interactive live teleconference, which focused on the Sisters of Mercy's ministries with women. This was a preview of what the new Institute might create. Justice coordinators, artists, theologians, scripture scholars and Mercy educators met on each level: elementary, secondary, and higher education.

Simultaneously with these activities, the Mercy Futures Task Force continued to carry out its mandate. In 1982, between September and December, the Federation sponsored presentations in sixty locations across the country to acquaint sisters with the reasons for change, to raise critical issues for discussion and to propose a model for the new government structure. More than 1800 sisters responded to a questionnaire; some made suggestions for modifying the model or submitted new models. The superiors and the Mercy Futures Task Force revised the model as a result of this questionnaire and developed two additional models.

By early 1983 a group of Rochester sisters (Clare Bollow, Patricia Flynn, Joan McAteer, Gaye Moorhead, and Jacqulyn Reichart) submitted to the Mercy Futures Task Force a model they had created called "The Assembly of the Sisters of Mercy of the Americas." This assembly model called for a central office with three sisters in full-time positions: a Social Justice Coordinator, a Ministry Resource person, and an Executive Coordinator. The central office staff was to be accountable to the major superiors. The proposal also called for a congress of sisters and a plan for decision-making. Forty-six additional Rochester sisters endorsed this model before it was sent on to the Federation task force on February 14, 1983.[17]

Sister Doris Gottemoeller, project director for Mercy Futures and later to become the new Institute's first president, wrote the following letter to the five Rochester sisters who had created this model. This letter was dated February 16, 1983:

Dear Sisters,

Thank you very much for the alternate model which you propose for Mercy reorganization. We will be very happy to have copies and to consider it at our meeting next week. Other proposals have also been submitted, and I feel we will have quite a bit of good material to work on—now is the time to get all of the ideas "in the pot"! Please pray for the

Spirit's guidance on our work and on whatever consultation we have after the February meeting.

Sincerely,

Doris Gottemoeller, RSM[18]

In a letter dated May 26, 1983, the Rochester group evaluated the other proposed models presented by the Mercy Futures Task Force and voiced these concerns about the models:

1. Broad, unlimited authority, with minimal guidelines, is vested in too few people; collegial responsibility among the members is absent. The autonomy of individual communities is in jeopardy under models of such absolute authority.

2. There is no stated benefit from or need of these governmental models which justifies the commitment of personnel and tremendous expense necessary to establish these models and make them operational, especially when those members who would be bound by these models have never been adequately involved in the process.

Seventy-two Sisters of Mercy of the Rochester community agreed with these statements and added their names to the letter. They also questioned the fairness of "one small group to wear both hats of designing and promoting sponsored models while apparently tabling, filtering or rejecting alternative models."[19] As planning and discussion went on within the Mercy congregations, the Rochester community continued to have a small but representative group that remained uncommitted to the proposed governmental structure that was to give future shape to the Sisters of Mercy.

Meanwhile, Sisters of Mercy in the United States and their designated leaders dialogued with the Constitutions Committee, consulted canonical advisors and visited Rome to speak directly with the members of the Congregation for Religious and Secular Institutes. CRIS (its popular name) had already approved the scheduling of a referendum among all Sisters of Mercy about the formation of a new Institute. This referendum, a written consultation, was planned for April 1988. The Rochester community scheduled their vote on April 17, 1988. The results of this non-binding, consultative vote in Rochester were 67% voting "yes" with 33% voting "no": 165 affirmative and 82 negative.

Rochester's official vote was taken at a special chapter gathering in July 1988. This was a delegate chapter which means that each sister did not vote personally, but instead voted for delegates (thirty-one in all) who were entrusted with making the decision for the congregation. There was only one decision to be made and it required a 2/3 vote of the delegates. The ballots contained this wording:

Do you want to petition the Holy See for our congregation to form part of the new Institute?

The thirty-one delegates cast their ballots on July 2, 1988, in the motherhouse chapel with the community in attendance. The vote was affirmative by a 2/3 majority. Twenty-one delegates voted Yes, ten voted No, and there were no abstentions. The Rochester Sisters of Mercy were to become part of the new Institute.

In September of that same year, a second written referendum was scheduled for all professed sisters, not just elected delegates. In this second referendum, 245 sisters were eligible to vote: 230 sisters, or 94.69%, voted in the affirmative. The results of the April and September referendums, as well as the July chapter vote, were sent to Cardinal Jean Jerome Hamer O.P., of the Congregation for Institutes of Consecrated Life. Sister Jean Marie Kearse, major superior, wrote the following petition:

September 30, 1988

Your Eminence,

The Religious Sisters of Mercy of Rochester, New York petition the Congregation for Institutes of Consecrated Life to establish the Institute of the Sisters of Mercy of the Americas and to include our congregation in this newly formed Institute.

The possibility of forming an Institute with other Sisters of Mercy of the United States was first placed before our congregation in 1980. In the years since 1980, the membership has participated actively in meetings, correspondence, consultations, surveys, straw-ballots and many other forums; they have offered recommendations, concerns, and alternatives; they have sought clarifications and greater depths of understanding and ownership. This congregation was very instrumental in contributing to the content and shaping of the process used by the Federation of the Sisters of Mercy of the Americas in their various consultations with the individual members. In these eight years each member of the congregation prayerfully and freely identified her personal response to the Institute in the light of the common good of the congregation.

Confident that throughout these years of discussion, discernment and decision, I and my Councils have given the members of our congregation all the information available to us, and have provided every type of personal and public forum, I feel that the following report represents the free, holy and informed response of each eligible sister of the Sisters of Mercy of Rochester.[20]

Sister Jean Marie Kearse

The Rochester Sisters of Mercy had struggled for a number of years with the concept of this Institute, but in the final vote they came together to affirm what was the chosen direction of a majority of sisters. Throughout these eight years, they were guided by the gentle administration of Sister Jean Marie Kearse, whose one desire was that each sister should choose prayerfully and freely what she believed was the best decision for the common good of the Rochester congregation. Just before the vote in the 1988 Chapter, she spoke to the sisters:

> Our history as Sisters of Mercy of Rochester is dynamically present to us. Let us remember past moments when we have struggled together for truth and accomplished with God's help that delicate but strong balance between unity and creative diversity. God has graced us in the challenges and defeats that we have experienced and we have been shaped by our history and culture in ways even Catherine with all her foresight never envisioned. Our story is not finished. We are writing the next chapter.[21]

Jean Marie's words were prophetic, not only for the Rochester congregation, but for herself. In March of 1991 she asked to begin a process of discernment in regard to her future as a Sister of Mercy. Eventually, she made the decision to journey in a new direction. In a letter written to the congregation on June 18, 1993, she shared these thoughts:

The congregation has been home and family for me and a source of great spiritual growth. I, in turn, have given my best to the Sisters of Mercy with a strong conviction and belief in the direction and mission. I will no longer be privileged to carry the name, Sister of Mercy, but my heart and soul are molded by and in the Mercy charism and tradition. Wherever I am, mercy will be present in compassionate and just ways.[22]

Transition Time (1989-1991)

In late June 1989, the newly-elected leadership team of the Rochester community traveled to Manchester, New Hampshire for the last meeting of the Federation of the Sisters of Mercy. The theme chosen for the meeting was "Gathered in Mercy" and over one hundred sisters from all parts of the United States gathered for the formal ending of the Federation, an outgrowth of the McAuley Conference.

The Rochester community was well represented in Manchester. Sister Ann Miller, the newly elected major superior, brought three members of the council—Sisters Kathleen Milliken, Judith Heberle, and Gaye Moorhead. Sister Joanne Lappetito, who had earlier served the Federation as its executive director, and Sister Audrey Synnott, as editor of its newsletter, attended as well. Also present was Sister Mary Sullivan, who delivered a talk on "Songs Prepared for the Journey: The Readings, Writings and Prayers of Catherine McAuley."[23]

The meeting began with the sharing of stories about Mercy, including the founding of the McAuley Conference in 1955. The business of the assembly began with the report of a Transition Task Force. In 1988 the Federation Governing Board had appointed this task force to develop an interim plan which would establish the processes and procedures needed to prepare for the new relationship among the Mercy communities in the Americas.

This task force recommended three women who would act as an administrative group to oversee the founding of the Institute: Sisters Judy Carle (Burlingame), Margaret Costa (New York), and Amy Hoey (New Hampshire). Sister Amy Hoey had lived in Rochester as the executive director of the Federation from 1986 to 1989, so she was well-known to the Rochester sisters. The group, called the Transition Administrative Group (TAG), was "to serve the developing Institute by providing a responsible and accountable body able to make and implement decisions necessary to prepare for the first Institute Chapter."[24] Consulting with and advising TAG on issues related to the transition and the development of the new Institute was a Transition Advisory Council, consisting of the major superior of each unit.

The task force also recommended that the administration offices for the new Institute be located in the Washington-Baltimore area. Other agenda items for the last meeting of the Federation included reports on the new *Constitutions*, the Mercy International Centre (Dublin), the collaborative novitiate, the committee preparing for the first Institute Chapter, and the visioning process designed to give the membership an opportunity to share their values and concerns about the new Institute of the Sisters of Mercy.

Before the meeting ended, the Sisters of Mercy of Newfoundland, who had been part of the Federation, shared their decision not to pursue membership in the Institute because of their small number, their distance from the States, and the difference in culture. The Federation members visited the grave of Frances Warde, an important American foundress of the Sisters of Mercy, to ask her blessing on the new Institute. Frances Warde had lived for twenty-five years in New Hampshire. She died there in 1884 in her 74th year.

From July 1989 until July 1991, the transition administrative group (TAG) worked with the twenty-five superiors to prepare for the founding moment. Their first meeting was at Holy Cross Hospital in Fort Lauderdale, Florida in January 1990. There were four more gatherings of these two groups during the transition years. The process for election of Institute leadership, the completion of the *Constitutions,* budget and finance issues, and other topics were the ongoing business of the two groups as they awaited approval from Rome for the formation of the Institute.

Simultaneously, the general membership was involved in the visioning process that would identify priorities for the future, share values and concerns, and shape the "new moment of Mercy." When each congregation/province's elected chapter delegates gathered in January 1991 in St. Louis to prepare for the July Founding Event, this material was affirmed as a starting point for direction-setting for the Institute.

CHAPTER TEN

THE FOUNDING OF THE INSTITUTE (1991)

On July 20, 1991, three thousand sisters and associates came together in Buffalo, New York to celebrate the founding of the new Institute of the Sisters of Mercy of the Americas. At the most solemn moment of the day, the women gathered to hear the official Decree of Establishment issued by Rome which formed one religious congregation out of seventeen. Over three thousand Mercy women signed the Founding Document proclaiming:

> We, women of Mercy, have discovered a new relationship among us. . . .
> We affirm this moment:
> we proclaim this reality
> and we found this
> Institute of the Sisters of Mercy
> of the Americas
> on this 20th day of July 1991.[1]

For the women present in Buffalo that day, "the dream of Mercy's tomorrow" came alive in story telling, singing, praying and sharing.[2]   Sister Pat Beairsto (Rochester) remembers that "there was such a sense of energy and power in the group of women in that place." Sister Kathleen Milliken, vice president in Rochester at that time, has never forgotten the rejoicing and celebration that "created a strong bond of unity, before we had even begun to talk about *Constitutions* or the election of leadership."

One hundred sixty-eight Rochester sisters boarded buses to travel home that night, energized by the events of the day. Six Rochester sisters remained in Buffalo to begin the official business of the Institute. These women had been elected by the community to act as the Rochester delegates to the two week chapter. Sisters Judith Heberle, Barbara Moore, Gaye Moorhead and Mary Sullivan were the elected delegates and Sister Ann Miller served ex-officio as superior of the Rochester community. Sister Janet Korn was present as a translator for Spanish speaking sisters.

1991 Chapter delegates: (first row) Sisters Mary Sullivan and Gaye Moorhead. (second row) Sisters Barbara Moore, Ann Miller, Janet Korn, Judith Heberle and M. Beatrice Curran.

The 1991 Chapter chose a windmill for its logo. Designed by Sister Estelle Martin of Rochester, it symbolized the hope that the Institute Chapter would

> --gather spirit-blown dreams from
>   the wide skies of Mercy
> --reach down into the wells of
>   150+ years of Mercy living
> --and transform this gathered wisdom into
>   the Institute of the Sisters of Mercy of the
>   Americas.

The "gathered wisdom" of the delegates created this transformation. They moved from reflection to discussion to approval of the *Constitutions* which would govern the new Institute; they chose the leaders of the new Institute; and they created a Direction Statement that committed all Sisters of Mercy to the same vision and actions. Elected to serve as the first president of the Institute was Sister Doris Gottemoeller from Cincinnati. Elected as members of the Council were Sisters Patricia McCann (Pittsburgh), Marie Chin (Cincinnati/Jamaica), Amy Hoey (New Hampshire), and Mary Waskowiak (Burlingame).

Early in the chapter, delegates participated in a direction-setting process. Three areas received unanimous support: commitment to the poor; education and solidarity around women's issues; and interconnectedness across the regional communities, with a special emphasis on our multi-cultural reality. When rough drafts were presented for debate, there was agreement that the chapter did, indeed, have the ingredients for a focus statement which would express the energy of the chapter. Nevertheless, the delegates took great care to choose words and phrases which would pull together their diverse cultures and experience. They wanted the statement to catch the life and energy of the chapter so that the membership would feel enlivened.[3]   Finally, the chapter delegates gave overwhelming approval to the *Direction Statement.*. A formal ritual of acceptance followed.   Sister Doris Gottemoeller, the new president, read the statement:

> Animated by the Gospel and Catherine McAuley's passion for the poor, we the Sisters of Mercy of the Americas, are impelled to commit our lives and resources for the next four years to act in solidarity with:
>   ❖ the economically poor of the world, especially women and children;
>
>   ❖ women seeking fullness of life and equality in church and society;
>
>   ❖ one another as we embrace our multi-cultural and international reality.
>
> This commitment will impel us to develop and act from a multi-cultural, international perspective; speak with a corporate voice; work for systemic change; and call ourselves to continual conversion in our lifestyle and ministries.

As the business of the chapter came to an end, the delegates were quiet and reflective; they knew their lives would never be the same. Sister Bette Moslander, a Sister of St. Joseph from Kansas City who had acted as a canonical advisor, reminded the group: "Future historians would wonder at your courage and daring."[4] Then Doris Gottemoeller, the new Institute president, announced the closing of the chapter and asked that the doors of the room be opened. The delegates stood and moved through the open doors singing:

Let us go forth carrying the promise
carrying out the promise
enfleshing the vision
incarnating the dream,
living the AMEN to the Truth,
to the Gospel, to the Christ,
Singing Mercy.[5]

The Journey Continued (1991-1995)

The years following the Buffalo Chapter were years of challenge and growth. By February of 1992 the Institute president and council, also called the Institute Leadership Team (ILT), had designed five goals for their four-year term. These goals coordinated planning around justice issues, sponsored ministries, the multi-cultural reality of the membership, the identity of the Sisters of Mercy and the stewardship of resources. The ILT met three times annually with the superiors of the twenty-five regional communities. "Regional community" is the name that replaced "province" and "congregation" as had been approved at the 1991 Chapter. These gatherings of the Institute Leadership Conference (ILC) allowed the coordination of common agendas and collaboration among all regions of the Institute.

Across the country sisters networked around the work of education, lifelong development, formation and ministry, to name only some of the networks established. In May 1992 as a result of a proposal presented at Chapter, the regional presidents approved the establishment of an Institute education office whose purpose was to demonstrate Mercy commitment to the ministry of education. Sister Judith Heberle, ministry director for the Rochester community, involved elementary and secondary school personnel in two Institute groups: Mercy Secondary Education Association (MSEA) and Mercy Elementary

Education Network (MEEN). She herself was an active leader in these movements, as was Sister Mary Alice O'Brien, who served on MEEN's executive board for many years.

At this same May meeting, the regional presidents also approved a proposal for an Institute Justice structure. This proposal was introduced at the March meeting by Patricia McCann from the Institute Leadership Team. The structure, according to Patricia, would keep justice concerns central to the life and mission of the Sisters of Mercy.

In 1993 the Institute Leadership Conference struggled with the concept of a specific Institute sponsored ministry. At the 1993 Chapter in Rochester, Sister Gaye Moorhead had presented a proposal to be considered by the chapter delegates. Her concern for migrant children had been heightened by her work as an attorney involved in children's legal issues. Turning her attention to their schooling, which was disrupted by the travels of their parents from one work site to another, she created the concept of a mobile staff of educators, outreach workers and health professionals who would travel with the migrant children in order to provide continuity of education for primary-aged youngsters. The Rochester Chapter recommended the proposal to the Institute leadership.

The Institute of the Sisters of Mercy eventually sponsored the Mercy Migrant Education Ministry, and many Mercy communities provided significant support through grants, donations and personnel who served in the ministry. The school, named La Escuela de San Jose, remained active and mobile between Ohio and Florida until May 1, 2001. During this time it educated more than 100 children and provided their families with health and outreach services. The faculty of the University of South Florida did a preliminary independent research study of the students who completed the primary grades at La Escuela de San Jose and entered the middle grades in the public schools. Their research proved that the school's premise was correct: children of migrant families can succeed in school if they have continuity of primary education and support services, and if their families value education and are full participants in the school program.

Several reasons necessitated the school's closing in 2001: a shift in migration patterns; frequent staff shortages and turnover; and lack of long-term funding. Sister Maria Luisa Vera, a member of the Institute Leadership Team, wrote at the time of the closing:

> Although insuperable obstacles have led to the decision to terminate the ministry, the Sisters of Mercy regard with pride the seven-year success of the Mercy Migrant Education Ministry. It has set a standard for meeting the unique needs of the children of migrant workers.[6]

In July 1994, the first convent of the Sisters of Mercy, the original House of Mercy on Baggot Street, Dublin, was rededicated as Mercy International Centre to serve as the spiritual center for the 10,000 Sisters of Mercy around the world. This project had been approved by the presidents of the worldwide congregations before the Buffalo chapter in 1991. Sister Mary Trainer of the Merion, Pennsylvania congregation had spearheaded this restoration and renovation project from its inception, involving all Sisters of Mercy worldwide in the planning and fundraising. Sister Nancy Whitley, the fund developer for the Rochester Sisters of Mercy, was actively involved in the project and later became a full-time staff member of the Centre from 1996 to 1999. Sister Barbara Stinard became a staff member in 2004. Over time, Rochester Sisters Catherine Pfleger, Janet Wahl and Ann Miller each gave two months service as volunteers at the Centre.

In November 1994 the Rochester regional community's advisory board, a group of nine elected women who served as consultants to the regional president and council, were asked "How do you think our community perceives the Institute now?" Their perceptions were positive. They felt the Rochester sisters saw the Institute as a rich source of hope for the future: it was enabling things to happen and was energizing many sisters, especially those who networked with other groups across the United States. At the same time, they looked for a stronger corporate voice from the Institute and more collaborative projects. Some wanted the Institute to sponsor common ministries, to exert greater influence on institutional ministries, and to promote a deeper awareness of the oppression of women.

The Institute began to prepare for a new chapter gathering in 1995. A study of the agendas of the past four years revealed the dedication and determination of the membership to commit their lives and resources to the direction they had embraced at the Buffalo Chapter.

Second Institute Chapter (1995)

"I look forward to Chapter 1995 to deepen my own personal and communal call to Mercy as well as our Institute's commitment to the Institute *Direction Statement* formulated in 1991."[7] These words of delegate Sister Barbara Moore echoed the feelings of the other delegates, as well as the general membership of the Rochester community, as they planned for the second chapter of the Institute.

Sister Doris Gottemoeller, president of the Institute, officially welcomed 141 delegates to the chapter on July 19, 1995, in Dayton, Ohio. Among the elected delegates from Rochester were Sisters Judith Heberle, Barbara Moore, Gaye Moorhead, Mary Sullivan and the community president Sister Ann Miller, who attended ex-officio. Sister

Janet Caufield and Sister Soledad Cantillana Calderón represented the Rochester members in Chile. Sister Anne Curtis was a member of both the Election Committee and the Chapter Steering Committee. Sister Jody Kearney was a member of the Ritual Committee, and Sister Patricia Beairsto created prayer services with an interregional team.

Sister Maryanne Stevens (Omaha), co-chair of the chapter steering committee, hoped the chapter would be an

> experience of Institute that touches every member, an expression of our multi-cultural and international reality, an opportunity to give an account of our Institute *Direction Statement*, a challenge to go to the heart of the call to conversion in our lives and in our ministries, a challenge to risk naming initiatives that enable conversion in our lives and ministries, and an experience of theological reflection.[8]

A process of "theological reflection" began on a personal level for each sister and associate, then moved to the regional community level and continued in cross-regional gatherings. The "material considered at chapter came directly from each of these levels, so there was a sense that the membership had really shared the Chapter's agenda."[9] These reflections also revealed how the membership had lived the *Direction Statement* during the four years since Buffalo. The reflection material was then sifted and refined by the delegates and the Institute leadership team until the fruit of their prayer, discussion and discernment became focused into five statements. These statements were named the Second Institute Chapter Initiatives, and called the membership to a deeper commitment to the *Direction Statement* (affirmed in Chapter 1991).

In brief, these initiatives challenged the members of the Institute to

❖ examine our life in Mercy and within the Church;

❖ promote our identity and development as a multicultural and international institute;

❖ reflect on sponsorship as a means of "witnessing to our enduring concerns";

❖ empower the Institute Leadership Conference to speak on behalf of issues related to our *Constitutions* and *Direction Statement* and challenge our membership to own and support these public statements; and

❖ walk together and share our journeys with those persons suffering from poverty in order that we might stand in solidarity with them.

In the 1995 Institute election, Sisters Doris Gottemoeller and Marie Chin were again called to leadership, as president and vice-president, and Sisters Mary Waskowiak, Maria Luisa Vera and Maureen Lowery were elected to complete the team. A motion was also approved, effective for the election of 1999, which changed the term of office for the Institute team from four years to six years. The *Direction Statement* was reaffirmed with two changes:

1. the phrase "for the next four years" was removed; and

2. a new challenge, "Act in harmony and interdependence with all creation," was added.

The Rochester delegation returned home to share

with the sisters and associates their insights and hopes for the future. The theme of the chapter, "Shaped by the Spirit's Fire," had evoked images of fire, light, warmth, passion and energy (represented in an image created by Sister Estelle Martin). The Rochester membership began to visualize how they would "tend the fire" of this community of Mercy. The process of interfacing the Institute agenda with the regional community agenda became a priority for everyone.

The theological reflection process which had been part of the Second Institute Chapter Initiatives was reinstituted in 1996 at the celebration of the feast of Our Lady of Mercy (September 24). This process called for reflection on the identity of the Sisters of Mercy as women, as members of the church, as vowed religious and as citizens of the earth. Rochester Sister Mary Ann Binsack served as chair of the Institute-wide committee that guided the reflection process.

Rochester sisters and associates also became active participants in three major undertakings sponsored by the Institute. In July 1996 they joined 160 other members at a gathering on "doing justice" and the vow of service. The University of Scranton was host to over 900 sisters/associates who met for the 1997 Education Congress: "Tending the Fire in the New Millennium." The purpose of this event was "to challenge sisters, associates and co-workers to further conversation around the elements of the Direction Statement."[10] That same year, Sister Karlien Bach from Rochester was a member of the planning committee for an August 1997 gathering of sisters who had entered the Sisters of Mercy after 1965.

In July 1998 the Institute published the Mercy prayer book, *Morning and Evening Prayer of the Sisters of Mercy*. Rochester's Sister Mary Sullivan served as editorial consultant to the Institute committee who prepared this prayer book over a period of three years. One part of the book contains "A Selection of Mercy Readings" (pp. 878-958). Eight of these readings came from Mary's published articles in *MAST*,[11] as well as from her book *Catherine McAuley and the Tradition of Mercy*. In the introduction of the prayer book, the editorial committee thanks Mary for "her special assistance throughout the project."[12]

Third Institute Chapter (1999)

In order to understand the agenda of the Third Institute Chapter (1999), it is important to look back to the year 1997 when the general membership of the Institute first heard about the project "Pathways Toward the Future."

The Institute Leadership Team appointed the Pathways committee in June 1996. Their purpose was to design a long-range planning process—"an interactive, creative and transformative process that would touch every member of the Institute in some way." During the years leading to the June 1999 Chapter, the goal of "Pathways Toward the Future" was to have each sister and associate answer the question: "What aspects of our Institute need to be strengthened, changed or created?"[13] The process asked members to complete surveys, attend meetings, participate in small group discussions, gather as regional communities and as international regions within the Americas. Two phases of the process set directions: (1) Assessing the Current Reality; and (2) Defining the Preferred Future. All sisters and associates were encouraged to participate in these phases.

In September 1997 each Mercy sister and associate received a membership profile designed by the Center for Applied Research in the Apostolate (CARA), a group affiliated with Georgetown University in Washington, D.C. The profile asked specific questions about the Mercy *Direction Statement* and other key aspects of life as a Sister of Mercy or associate. When the data were collected and analyzed, it gave considerable insight into the current reality of Mercy life. Opportunities for the membership to meet and dialogue about the data helped create the "preferred future" of the Institute. Theological reflection, video-teleconferencing and cross-regional gatherings refined the vision which became the content of the 1999 Chapter.[14]

The Third Institute Chapter opened on June 21, 1999, in St. Louis, Missouri with 141 delegates from the United States and countries beyond the U.S. These delegates assembled on the "threshold of a new millennium," as the chapter logo proclaimed. Rochester's Sister Estelle Martin was again selected to design the chapter logo. Her sweeping arch symbolized both the new millennium and the city of St. Louis—the setting for the chapter.

Sister Sheila Stevenson, president of the Rochester community (1997-2004), reflected on her experience of the chapter gathering:

> After the experience of two previous Chapters, cross-regional meetings, network meetings and all manner of Institute ways to relate, including our various publications and preparations for this Chapter, we came together with eight years of knowledge of one another in various ways. This was a different reality from previous Chapters and it added to the easier flow and spontaneity of this gathering. You could feel it from the first night, and it continued throughout the ten days. We have worked hard at becoming an Institute, and it is beginning to show, not just among leadership, but among the grassroots sisters and associates from across all twelve countries where we are located.[15]

As the delegates deliberated on the preferred future for the Sisters of Mercy, they focused on the questions: "What gives you energy? How would you like to see this evolve? What are your leanings regarding the emerging content of the chapter?" After some quiet time, delegates and alternates were invited to share their concepts of our preferred future and what led them to these views. The delegates then placed their ideas on newsprint, keeping in mind the *Direction Statement* and the *Constitutions*. The statements were synthesized into six themes: finances, passion for the poor, planet Earth, racism, right relationships, and women in the Church. In small groups, the delegates and alternates designed action steps for each of these issues. Thirty-three groups presented ideas. These ideas were then given to a Writing Committee, who synthesized, polished and presented them to the delegates for review. When this draft, in general language, did not meet with the delegates' approval, several groups of delegates undertook to prepare more specific parts of a new draft, reflecting the concrete detail the delegates desired. Sister Margaret Farley, a spokesperson for these groups, explained that the new "material was organized under five topics corresponding to five points in the Institute *Direction Statement*." The final document was approved by the delegates, section by section, and became the Sisters of Mercy *Action Plan (1999-2005)*.

The introduction to the *Action Plan* explains that "these issues all flow from our *Direction Statement*. They touch our hearts, our aspirations and our daily lives. They hold power for personal conversion and Gospel witness as they focus and advance the life and mission of our Institute over the next six years."[16]

The second major task of the delegates was to elect the new Institute Leadership Team. The election process began on Monday, June 28, 1999, with 141 delegates present for the election. From the five nominees for president, Sister Marie Chin was elected president on the fourth ballot. From the seven nominees for members of the Council, the following four sisters, in order of choice, were elected: Sisters Helen Marie Burns, Patricia McDermott, Sheila Carney, and Maria Luisa Vera. As agreed in Chapter 1995, the new term of service was six years rather than four years.

At the closing ritual of the Chapter, Sister Marie Chin summarized in both English and Spanish what had happened during these Chapter days:

> In this sacred time and space, we have heard God speak in one another. We have heard God's eternal love for persons who are poor and the call to deepen our hearts' response to their transforming presence. We have heard God's call to be revealed and celebrated in all creation and the call to recognize that revelation, especially in women and children. We have heard God's tender and creative presence in the cosmos and the call to revere God's vital power by gentle living and respectful relationships.
>
> We have heard God's pain at the fragmentation of the Divine Image because of racism and prejudice and the call to love each other with dynamic inclusivity. We have heard God's promise for a new heaven and new earth and the call to witness God's dream by living our lives in communities of right relationships. In the name of Mercy, I call us now to act on what we have heard.[17]

The Rochester delegates came home ready to act on what they had heard at the St. Louis Chapter. With Sister Sheila Stevenson as facilitator, Rochester delegates Sisters Karlien Bach, Janet Korn, Gaye Moorhead and Mary Sullivan joined alternates Anne Curtis, Jody Kearney and

Pat Prinzing to plan ways of bringing the chapter experience to life for the sisters and associates at home.

Implementation of the *Action Plan* (1999-2005)

In September 1999 the newly-elected Institute president, Sister Marie Chin, was the main speaker at Rochester's celebration of the feast of Our Lady of Mercy. Her topic, "Community: A Gift Given Us," was chosen as an introduction to the Chapter *Action Plan* which focused efforts on three major areas of life: spirituality, community, and ministry. The section on "Community and Shared Resources" states: "We affirm that the biblical demand for right relationship calls each of us to balance community, spirituality and ministry in order to achieve the quality of community needed for apostolic life today."[18] The annual community planning materials and reflection group agendas for the following year focused on community.

Chapter follow-up meetings held in various areas invited sisters and associates to listen, discuss and reflect on the Chapter *Action Plan* that would guide their lives over the next six years. That same year, the Mercy Elementary Education Network (MEEN) met in Philadelphia to dialogue around the question: "On what level can we enter into the initiatives proposed by the Institute Chapter, and how do we address these issues in a Mercy conversation that is ongoing and heard by those outside the education community?"

In November 2000 the Rochester community gathered for a weekend meeting to begin to "revise our Strategic Plan in the light of the Institute *Action Plan.*" The results from previous assemblies on ministry, stewardship, and community were considered in this planning. Sisters and associates, aided by a facilitator, worked through the necessary drafting and revision and identified five areas that became goals for 2001-2005. These five areas were:

1. Aging and Life Transition
2. Housing and Community Life
3. Solidarity With the Economically Poor
4. Relationship with the Church
5. Cultural Diversity

Sister Sheila Stevenson reminded the community that

> the Spirit moves among us in a special way when we gather, and all of our deliberations are influenced by our relationship to the Church, to the community and to our ever-shrinking world, as well as to our Institute.

In completing the *Strategic Plan*, the Rochester community confirmed where it needed to place its energy for the next four years (2001-2005). The written document now needed to come to life in the words and actions of the sisters and associates.

In July 2001 the Institute celebrated the tenth anniversary of its founding. To begin this commemoration, the sisters were asked to reflect on the question "What does the Institute mean in my life?" Sister M. Walter Hickey (Rochester) wrote:

> The Institute has meant a broader vision and a sense of "Mercy" strength. It has united me with a greater number of sisters whose values and ideals are the same as mine. We have together a voice that can make a difference in our service to those who are marginated.

> As a secondary school administrator, I am hopeful

that the Network for Mercy Secondary Education
will keep the values and ideals of our foundress
alive in our institutions, as fewer sisters are
involved in this critical ministry. This network has
kept us connected.

Sister Susan Cain (Rochester) believed:

that being a member of the Institute has meant new
life for me. My horizons have broadened . . . and
I'm loving it! The most direct impact of the
Institute on me has been through my involvement as
a volunteer with Mercy Volunteer Corps. Mercy
Corps began as a project of the Merion,
Pennsylvania regional community twenty-two years
ago and has become a sponsored ministry of the
Institute. As such all the regional communities now
embrace it.

These encounters have brought such added richness
in my life. The activity generated here on behalf of
Mercy Volunteer Corps and the kingdom of God is
creative, varied, impressive and extensive, and I am
privileged to be witness to this and to be a part of it.
Thank you, Institute!

When the Institute celebrated its twelfth
anniversary, President Marie Chin and the four leadership
members wrote this message for the future:

We greet you on this twelfth anniversary of our
Institute. In the years leading to our founding
event, we engaged one another in varied and
creative ways in order to design a future together.
This year we stand in a similar place, asking
ourselves once again how best to shape our lives

and structures in order to foster mission and sisterhood. As we approached our founding moment, we were twenty-five seeking to become one. Now we are one and we look for new ways to realize and organize the oneness for the sake of our future and God's reign.[19]

These words echoed the Institute *Action Plan* that challenged us "to explore opportunities for collaboration among Regional Communities (e.g., in co-sponsorship and in reconfiguration of Regional Communities) as well as sharing, reallocating, pooling and/or centralizing financial resources, because we desire to use our resources for mission and for the common good."[20]

The Institute Leadership Team, the twenty-five regional presidents, and the membership of these communities are now actively engaged in this process, aptly named "Reimagining, Reconfiguring Our Life as Institute."

CHAPTER ELEVEN

ROCHESTER PLANS FOR RECONFIGURATION

L ong before the Institute *Action Plan* called for exploring opportunities for reconfiguration of the regional communities, Rochester had already been collaborating with three other Mercy communities: Buffalo, New York; Erie, Pennsylvania; and Pittsburgh, Pennsylvania. These four regional communities have roots dating back to the nineteenth century. The first Sisters of Mercy who founded St. Bridget School in Buffalo in 1858 came from St. Mary's community in Rochester, just eight months after their own founding. In a similar fashion, the Sisters of Mercy from Pittsburgh, founded in 1843, started a mission in Titusville, Pennsylvania in 1870 and from this mission the Erie community began in 1926. These four regional communities are also linked by their geography: Buffalo and Rochester are located in western New York State; Erie and Pittsburgh in western Pennsylvania. They are neighbors who share the Great Lakes and the rivers of Pennsylvania.

Since the beginning of the Institute in 1991,

members of the leadership teams of all the regional communities had been discussing ways to collaborate more effectively across the twenty-five regional communities. One of the first topics to engage interest was vocations and formation. The leadership teams from Buffalo, Erie and Rochester met together in the fall of 1993 to discuss the idea of shared personnel, programs and finances in the formation of new members. At that meeting they agreed to the following:

> We support, in terms of incorporation (formation), the idea of sharing personnel, finances, programming and more involvement of members of our three communities.[1]

A committee was formed to plan a meeting of all sisters to introduce these ideas. Later the committee decided that it would not be beneficial to have the meeting as anticipated because of developments on an Institute level regarding formation. However, the desire to continue the Buffalo, Erie, Rochester collaborative efforts around vocations-formation remained.

The leadership teams met again on November 28, 1994 and agreed on two important points: the leadership teams needed to meet regularly to discuss increased collaboration; and Sister Peggy Gorman (Buffalo president) would contact Sister Sheila Carney (Pittsburgh president) to invite the Pittsburgh community to join in these meetings. On February 28, 1995, with the Pittsburgh leadership team present, the four communities agreed to share two full-time vocation directors by September 1995—a time line that proved unfeasible. However, in June 1996 the leaders welcomed Sister Jeanne Thomas Danahy (Buffalo) and Sister Geri Rosinski (Pittsburgh) as the first directors of vocation efforts for Buffalo, Erie,

Pittsburgh and Rochester. In September 1996 they organized their vocation headquarters in Buffalo. Plans included assisting women discerning a call to membership in the Institute, supporting the four regional community vocation teams, and developing programs for vocation awareness. Sister Jeanne promised: "We want to get to know the names and faces and history of each regional community. Mercy is Mercy, but the flavor is different in each regional community."[2]

Originally, the four communities referred to themselves as the Great Lakes-Appalachian region because of their geographical location; however, by October 1996 they had decided on a new title: Sisters of Mercy, New York/Pennsylvania West (NyPaW). The name never totally satisfied the membership, but it has so far persisted for lack of a better suggestion.

Sister Estelle Martin (Rochester) designed a logo to represent the four regional communities. In reflecting on what they shared in common, she chose the image of water, since all four groups have large bodies of water within their regions: the Finger Lakes and the Great Lakes, and the Allegheny, Genesee, Susquehanna and Monongahela Rivers. In the logo, water was represented by four curved lines in the center, free flowing and showing movement. It was a symbol of new life but also a symbol of continuity, as Sister Estelle described it. An open circle of Mercy united the four communities. Sister Estelle explained: "Others may see different connections and have different ideas—and isn't that what our cross-regional collaboration is all about, sharing different ideas and new ways of doing things?"

In June 1996 two of the regional communities elected new leaders: Sister Georgine Scarpino replaced Sister Sheila Carney in Pittsburgh and Sister Joanne Courneen replaced Sister Maura Smith in Erie. Sister Peggy Gorman and Sister Ann Miller still represented

Buffalo and Rochester. During the preceding year, these leadership teams became familiar with one another's communities, encouraged members to understand their part in vocation ministry, and provided opportunities for everyone to attend a cross-regional gathering in one of the four regional communities.

The year 1997 was a year of additional growth for the four communities. They explored collaborative models for such issues as leadership, finances, new membership programs, and sponsorship of ministries. Sharing ways to implement the Institute *Direction Statement* and Chapter 1995 Initiatives, planning cross-regional meetings, integrating and networking among the four regions were all avenues for looking to the future as geographic neighbors and members of the Institute of the Sisters of Mercy of the Americas.

During this time the communication directors became a vital and necessary component of the NyPaW collaboration. In retrospect, communication among and within the four communities was a major factor in their growth toward a shared future. The archivists from each regional community also met, first in 1997 and five years later in 2002. A central archives was established in Pittsburgh with Sister Patricia Hodge (Pittsburgh) as archivist. Sister Jeanne Reichart, the Rochester archivist, shared the four archivists' belief that "the difference among their communities consisted only in the names and places in their history; the mission and spirit which motivates, unites and inspires them is the same."[3]

At a February 1997 meeting in Erie, the presidents of the four regional communities reflected on the crucial question: "What do we want as an end result? Do we want networking or collaboration?" The group unanimously agreed they were all looking toward collaboration and reaffirmed their commitment in a statement drafted by Sister Patricia McCann (Pittsburgh):

We have a commitment to creative collaboration which will lead us into deeper relationships with one another in order to strengthen mission, use our resources more effectively, and render our structures more simple and tightly unified.[4]

Leadership Team 1997-2001
Sisters Sheila Stevenson, president; Sister Fran Wegman, vice president,
Mary Ann Binsack and Patricia Prinzing councilors.

In May and June 1997 the four presidents traveled together to each of the four regions to present updates on NyPaW and open the floor for questions and suggestions. The agenda included a slide presentation on each region which explained the history of its founding, its ministries, its missions beyond the United States, its membership, and other common interests. After the presentation, the assembled sisters shared their hopes and concerns about the future. As the newly elected president of the Rochester community, Sister Sheila Stevenson participated in these gatherings along with Sister Ann Miller.

Collaboration in vocation and incorporation ministry continued to grow stronger in the next years. This was particularly rewarding because these efforts had brought the regions together for the first time in 1993. Two

Rochester sisters, Kathleen Wayne and Kathryn Wahl, were actively involved in new membership ministry. Sisters Nancy Hoff (Buffalo president) and Kathryn Wahl welcomed Sister Kathleen Sisson (Buffalo) into the Mercy novitiate at a reception ceremony in July 2001 at Erie, as all four communities gathered to celebrate the tenth anniversary of the founding of the Institute of the Sisters of Mercy of the Americas.

Exploring Future Leadership

From 1998 to 2002 these regional communities continued to convene, communicate and celebrate together as often as possible, but they intensified their efforts to move toward a shared future. In February 1999 the leadership teams charged a committee to explore the potential of "Shared Governance." The committee was organized as the Coordinating Committee of NyPaW on Shared Governance, but the committee members wanted to move beyond the idea of coordination to an image that invoked action. Thus they chose to rename themselves the NyPaW Task Force on Exploring Future Administrative Relationships. However, by May 1999 they had evolved into the committee on Exploring Future Leadership Structures.

This task force convened the four regional communities in the fall of that year to test community readiness to engage the question of shared leadership structures. This was an important step because implementation of a new leadership structure could not occur without the involvement and discussion of all the communities. Any change in leadership structures needed the approval of the communities' chapters or assemblies as well as approval by the Institute Leadership Team. The four communities responded positively to the possibility of exploring a shared leadership structure. Sisters Mary Ann

Binsack and Patricia Beairsto represented Rochester on this task force, Mary Ann serving as chair.

To celebrate six years of working together as communities, the communications personnel: Sister Bernadette Bell, Sister Elenore Kam, Micaela Young and Tami Bohannon developed the idea for a NyPaW newsletter named *In Harmony*. It did not replace regional newsletters, but was published several times a year to focus on common efforts within NyPaW. The first edition in January 2000 recapped the program on shared leadership.

In the fall of 2000 the task force on leadership structures reconvened the four communities to share ideas about the roles of leadership and to name guiding principles for further collaboration; seventy-five percent of the active members of the four communities attended these meetings. The task force stressed the need for education and involvement of all members in the decision-making process. They also wanted the structure to represent each regional community and to preserve the unique culture of each region. This call for grassroots involvement in the process led to the formation of a Design Team to produce models of shared governance. Two members from each community were chosen for this task and were given eighteen months to accomplish their work, from January 2001 to mid-year of 2002. Sisters Kathleen Wayne and Kathleen Mary O'Connell served for Rochester and Sister Mary Ann Binsack, chair of the Task Force on Exploring Future Leadership Structures, was liaison to the Design Team.

In May 2002 the Design Team presented a proposed leadership model to the regional communities through their common newsletter, *In Harmony,* and invited the membership to gather on June 1, 2002 to critique the model. The model recommended that one regional community be formed by 2008 from the combined communities of Buffalo, Erie, Pittsburgh and Rochester.

From 2004 on, the four regional presidents, working as a team, would oversee the NyPaW mission and develop the detailed model for the formation of the one regional community.

On September 21, 2002, a vote was taken in each community on the following statement:

> The four NyPaW regional communities will continue working together in a process that is intended to lead to the creation of one regional community by 2008, advance the charism and Institute reimagining, and enhance spirituality, ministry, and leadership. A shared leadership structure will be refined and tested before implementation in 2004.[5]

In Rochester, Sister Sheila Stevenson presided as 158 sisters met at the motherhouse for the voting; this included the sisters in Chile who gathered at San Luis in Santiago and communicated by fax. The vote was an overwhelming "yes," with 154 sisters voting in the affirmative and three in the negative. (It is interesting to recall that in 1929, when 152 Rochester sisters voted on the union of all Sisters of Mercy in the United States, 142 voted against the idea and ten voted in favor.) The sisters from Buffalo, Erie and Pittsburgh also chose to move toward one regional community. Thus, the membership of the four communities continued to contribute guidance and support as they moved forward. In 2004 the Sisters of Mercy in the Philippines, who had been founded as a branch community from Buffalo, voted to become a separate part of NyPaW.

The success of the NyPaW endeavor to date is a tribute to the four leadership teams, the communications directors, the sisters and associates who collaborated on committees and events, and the overall membership who read, listened, discussed and continued to believe in NyPaW's potential for advancing the charism of Catherine McAuley and the mission of the Sisters of Mercy.

Chile Plans for Reconfiguration

The Sisters of Mercy in South and Central America and the Caribbean have shared a friendship with one another for a quarter of a century. They have come together on a regular basis since 1980 to discuss the realities of the Third World within the context of the Mercy heritage.

In 1978 the General Administrative Team of the Sisters of Mercy of the Union sought ways of supporting and collaborating with sisters serving outside the United States. A questionnaire sent to these sisters revealed the need for networking across the Caribbean and South and Central America. A planning meeting was held in Guyana in 1979. In February 1980 twenty-two Sisters of Mercy from ten countries met in Jamaica for the first Mercy Latin American/Caribbean Conference. Jane Kenrick from Chile and Noreen Graney, a member of the Rochester leadership team, attended. The Conference, conceived by the Sisters of Mercy of the Union, came to life as a meeting of all the missionary groups of Mercys in the Federation as it existed in 1980.

The women gathered to share the Mercy charism and spirituality. Solidarity with poor and oppressed people, enculturation, initial formation, communication among sisters and the sharing of resources were identified as priorities.[6] As the Conference moved into the 1980s, the participants decided to respect the diversity of the various regions by holding the full Conference only once every three years and gathering as regions in the alternate years. In February 2000 the Conference met in Chile to celebrate its twentieth anniversary. Sister Marion Collins

(Peru/Cincinnati) reflected on the meaning of this anniversary for the participants: "The journey that began twenty years ago continues to challenge and strengthen us for further growth and commitment."[7]

Four years later, in 2004, the Mercy sisters in Peru, Chile, Argentina, Honduras, Guatemala, Panama, Belize and Guyana gathered for the eleventh Latin American/Caribbean Conference (LACC) in San Pedro Sula, Honduras. From February 1 to February 7, they prayed, shared, and searched for concrete ways of "Walking with Integrity into the Third Millennium." Similar problems and challenges were presented by each country.[8]

When the Conference ended, twenty-eight sisters from these countries remained for two more days to explore the reimagining and reconfiguring goals that the Institute leadership was asking them to consider. After discussion, the group tentatively agreed to work toward one regional community (or area) for the eight countries. The years they had shared as the Latin American/Caribbean Conference no doubt made the decision—reaffirmed in February 2005—easier; they were already a part of one another in spirit. However, in Rochester there was both joy and sorrow—joy that the Chileans accepted the challenge to walk into the future with these other countries, but sorrow that they would no longer be a special and integral part of the Rochester community.

EPILOGUE

> History doesn't just happen. It is made, created, shaped.
> And it helps if somebody writes it down—candidly,
> factually and with a bit of flair.
>
> Joe Feuerherd[1]

At the threshold of the twenty-first century, the Sisters of Mercy could look back on the people and events that had helped to shape their history and create a vigorous group of women religious who had persevered through a century of change, remaining faithful to God's call to serve the poor, the sick and the uneducated. As Father Robert McNamara writes in his book on the Diocese of Rochester, "Bishop McQuaid's reserved attitude did have the good effect of creating among his Sisters of Mercy a patient and persevering self-reliance which eventually received its reward."[2]

Bishop Matthew Clark, after attending a Mercy Day

celebration at the Blossom Road motherhouse in 1990, wrote in the *Catholic Courier*, the diocesan newspaper:

> I am ever aware at such celebrations of the enormous contribution the Sisters of Mercy now make and have made to the people of this region for more years than our diocese has existed. In the 1850s, when we were still part of the Diocese of Buffalo, these daughters of Catherine McAuley were doing the works of mercy in this area.[3]

Bishop Clark headlined his story "Mercy Sisters Have Made Mark in Diocese." Let us hope, Bishop McQuaid reads the Rochester diocesan newspaper in heaven.

The twentieth century transformed religious life. The Sister Formation Movement, the Second Vatican Council and the years that followed were a time of challenge and grace. Women religious, some of whom had for years simply walked from the convent door to the school (or hospital) door, were plunged into a new world that was developing a global perspective on the works of mercy. The horizons of their life expanded beyond the parish property to wider vistas. In addition, they faced the phenomena of declining membership, school and convent closings, hospital mergers and the need for lay people to assume responsibility for some of their sponsored ministries that had once been staffed almost completely by sisters.

As the new millennium began, the Rochester sisters were older and fewer, but profoundly grateful and hopeful. In the period 1990-2005, nine women had entered the community. Their membership averaged 200 professed sisters, with a median age of 69, and they experienced an annual increase in associate membership: 151 lay men and women had chosen to walk with the sisters to further the mission of mercy.

In April of 2004 they had gathered to elect the leadership team who would lead them through the last phase of reconfiguring their thirteen-year-old Institute. The new team: Sisters Gaye L. Moorhead, Jane Schur, Kathleen Ann Kolb and Kathryn Wahl, would work with other elected leaders to create a new regional area with the necessary government structures. As the sisters wrote their ballots, they were aware that this was to be the last election solely for the Rochester community. Four years later, in 2008, the leaders will be elected from the combined communities of Buffalo, Erie, Pittsburgh, the Philippines and Rochester, and there will be only one leadership team for the entire area.

The Rochester Mercys celebrate two major anniversaries in the future. On December 24, 2005, they commemorate forty years of service in Chile. Five Rochester sisters minister there as well as five Chileans who are members of the Rochester community. This celebration will be a significant one as the Chilean community now begins the process of becoming a new area of the Institute that will not involve them directly with the Rochester community.

On June 9, 2007, the community will commemorate 150 years of service in Rochester For the first eleven of those years, they were part of the Diocese of Buffalo. Just eight months after opening the Rochester foundation, the community sent four sisters to serve St. Bridget's parish in Buffalo; in 1862 four more left Rochester for a mission in Batavia. As the sisters and associates celebrate this anniversary, they will be in the final planning phase of the Institute's reconfiguration that will unite them once again with the Buffalo Sisters of Mercy.

The Rochester community rejoices in remembering its past during this time of celebration, but the future is what the sisters look to build. Where is the Holy Spirit sending them in order to do greater service? "There is among them an expectant hope in the future, not only of religious life in the church but most especially in that of the Institute of the Sisters of Mercy of the Americas and its many waiting configurations." With all the women of this Institute, "we deeply trust we will discover a new map for our journey together, new relationships to sustain the journey, and new structures to facilitate the mission of our deep story. We hope we will come to understand once more God's promise: Behold, I am doing something new. I am creating a new heart within you."[4]

Leadership Team 2004-2008
(left to right) Sisters Gaye L. Moorhead, president; Kathryn Wahl, councilor;
Jane Schur, vice president; Kathleen Ann Kolb, councilor

NOTES

In the notes the following abbreviations are used: DR, for the Roman Catholic Diocese of Rochester, as in Archives DR; SMR, for the Sisters of Mercy of Rochester, as in Archives SMR.

Chapter One

[1]Mary Florence Sullivan, *Mercy Comes to Rochester*, 2nd ed. (Rochester, NY: Sisters of Mercy, 1985), 57.

[2]A Sister of St. Joseph, *Sisters of St. Joseph of Rochester* (Rochester, NY: Sisters of St. Joseph of Rochester, 1950), 50-51.

[3]*The Rule and Constitutions of the Religious Called Sisters of Mercy* (Dublin: Browne & Nolan, Ltd., 1863), 68, art. 114.

[4]Robert F. McNamara, *The Diocese of Rochester in America 1868-1993,* 2nd ed. (Rochester, NY: Roman Catholic Diocese of Rochester, 1998), 135.

[5]Mary Florence Sullivan, *Mercy*, 45.

[6]Mary C. Sullivan, *The Correspondence of Catherine McAuley, 1818-1841* (Washington: The Catholic University of America Press, 2004), 365.

[7]Frederick J. Zwierlien, *Life and Letters of Bishop McQuaid*, vol. 2 (Rochester, NY: The Art Print Shop, 1926), 13.

[8]Bernard J. McQuaid to Michael Corrigan, 22 April 1902 (hand copy), Archives SMR.

[9]McNamara, 185.

[10]Mary Florence Sullivan, *Mercy*, 79.

[11]McNamara, 263.

[12]Bonaventure Brennan, *According to Catherine: Words of Wisdom from Catherine McAuley, A Thematic Approach* (Dublin, Ireland: Congregation of the Sisters of Mercy, 2003), 102.

[13]*Familiar Instructions of Rev. Mother McAuley*, ed. Sisters of Mercy of St. Louis, Missouri, new and rev. ed. (St. Louis: Vincentian Press, 1927), 16.

[14]*St. James Mercy Hospital 1890-1985. The First 95 Years*. Booklet printed for anniversary by the hospital, Archives SMR, Box 670.1.

[15]"Parochial Schools to Open Monday," *Catholic Journal* (Rochester, New York): 18 November 1918, Archives DR.

[16]Minutes, Board of Trustees, Sisters of Mercy of Rochester, 25 August 1927, Archives SMR.

[17]Mary Borgia O'Keefe to Mary Carmelita Hartman, 30 December 1927 (hand copy), Archives SMR.

[18]Mary Evangelist Meyer, interview by author, 5 June 1996, Archives SMR.

[19]"Mothers General," Book C, Archives SMR.
[20]"Opening of Our Lady of Mercy High School," *Catholic Journal*, 8 September 1928, Archives SMR.
[21]Margaret Grimes Lynch to author, 30 June 1997, Archives SMR.
[22]Marie Lavelle Hanss to author, 29 June 1997, Archives SMR.
[23]Eunice Aman, interview by author, June 1997, Archives SMR.
[24]Mary C. Sullivan, *Catherine McAuley and the Tradition of Mercy* (Notre Dame, Indiana: University of Notre Dame Press, 1995), 297.

Chapter Two

[1]Mary Florence Sullivan, *Mercy*, 84.
[2]Mary Carmelita Hartman to Mary Liguori McHale, 1 April 1928, Archives SMR.
[3]Mary Borgia O'Keefe to Mary Carmelita Hartman, 5 April 1928 (hand copy), Archives SMR.
[4]Mary Liguori McHale to Apostolic Delegate, July 1929 (hand copy), Archives SMR.
[5]Mary Evangelist Meyer, interview by author, 5 June 1996, Archives SMR.
[6]Mary Colette Frank, interview by author, 11 June 1996, Archives SMR.
[7]Mary Carmella Coene, interview by author, 17 June 1996, Archives SMR.
[8]Mary Justin Morris, interview by author, 18 June 1996, Archives SMR.
[9][Mary Antonia Hyde], *Mercy* (Rochester, New York: George P. Burns Press, 1932), 54.
[10]Mary Beatrice Curran, interview with author, 15 May 1997, Archives SMR.
[11]Hyde, 55.
[12]Hyde, 56.
[13]Hyde, 58.
[14]Hyde, 12, 13.
[15]Minutes, Board of Trustees, Sisters of Mercy of Rochester, 29 June 1940, Archives SMR.
[16]Mary Jo Lanphear, Town of Brighton Historian, interview by Patricia Donovan, 22 May 2002, Archives SMR.
[17]Mary Eymard Hyland, "History of Mercy High School," Archives SMR, Box 613.
[18]"Mothers General," Book C, Archives SMR.
[19]Ibid.
[20]Mary Sullivan, *Catherine McAuley*, 286.
[21]The Sacred Congregation of Religious, Document III N 3709/54, 16 July 1954, Archives SMR, Box 550.
[22]Mary Camilla McGuire to Rochester Congregation, July 1953, Archives SMR.
[23]*The Rule and Constitutions of the Religious Called Sisters of Mercy*

(Dublin: Browne & Nolan, Ltd., 1926), 90, Art. 154.

[24]Mother M. Magdalene Schenck to Friends of the Sisters of Mercy, 25 March 1957, Archives SMR.

[25]Patricia Donovan, interview by author, Archives SMR.

[26]Anniversary Programs and Celebrations, Archives, SMR, Box 450.

[27]Homily of Bishop Lawrence B. Casey, 1 June 1957, Archives, SMR.

[28]"Mercy Echoes," (Newsletter of St. James Mercy Hospital) June 1957, Archives, SMR.

[29]Ibid.

[30]Frederick J. Shortall to Mary Magdalene Schenck, 1 June 1957, Archives SMR.

Chapter Three

[1]Mary C. Sullivan, *Catherine McAuley*, 330

[2]*The Rule and Constitutions of the Sisters of Mercy,* written by Catherine McAuley and revised by Daniel Murray, Archbishop of Dublin. Quoted in Sullivan, *Catherine McAuley*, 296.

[3]John J. Fialka, *Sisters: Catholic Nuns and the Making of America* (New York: St. Martin's Press, 2003), 3.

[4]Holy Cross Church, *Centennial 1873-1973*, Archives SMR.

[5]Robert J. Kialey, Executive Director, Department of Elementary Schools to Mary Alice O'Brien, 15 December 1997, Archives SMR.

[6]*Mercy Focus*, (Newsletter of the Rochester Sisters of Mercy), 6 November 1998, Archives SMR.

[7]McNamara, 157.

[8]Jane Hasbrouck, interview by author, 2 November 2000, Archives SMR.

[9]*Holy Family High School 1930-1957* (Auburn, NY: Holy Family High School Alumni, 1997), 5.

[10]Notre Dame High School File, Archives SMR, Box 612.

[11]Mary Carmella Coene, telephone interview by author, 14 June 2001, Archives SMR.

[12]"Notre Dame High School Dedication Supplement" *Catholic Courier-Journal*, September 23 , 1955, 5.

[13]Mary Edwina Butler and Mary Carmella Coene, telephone interview by author, 14 June 2001, Archives SMR.

[14]Mary Eymard Hyland, interview by author, 5 March 2003, Archives SMR.

[15]Catherine McAuley College File, Archives SMR, Box 410.

[16]Edward Mooney, Associate for Teacher Education, to Mary Liguori McHale, 1 June 1940, Archives SMR, Box 410.

[17]Catherine McAuley College File, Archives SMR, Box 410.

[18]Reading Laboratory File, Archives SMR, Box 490.

[19]Marilyn Williams, interview by author, 27 January 2004, Archives SMR.

[20]Pope Pius XII, International Meeting of Superiors 1950, cited in Minutes of Catherine McAuley College Faculty, Spring 1960, Archives SMR, Box 410.

[21]Doris Gottemoeller, Statement quoted in *The Quality of Mercy*, Claudette Dwyer, ed. (Sisters of Mercy, Regional Community of Chicago, 1996), 57.

[22]Mary Edwardine Weaver, interview by author, 19 November 2002, Archives SMR.

Chapter Four

[1]Mary Augustine Roth, RSM, *The McAuley Conference 1955-1965* (Potomac, Maryland: Federation of the Sisters of Mercy of the Americas, 1978), 5.

[2]Mary. Camilla McGuire to Mothers General of the Independent Congregations of Sisters of Mercy, 7 September 1954, Archives SMR.

[3]Roth, 2.

[4]Roth, 3

[5]Roth, 15.

[6]Roth, 21.

[7]Roth, 23.

[8]*Perfectae Caritatis (Decree on the Adaptation and Renewal of Religious Life)*, second Vatican Council, 29 October 1965, art. 8.

[9]Ibid., art. 2.

[10]Ibid., art. 2c.

[11]Chapter Minutes 1967-68, Archives, SMR, Box 540.

[12]Ibid.

[13]*Perfectae* Caritatis, art. 2c.

[14]Chapter Minutes 1967-69, Archives SMR, Box 540.

[15]Ibid.

[16]Ibid.

[17]*The Customs of the Sisters of Mercy in the Diocese of Rochester, New York* (Rochester, NY: Sisters of Mercy, 1938), 52-54.

[18]Roth, 18.

[19]Mary Gabriel Oster to the Rochester Sisters of Mercy, 16 January 1964, Archives SMR, Box 250.

[20]Ibid.

[21]Mary Florence Sullivan to the Mercy High Students, December 1965, Archives SMR, Box 250.

[22]Ibid.

[23]Patricia A. Donovan, interview by author, 8 September 2003.

[24]*MAST Journal* 8.1 (Fall 1997) 8, 2.

[25]Kathleen Milliken, interview by archivist, 4 April 2004, Archives SMR

[26]Doris Gottemoeller, quoted in *The Quality of Mercy, ed.* Claudette Dwyer (Sisters of Mercy, Regional Community of Chicago, 1966), 56.

[27]Kathleen Milliken, interview by Archivist, 4 April 2004, Archives SMR.

[28]*Perfectae Caritatis*, art. 3.

[29]Chapter Minutes 1967-69, Archives SMR, Box 540.

[30]Ibid.

[31]*Interim Constitutions* (Sisters of Mercy of Rochester, 1971), 32, art. 46.

[32]"Proposal to Live in a Rented House," Sisters of Mercy, Hornell, New York, September 1975, Archives SMR, Box 250.

[33]Housing Task Force File, Archives SMR, Box 250.

[34]Martin Tracy to Jean Marie Kearse, 21 May 1991, Archives SMR.

[35]Jean Marie Kearse, "Open Forum" with Matthew H. Clark, November 1983, Archives SMR.

[36]*Perfectae Caritatis, art. 2d.*

[37]Minutes of Social Justice Commission, 24 November 1968, Archives SMR, Box 525.

[38]Minutes of Chapter 1975, Archives SMR, Box 540.2.

[39]Minutes of Mercy and Justice Committee, 29 January 1976, Archives SMR, Box 640.

[40]*Perfectae Caritatis*, art. 2d.

[41]Jean Marie Kearse to Rochester Congregation, April 1986, Archives SMR, Box 640.1.

[42]By-Laws, Mercy and Justice Committee, December 1976, Archives SMR, Box 640.

[43]Sheila Miller to Rochester Congregation, 3 February 1989, Archives SMR, Box 640.1.

[44]*Interim Constitutions* (Sisters of Mercy of Rochester, 1975), 15, Archives SMR, Box 550.

Chapter Five

[1]Desmond Stone, quoted by Mark Hare, Rochester *Democrat and Chronicle*, 30 December 1998, Archives SMR.

[2]House of Mercy File, Archives SMR, Box 630.

[3]Ibid.

[4]Tioga County Rural Ministry File, Archives SMR, Box 602.

[5]Ibid.

[6]Margaret Louise Snider, interview by author, February 2005, Archives SMR.

[7]St. Mary's House of Prayer File, Archives SMR, Box 650.

[8]Ibid.

[9]Ibid.

[10]Ibid.

[11]Judith Heberle to Rochester Congregation, 11 June 1976, Archives SMR.

[12]Judith Heberle to Rochester Congregation, June 1978, Archives SMR.

[13]Ibid.

[14]Mission Statement of Mercy Prayer Center, Archives SMR, Box

650.

[15]Donald A. Lawler to Betty Hughes, 26 April 1968, Archives SMR.

[16]Andrews Center File, Archives SMR, Box 600.

[17]A note in Judith Heberle's handwriting in the margin of the material on Andrews Center, Archives SMR, Box 600.

[18]Mercy Care Center File, Archives SMR, Box 620.

[19]Joseph L. Hogan to Rochester parishes, "The Religious Education Coordinator: Role and Placement," Summer 1972, Archives SMR.

[20]Joseph L. Hogan to Carol Fox, 4 September 1975, Personnel File, Archives SMR.

[21]George A. Cocuzzi to Hispanic community, St. Patrick parish, Diocese of Rochester, 22 December 1976, Personnel File, Archives SMR.

[22]"History of Camp Stella Maris and the Sisters of Mercy," Archives SMR, Book F.

[23]Marilyn Williams, interview by author, 15 March 2003, Archives SMR.

Chapter Six

[1]Kevin O'Boyle included this information in a Letter of Appeal he wrote in 1963. He sent a copy of this letter to Mary Bride Claire, Archives SMR, Box 690.

[2]Mary Bride Claire's words written for the celebration of the twentieth anniversary of the Chile foundation, December 1985, Archives SMR, Box 690.

[3]Kevin O'Boyle to Mary Bride Claire, February 1965, Archives SMR, Box 690.

[4]Mary Bride Claire to Rochester Congregation, 27 February 1965, Archives SMR, Box 690.

[5]These comments were told to Janet Caufield by Mary Bride Claire sometime in 1965. There is no record in the Archives of this exchange.

[6]Missionary sisters to Mary Bride Claire, 27 December 1965, Archives SMR, Box 690.

[7]"A Day in a Missionary's Life," *The Beacon* (Patterson, New Jersey, 15 February 1968), Archives SMR, Scrap Book #1, 15.

[8]Graced History Assembly, 21 October 1987, Archives SMR, Box 693.

[9]Janet Korn to Mary Florence Sullivan, Archives SMR, Box 690.

[10]Margaret Mungovan to Elaine Kolesnik, July 1985, Archives SMR, Box 690.

[11]"Light History," Graced History Assembly, 21 October 1987, Archives SMR, Box 693.

[12]Jesús Rodrígue Iglesias to Rochester Sisters of Mercy, 14 April 1977, Archives SMR, Box 692.

[13]Chilean Missionaries to Gerald R. Ford, 9 October 1974, "Congressional Record," Archives SMR, Box 691.

[14]"Dark History," Graced History Assembly, 22 October 1987,

Archives SMR, Box 693.

[15]Ibid.

[16]Kay Schwenzer to Rochester Sisters, Chilean Correspondence, Archives SMR, Box 690.

[17] "Dark History," Graced History Assembly, 22 October 1987, Archives SMR, Box 690.

[18]"Hope," Graced History Assembly, 23 October 1987, Archives SMR, Box 693.

[19]*Mercy Outreach* (Newsletter of the Sisters of Mercy), January 1989, vol. 8, no. 3, Archives SMR.

[20]Graced History Assembly, 23 October 1987, Archives SMR, Box 693.

[21]Words of an unidentified Chilean Woman, *Chile Update*, December 1987, Archives SMR, Box 692.

[22]*Chile Update* (undated material), Archives SMR, Box 692.

[23]Ibid.

[24]Chilean Sisters, interview by Louise Dantzig, June 1993, Archives SMR, Box 693.

[25]Ibid.

[26] *Vita*, (Newsletter of the Institute of the Sisters of Mercy of the Americas), September 1992, Archives SMR.

[27]Theresa Rutty to Rochester Sisters/Associates, December 1996, Archives SMR.

[28]*Mercy Focus* (Newsletter of the Sisters of Mercy of Rochester), 2 February 1996, vol. 8, no. 2, Archives SMR.

[29]*Courier Journal* (Rochester, NY), 6 May 1993, Archives DR.

[30] Joseph L. Hogan to Diocese of Rochester, *Courier Journal*, 19 April 1976, Archives DR.

[31]*Courier Journal*, 4 February 1981, Archives DR.

[32] Janet Korn to Rochester Sisters of Mercy, 20th anniversary of Chile, 24 December 1985, Archives SMR, Box 690.

[33] Graced History Assembly in Chile, 23 October 1987, Archives SMR, Box 693.

Chapter Seven

[1]Frederick J. Zwierlein, *The Life and Letters of Bishop McQuaid* (Rochester, NY: Art Print Shop, 1926), vol. II, 1.

[2]Honorable Harlo Hakes, ed., *Landmarks of Steuben County* (Syracuse, NY: D. Mason and Company, 1896), 286, 287.

[3]St. James Mercy Hospital File, Archives SMR, Box 670.

[4]"Organization and By-Laws of St. James Mercy Hospital," 2 April 1896, 2, 8, Archives SMR.

[5]W.R. Wakeman, "History of the Hospital," Archives SMR, Box 670.

[6]Adam J. Maida, Memorandum to the Sisters of Mercy re: St. James Mercy Hospital, 23 November 1976, Archives SMR, Box 670.

[7]Mary René McNiff to Central Administration, Sisters of Mercy,

December 1977, Archives SMR, Box 520.

[8]Paul Shephard to Nursing School Graduates, 27 June 1997, Archives SMR.

[9]Paul Shephard, *Catholic Courier,* (Rochester, NY: 2 February 1995), Archives SMR.

[10]Chapter 1989, Rochester Sisters of Mercy, June 1989, Archives SMR, Box 540.5.

[11]Clarence (Ted) La Liberty, Sisters of Mercy Assembly, 27 June 2003, Archives SMR, Box 511.

[12]Francis P. Hogan, *Mercy Echoes* (Newsletter of St. James Mercy Hospital), August 1955, Archives SMR.

[13]Arthur J. Karl, M.D. to Mary deSales Reilly, 15 August 1955, Golden Jubilee, Archives SMR.

[14]Mary Howard Cowan and Mary Rose Schum to Judith Heberle, November 1970, Archives SMR, Box 460.

[15]Joseph L. Hogan to Rochester parishes, March 1976, Archives SMR, Box 460.

[16]Mary Frances Wegman, interview by author, 8 February 2005, Archives SMR, Box 330.

[17]*Constitutions* (Silver Spring, MD: Institute of the Sisters of Mercy of the Americas, 1992), 6.

Chapter Eight

[1]Fund Raising File, Archives SMR, Box 313.

[2]Mercy Guild File, Archives SMR, Boxes 470, 470.1.

[3]Mary Bride Claire to Friends of the Sisters of Mercy, 30 August 1968, Archives SMR, Box 313.

[4]Judith Heberle to Rochester Sisters of Mercy, 5 December 1970, Archives SMR, Box 313.

[5]Founders Club File, Archives SMR, Box 313.

[6]Ibid.

[7]Ibid.

[8]Jean Marie Kearse to Friends of the Sisters of Mercy, *Mercy Outreach,* June 1987, Archives SMR.

[9]Minutes of Intercongregational Council, 7 January 1971, Archives SMR, Box 123.

[10]"Diocesan Study of the Role of Vicar for Religious," 12 July 1993, Archives SMR, Box 123.

[11]Minutes of Intercongregational Council (1971-2000), Archives SMR, Boxes 123, 123.1.

[12]Ibid.

[13]*The Fire in the Thornbush: A Pastoral Letter on Women in the Church* (Rochester, NY: *Courier Journal* 29 April 1982), Section VIII, No. 92.

[14]"Bishop Matthew Clark to the Leadership of the Sisters of Mercy, " March 1995.

[15]Mary Ellen Fischer, interview by author, 12 February 2004, Archives SMR.

[16] Joanna Regan and Isabelle Keiss, *Tender Courage* (Chicago: Franciscan Herald Press, 1988), viii.

[17] Nancy Whitley, interview by author, 12 February 2004, Archives SMR.

[18] *Mercy Focus* (Newsletter of the Sisters of Mercy of Rochester), 21 January 1994, Archives SMR, Box 910.

[19] Minutes of the Senate, 1969-1971, Archives SMR, Box 529.

[20] Sullivan, *Mercy*, 99.

[21] Minutes of the Senate, 1969-1971, Archives SMR, Box 529.

[22] Minutes of Governance Task Force, 18 May 1985, Archives SMR, Box 522.

[23] *Bylaws*, Advisory Board, Archives SMR, Box 522.

[24] Jean Marie Kearse to Rochester Community, Archives SMR, Box 522.

[25] Minutes of Chapter 1997, November Session 1997, Archives SMR, Box 540.5.

[26] *Governance Plan* (Regional Community of Rochester, 1997), 4.

[27] *Governance Plan*, 9.

[28] *Governance Plan*, 3.

Chapter Nine

[1] Marie Kennedy, *Federation of the Sisters of Mercy of the Americas* (1966-1980). Published by the Federation, 1981, 3.

[2] Minutes of the Federation, 9 June 1966, Archives SMR, Box 560.1.

[3] Ibid.

[4] Ibid.

[5] Federation File, Archives SMR, Box 560.1.

[6] Ibid.

[7] Kennedy, 12.

[8] Kennedy, 16.

[9] Kennedy, 19.

[10] Kennedy, 20.

[11] United States Bishops, Pastoral Letter on Justice, Archives SMR, Box 549.1.

[12] Kennedy, 21.

[13] Kennedy, 23.

[14] Minutes of the Federation, 27 June 1981, Archives SMR, Box 570.

[15] Ibid.

[16] Judith Heberle to Rochester Sisters of Mercy, 6 March 1982, Archives SMR, Box 560.2.

[17] Mercy Futures File, Archives SMR, Box 560.2.

[18] Ibid.

[19] Ibid.

[20] Ibid.

[21] Ibid.

[22] Jean Marie Kearse to Rochester Congregation, 18 June 1993, Archives SMR, File B.

[23]Minutes of Federation Meeting, 23-27 June 1989, Archives SMR, Box 570.
[24]Ibid.

Chapter Ten

[1]*Constitutions* (Institute of the Sisters of Mercy of the Americas, 1992). Appendix B, 30.

[2]Jeanette Goglia, "In the Joy of God's Love," *Music and Rituals for the Founding Event* (Institute of the Sisters of Mercy of the Americas, 1991), Archives SMR, Box 570.

[3]Minutes of Institute Chapter, July 1991, Archives SMR, Box 570.

[4]Ibid.

[5]Claudette Schiratti, "Trocaire," *Music and Rituals for the Founding Event* (Institute of the Sisters of Mercy of the Americas, 1991), Archives SMR, Box 570.

[6]Mercy Migrant Education File, Archives SMR, Box 610.1.

[7]Barbara Moore, interview by Public Relations Director, 6 June 1995, Archives SMR, Box 570.1.

[8]Minutes of Institute Chapter, July 1995, Archives SMR, Box 570.1.

[9]Carol Jussaume, *Chapter Bulletin*, July 1995, Archives SMR, Box 570.1.

[10]*Mercy Focus*, (Newsletter of the Sisters of Mercy Rochester), 10 January 1997, Archives SMR.

[11]*MAST Journal* is a publication of the Mercy Association in Scripture and Theology.

[12]*Morning and Evening Prayer of the Sisters of Mercy* (Sisters of Mercy of the Americas, 1998), viii.

[13]Minutes of Third Institute Chapter, 21-30 June 1999, Archives SMR, Box 570.1

[14]Ibid.

[15]Sheila Stevenson to Rochester Community, 26 September 2001, Archives SMR.

[16]*Sisters of Mercy Action Plan 1999-2005*, Document from Institute Chapter, June 1999, Archives SMR, Box 570.1.

[17]Minutes of Third Institute Chapter, 21-30 June 1999, Archives SMR, Box 570.1.

[18]*Sisters of Mercy Action Plan 1999-2005*.

[19]Institute Leadership Team to Institute Membership, 20 July 2003, Archives SMR.

[20]*Sisters of Mercy Action Plan 1999-2005*.

Chapter Eleven

[1]NyPaW Minutes of 28 November 1994, Archives SMR, Box 580.

[2]Jeanne Thomas Dansby, interview by NyPaW presidents, September 1996, Archives SMR, Box 580.

[3] Jeanne Reichart, interview by author, 6 June 2003, Archives SMR.

[4]NyPaW Minutes of 13 February 1997, Archives SMR, Box 580.
[5]NyPaW Approved Documents, Archives SMR, File F.
[6]Minutes of the Latin American/Caribbean Conference, February 1980, Archives SMR, Box 693.
[7]Minutes of the Latin American/Caribbean Conference, February 2000, Archives SMR, Box 693.
[8]*Vita* (Newsletter of the Institute of the Sisters of Mercy), March 2004, Archives SMR, Box 931.1.

Epilogue

[1] Joe Feuerherd, *National Catholic Reporter*, 21 January 2005.
[2] McNamara, 263.
[3] *Catholic Courier*, 27 September 1990, Archives DR.
[4]"Accountability Report, Phase II," Easter 2005, Institute of the Sisters of Mercy of the Americas, Archives SMR.

SELECT BIBLIOGRAPHY

1. Manuscript Sources

Archives of the Sisters of Mercy, 1437 Blossom Road, Rochester, New
York 14610: correspondence, newsletters, unpublished
manuscripts, minutes, reports, hand copied and photocopied
letters, interviews by the author, newspaper clippings, chapter
documents, and personal memoirs. All references to these
manuscript sources are fully documented in the endnotes to
each chapter.

Archives of the Roman Catholic Diocese of Rochester, New York, 1150
Buffalo Road, Rochester, New York 14624: correspondence,
diocesan reports, Catholic newspaper clippings, and other
diocesan archival holdings. All references to these manuscript
sources are fully documented in the endnotes to each chapter.

2. Books and Other Publications Cited:

A Sister of St. Joseph. *Sisters of St. Joseph of Rochester*. Rochester,
New York: Sisters of St. Joseph of Rochester, 1950.

Brennan, Bonaventure, RSM. *According to Catherine: Words of
Wisdom from Catherine McAuley, A Thematic Approach*.
Dublin, Ireland: Congregation of the Sisters of Mercy, 2003.

*Constitutions of the Congregation of the Religious Sisters of Mercy of
Rochester, New York*. Rochester, New York: Sisters of
Mercy, 1954.

Customs of the Sisters of Mercy in the Diocese of Rochester, New York.
Sisters of Mercy of Rochester, 1938.

Dwyer, Claudette, ed. *The Quality of Mercy*. Chicago, Illinois: Sisters
of Mercy, Regional Community of Chicago, Illinois, 1996.

Familiar Instructions of Rev. Mother McAuley. New and rev. ed. St.
Louis, Missouri: Vincentian Press, 1927.

[Hyde, Sister M. Antonia, RSM]. *Mercy*. Rochester, New York:
George P. Burns Press, 1932.

Institute of the Sisters of Mercy of the Americas. *Constitutions*. Silver
Spring, Maryland: Sisters of Mercy of the Americas, 1991.

Kennedy, Marie, RSM. *Federation of the Sisters of Mercy of the
Americas 1966-1980*. Privately printed, 1981.

McNamara, Robert F. *The Diocese of Rochester 1968-1993*. 2d ed.
Rochester, New York: Roman Catholic Diocese, 1998.

Neumann, Sister Mary Ignatia, RSM, ed. *Letters of Catherine McAuley*. Baltimore, Maryland: Helicon Press, 1969.

Perfectae Caritatis (Decree on Adaptation and Renewal of Religious Life). Second Vatican Council, October 1965.

Regan, Joanna, RSM and Isabelle Keiss, RSM. *Tender Courage*. Chicago, Illinois: Franciscan Herald Press, 1988.

Roth, Sister M. Augustine, RSM. *The McAuley Conference 1955-1965*. Potomac, Maryland: Federation of the Sisters of Mercy of the Americas, 1978.

Sisters of Mercy of Rochester. *Interim Constitutions*. Rochester, New York: Sisters of Mercy, 1971.

Sullivan, Mary C., RSM. *Catherine McAuley and the Tradition of Mercy*. Notre Dame, Indiana: University of Notre Dame Press, 1995.

Sullivan, Sister M. Florence, RSM. *Mercy Comes to Rochester.* 2d ed. Rochester, New York: Sisters of Mercy of Rochester, 1985.

Zwierlein, Frederick J. *The Life and Letters of Bishop McQuaid*. 2 vols. Rochester, New York: Art Print Shop, 1926.

INDEX

266